Clown Shoes

CLOWN SHOES

ROBERT MARKOWITZ

 Heliotrope Books

New York

Heliotrope Books LLC
heliotropebooks@gmail.com

ISBN 978-1-956474-30-5
ISBN 978-1-956474-31-2 eBook

Cover design by Naomi Rosenblatt with AJ&J Design
Typeset by Naomi Rosenblatt with AJ&J Design

To my parents, Selma and Joe Markowitz,
my wife, Linda Kelly, and my daughter, Kate Markowitz.

Also, Lorraine Gengo, whose help with this project was indispensable;
Susan Shapiro, who mentored me;
and Naomi Rosenblatt, founder and manager of Heliotrope Books,
who shepherded *Clown Shoes*.

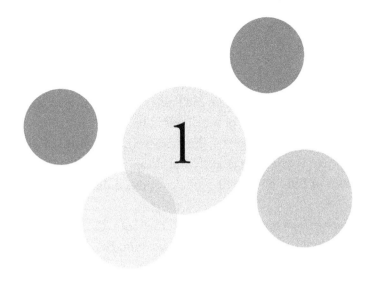

1

My inner matador woke me at three a.m., as he usually did on trial days. He poked me with his banderillas. I ascribed it to a nervous temperament but in talking to other attorneys a lot of them had their own internal tyrants. It's amazing how many future lawyers are swayed by "Perry Mason," "L.A. Law," or "The Good Wife" without knowing what the profession really entails. It's like falling under the sway of a fast-talking pitchman on late-night TV: Do you want high status but have little idea of what to do with your life? Would you like people to stop asking you questions about your career path? Law school may be for you!

My first wakeful act was to meditate and pray at my makeshift altar, briefly falling back to sleep twice. Shaded by a brass tree of life, the Divine mother and meditating Jesus were all in favor of me getting more rest, but Sekhmet and Ganesh brooked no nonsense.

I got up and stood under the shower, red-eyed from lack of rest. At least, I'd noticed as I glanced around the room, there was no evidence of sleepwalking. After drying off, I dressed in shirt and tie, cool from the closet. Returning to the bathroom to brush my teeth and shave, I nicked myself and clotted the trickle of blood with toilet paper. Frustrated, I waded socks-on into a puddle, and plodded all over the bedroom carpet, leaving footprints. There were no clean socks so I emptied the dirty laundry and matched a pair.

Once in my White Plains office, the keys of my MacBook clicked over the hum of the HVAC system. No lights on. Only the gray glow of the screen to keep the wolves of loneliness at bay. I was loath to admit loneliness. I took pride in never feeling that way. Except that I'd been lonely as hell. Reviewing a practically-hopeless, pre-trial motion to exclude 158 tabs of LSD on constitutional grounds didn't help much, by the way.

My paper-strewn oak desk dominated the room. I'd bought it years ago for $180 when I only had $700 in my account. Bookcases lined the walls. Most of the volumes were out-of-date case law reporters or legal encyclopedias that I'd picked up for free. Diplomas framed in black, gray, and red were arranged for easy observation from the client chairs.

It may have been some time before I noticed that another sound had blended with the staccato clicks and droning whir. The soft beeping of my phone alarm. Time to go. Without thinking, I picked at the specks of toilet paper still glued to my face, then spit on my finger to remove them.

Breakfast was an Egg McMuffin and coffee purchased on the way to court at a drive-thru window. *You deserve a break today.* Who speeds into a drive-thru when they have time for a break? As I pulled away with my hot little bag, I felt an outburst coming and sealed the open window.

"I hate being a damn lawyer," I wailed. "Objection, your honor, I don't like your smug face! Objection, prosecutor—I hate your blue suit!"

Still driving, I threw my phone at the windshield and it rebounded to the passenger-seat floor.

"I hate fighting losing battles! I'm tired of the weight. It's too damn heavy! When do I get my reward? I want my fucking reward!" I didn't even know what that would look like.

I was weeping as I drove down the tunnel to underground parking, found a space, then lay across the front seats, knees bent toward my chest.

My anger turned to cold fear like breathing dry ice. I was pushing back a panic attack.

These seismic waves of dread had increased since Joshua's death.

His mother had been a client, and a mistaken judgment of mine had led to him dying at her hands. Maybe now I could just give in. Allow myself to be afraid and deterred.

But my current client was waiting upstairs, the acid head. Trippers were curious types—nerdy explorers. This one had made the mistake of Instagramming the location of his adventure in real time and the police found him with 158 tabs.

Part of me—the wily, scrappy little savage—was tired of being coerced. He saw his opportunity to strong-arm a bargain. This would be the last trial. No more.

Don't take advantage, the adult in me chided.

Take advantage? You've run us into the ground, buddy. You want me to get up? Give in.

Are you willing to waste fourteen years? This was the adult's pet refrain. Four years of law school, including a year's leave, three failed bar exams in three years, and now seven of practicing law.

Shove those fourteen years up your ass, counsel. Else, I won't move.

The punk hammered the car window until his knuckles were raw. This was no bluff.

Fourteen years. This argument had always prevailed even when it had been thirteen, twelve, eleven, ten. You can't argue with fourteen years.

The kid reared back to smash his fist once more against the window. The stakes were life.

The adult sighed. *I capitulate.* The fancy word was a last attempt to pull rank.

Deal, grunted the child.

Of course the adult could always renege. But there are dangers when an urchin loses all faith. He really does have the power to bring down the whole operation.

The battle had the effect of anesthetizing me. I felt numb rather than scared. I drank my coffee and ate my Egg McMuffin, then took my briefcase and walked toward the courthouse.

In the lobby I spied my client. He wore a black top hat, green lion-tamer's jacket with oversized buttons, orange vest, white gloves, and a purple bowtie which resembled the floppy ears of a beagle. Since he sported a full beard, clown white was applied only around his eyes, setting off the red-ball nose. He was practicing with a color-changing handkerchief.

"Peter," I said. "You're not dressed for trial." I guided him by the elbow toward the exit, talking in a hushed tone. "I can't try your case. I'm going to have to settle it in chambers before anyone sees you."

He grinned, as if upsetting my expectations constituted a win.

This was actually a relief. I could probably cut a favorable plea bargain. LSD is an upscale drug of white suburbanites—and don't think that doesn't prompt judicial mercy.

"Look," I continued, ushering him outside. "Why are you dressed like this?"

"These are my work clothes," he said blithely. "You told me not to speak in court unless I'm asked questions. This," he gestured to his outfit, "is my message: The judicial system is the oppressive hand of the bourgeoisie that lashes out at anything it doesn't understand and attempts to apprehend the human soul by incarcerating bodies. Doesn't my costume convey that eloquently, Mr. Ross?"

His body language said, *Let the little people sweep up, I'm too busy being me.*

"How dare you show contempt for this esteemed institution," I said, constraining my volume through clenched teeth. "Do you realize that I've spent fourteen years—fourteen years—who do you think you are? Timothy Leary? Wavy Gravy? Who are *you* to ridicule a system that is the very core of democracy? Wear a humble blue suit, Sir! The men in orange jumpers will be throwing a party for you."

His face fell. "Am I really going to jail, Mr. Ross? I can't. I'm no fighter. They'll carve me up. I don't do well in close places!" His eyes throbbed blue against clown white. He searched me pleadingly, eyes resting on my bruised knuckles. I, too, did not do well in close places. Taking a deep breath, I steadied myself.

"Look, if you're willing to plead guilty, I might get you off with a stiff fine and work detail—picking up trash by the highway in a dayglow vest."

"I'll plead guilty," he said. "No jail. I'll die in there. I know it."

Rather than feeling superior to Peter, the opposite was true. I was jealous.

"Okay," I nodded. "Just tell me one thing." I dipped my head. My voice dropped to a murmur. "Where did you learn to be a party clown?"

He told me about an outfit in lower Manhattan that equipped and trained you in one night. I asked for details as if it were just a vague curiosity to me. It was no frills, he said, glancing at my expensive suit and shaking his head doubtfully. "The class was in a basement on the Lower East Side."

"Have you worked any parties?" I asked.

"Oh yeah," he replied, smiling.

"Did you love it?" I couldn't conceal my keenness on this point so I lowered my eyes to his lime-green shoes.

"You really want to know?" he asked. "I've tried LSD, clowning, zip-lining, almost everything. You can't change your insides with something on the outside."

Maybe so. But I felt like my feet weren't quite touching the ground—as if I could rise to the ceiling, weightless. Give up my law practice to become a children's party performer? It was ridiculous. How could I make a living at it? But I hadn't felt my blood quicken like this in a very long time, and if I didn't honor it in some way, I may never again.

I negotiated a favorable plea with the prosecutor. Then it came to me—*fourteen years*. Damned if I was going to throw it all away for some shlock clown training.

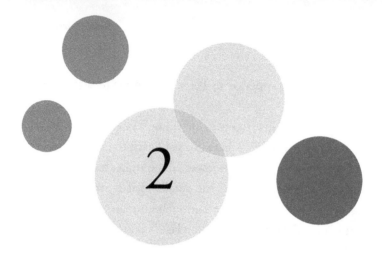

2

Wednesday, May 27, 2009 South Salem, NY

Norma Wilkes was ranting to the guards and a couple of hand-cuffed, tangerine-suited inmates in earshot. "I don't remember cutting Joshua. I must be crazy. Can't remember anything."

I was her attorney-of-record, having helped her beat misdemeanor child abuse just a month ago. Acquitted by a jury. Her present charge was murder.

I sat in the see-through meeting room watching her approach. She was lean and compact, appearing much younger at a distance. Up close, crow's feet and marionette lines were etched deeply. Her waxy face framed by straggly dishwater-blonde hair.

She scowled. "I got nobody to help me except you. I'm all alone."

The guard locked us in and we sat on plastic chairs at the stainless-steel table. The room had plexiglass walls from which you could see the guard booth and the corridor out to the world. I took a deep breath—never liked to be closed in.

I hated her more than I ever remembered hating anyone except maybe Tony Pappalardo, who I'd fought with after every freshman football practice in ninth grade.

I forced myself to look at her. "Why did you do it, Norma?"

She straightened her back. "I don't need no story for an insanity defense, Mr. Ross."

The futility of ever getting the truth left an acid taste in my mouth.

I met her eyes.

"Did you do it because Joshua went to the police?"

"I remember nothing." She hesitated. "Nothing."

That was a lie. But one thing was clear. If I hadn't secured Norma Wilkes's acquittal from charges of inflicting cruel and inhuman punishment on her son, CPS would have removed Joshua from the home. The boy would be alive. I wanted to blot myself out, dig a ten-foot hole in the ground and hide.

Her jaw set, lips grew tight. The whites of her eyes were visible below milky-green irises. Her stare was unnerving. I felt my resolve melt like wax from a candle. Why did I grow timid just when I needed to be forceful? Her hand twitched on the steel table. A flash of rage gripped me. I reached out, grabbed her little finger and bent it back.

Blood roared in my ears. "Did you do it because he went to the police?"

"Let go of me!"

She slow-blinked like a cat. That was my answer. I released her. Had I lost my sanity?

Never mind that what I'd just done could get me disbarred—forget that it was cruel. I had become desperate. Desperate men quit trying to be good, believing it's impossible.

I dropped my shoulders. "I should have counseled you to plead guilty."

"Why didn't you?" A sarcastic smile played on her lips. Her voice was low, teasing.

"I believed your story." She had been very persuasive. Norma's testimony, more than anything else, won over the jury. She'd stared them down and sold them.

"Believe me now," she said firmly.

We had won the trial. It had never occurred to me that I was obliged to get the human part right, too.

"Why did you do this to me?" I asked.

She peered up cradling the finger I'd bent back as if it were an IOU. "Help me."

Reaching for a document in her waistband, she unfolded it, and forced it into my hand. Power of Attorney. "Go to my bank. Take all the money."

She had been my client. Was I obligated?

Again, she lifted the finger I'd tried to damage. "You punished me." Kneeling on the concrete floor, she put her hands together in supplication. The fluorescent light made her blonde hair almost colorless. Furrows on her face cast grease-pencil shadows. It was a wretched sight. Despite my promise to myself, despite my anger, I was in danger of acquiescing. But something inside wouldn't quite yield.

There was a change in Norma's pearly green eyes. They clouded. Then she looked down at her body as if she hadn't been aware of her servile posture. Her mouth opened in disbelief, nostrils flared. She slapped her bended knee like she was disciplining a disobedient child. Rage lit her eyes and she glared like a wolf at my throat.

"Get out!" she screamed. "I don't want you!"

The guard opened the door. My head throbbed. I pressed my right temple to make it stop. I felt ashamed for hurting her.

Norma stared at me from the floor, a sliver of white below the iris. God help a vulnerable boy looking into those eyes. Even as I turned away, I felt them bore into the back of my neck, and track me down the hall.

I was still willing to suffer. That hadn't changed. I was prepared to labor on, day after day, despising my work. It was ever in the back of my mind that as a lawyer, if not careful, I could do harm. No more was this an abstract notion. I had contributed to a boy's death.

Outside, rust-colored buildings and barbed wire glimmered in the sun. There had been no choice but to park in the direct rays. A chocolate bar I'd bought at lunch was softening on the passenger seat. I ate it. The sugar daze and stomach ache were darkly satisfying.

Oh to be a clown! Agile, light-footed, effervescent, before an audience of children. Spontaneity had always been the deepest longing of my heart.

But whimsy would not make my mortgage or car payments. No doubt my soul was at risk.

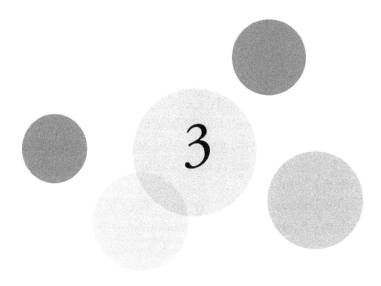

3

My best friend, Ray, was the closest thing I knew to a clown, and he made his living, such as it was, by playing music for children. We'd met at Mamaroneck High School, and became friends when he'd watched my back as I fought a kid who'd thrown a basketball at my head. Ray was the poster child for the wages of sin. Sin, in the gospel of my parents, was refusing to tailor yourself to the world. He lived in Kerhonkson, a little town in the Catskills, an hour-and-a-half north of White Plains. I picked up the phone and asked him if he would tell me what he knew about playing gigs for kids.

"Why?" he asked. "I thought you settled that LSD clown case."

"No, for me." The admission barely cleared my throat.

"You poor bastard. You're going to quit on account of that boy?"

So, on a rainy Saturday morning I made my Catskills pilgrimage. I drove north with the light bending through the clouds, casting the trees as warlocks, along a snakelike Taconic Parkway. Ray had given me written directions like it was 1982 or something. *Turn left at Stewart Gas and then veer right at the next fork.* You couldn't always get a GPS cell phone connection up there.

When I reached his place, I took my guitar around back and entered from the patio as instructed. Ray waved me in through the glass door. I slid it open and stepped into a living room. There he was: greasy hair, disheveled, lying on a couch, half-wrapped in a white cotton blanket, his guitar on the floor. Not a great ad for living the intuitive, spontaneous life. Back in high school, I'd considered an artistic path. Ray's plight was the outcome I chose to avoid—living broke and alone in a couple of rented rooms. I willingly assumed my parents' worldview, once boasting to Ray, "Right out of school, I'll make more money than my father ever did." Hubris.

A cotton blanket was just one step down from Ray's usual outfit. When I saw him perform once, he donned the stage with frayed cut-offs, and a bleach-damaged Camp Greylock T-shirt. His hair looked like it had been combed with the jawbone of a walrus. But his guitar work was masterful and his style, mocking, but in good humor. He was so talented he didn't need to woo the crowd. But I'd already known that from playing gigs with him in high school.

Ray blinked. "I'm sick," he said, and he looked it—glassy eyes, chin stubble, black hair pasted to his temple, shirt wrinkled like he'd slept in it.

He squirmed on the couch. "Can you make me a cup of tea?"

"Sure." I was relieved to have something to do. "Has your girlfriend seen the place like this?" I asked.

"No." He blinked twice as if he'd been sleeping. "She's visiting relatives in Guyana for two weeks."

The kitchen adjoined the living room. There was a cast-iron tea pot on a porcelain gas range. I filled the pot from the sink. Tea bags lay across a wood-block cutting board and there was an open jar of Orange Blossom Honey with a spoon buried in it. I held it to the window, examining for ants, then washed two tea cups from the sink.

Ray blew air through pressed lips and shook his head. "It's a midden pile," he said apologetically.

"No worries," I said, waving it off. But I felt embarrassed for him. One more way Ray relied on the world to adapt to *him*.

"This boy's death," he said. "It's not your fault. You know that, right?" He narrowed his blue eyes. I nodded. But logic was irrelevant. I felt Joshua's death viscerally, like a weighted vest, the kind they use to contain autistic kids at a juvenile facility I'd visited.

Ray's house had some elegant features like high ceilings and ornamental molding, but the paint on the ceiling was discolored from water damage. A makeshift wall erected in the living room suggested that this former one-family house had been haphazardly divided into apartments. This explained the patio entrance.

Ray leaned forward. "How's David?"

"Oh, he's fine," I said. "He's making a fortune in real estate law."

Ray had always liked my brother. Each was adventurous in his own way: Ray's nonconformity and unique talent, David's 2002 Harley VRSC V-Rod and his dream of living in Switzerland.

"Our very own Jay Gatsby," Ray quipped. He was fond of literary references.

I poured boiling water into cups set with tea bags, rescued the spoon from the honey, and loaded a heaping glob into each, handing Ray a cup.

He nodded thank-you. "Luckily, I have no gigs today." He drank some tea, balanced the cup on the floor, then slumped back on the couch.

I tasted the tea. Too sweet. "Have you ever performed feeling like this?"

Ray frowned. "The libraries won't have you back if you don't show. And you can't disappoint a birthday child. I once played four gigs in seven hours feeling worse."

This life clearly had its own demands. "How did you do it?"

"You find a way." Ray smiled. "I like to keep promises."

"You played the leads, I strummed the chords," I said, remembering our teenage band, Bad Chemicals. "You're a virtuoso guitar player. I'm not."

I was doing it again. Rationalizing why other people could live artistic lives but not me.

Ray shook his head. "It's never the guitar playing or the props. Once I went on stage with a borrowed 12-string. I didn't know where to fit my fingers. One of the best shows I ever did."

I leaned forward. "Why?"

Ray arched one eyebrow in that Captain Spock way. "Because it's *me*," he said, touching a finger to his throat, "not the guitar." He sipped the tea. "What would you charge?"

I shrugged. "I don't know. Fifty dollars a show?"

Ray snapped his fingers. "Start with $150."

That seemed impossible.

He read my face. "Price is a funny thing. I've seen amazing performers charge $250 a show, and along comes a guy at $500 or $600 and he's getting it. But the $250 guy is better."

I scratched my head. "So how is the other one getting $500 a show?"

Ray reclined on the couch and mirrored my action, scratching his pasty scalp. "He's *owning* it. He's comfortable with the $500."

"How do you get that way?"

"I'm not sure," Ray said. "I've gone up gradually."

"May I ask?"

"Four hundred and I get it. But I'm not immune to dry spells. In fact, last year I was going to quit and my girlfriend begged me not to. So I hung in there."

I winced to think that it was still so precarious after all the years Ray had put in.

"Feels like quite a jump to make a living at this," I said.

He repositioned himself on the couch and pointed a finger. "Book yourself a library tour and by the end of it you'll be in a different place."

"But what if —"

"Do it." Ray's eyes pulsed. "When you get home, pick up the phone."

"But I hardly remember the chords." I reached for my guitar.

Ray motioned me to put it down. "It doesn't matter."

He must have seen the disbelief in my eyes because he leveled me with a stare.

"It's really about claiming your turf. At first the world might think you're bluffing, and refuse to budge. But the moment *you* know that this is no act, that you're serious, it will open up."

My best friend was a bedridden musician cooped up in a godforsaken upstate town but somehow it all felt possible. A warm glow, like birthday-cake candles, filled my chest. It would not have been possible to make peace with this kind of life, never mind get serious about it, before Joshua's death.

"Can I make you something to eat?" I asked.

Ray motioned to the refrigerator. "There's not much in there."

"How about a grilled cheese sandwich? I bet I can find that."

I scavenged the fridge for bread, butter and cheese. Minutes later, I clapped slick, toasted bread onto some brittle Swiss. A cast iron frying pan on the front burner looked clean enough. I cut another chunk of butter into the pan and fried the sandwich on both sides.

Ray took a slug of tea. "It's tricky to find your passion. And *keep* finding it," he said. "That's *really* why I wanted to quit. Nothing got me excited. But now it's good. I'm into Andean music." He put down the cup and played something on the guitar that sounded like "El Condor Pasa" by Simon and Garfunkel. Airy. Easy to imagine Andean flutes. It frightened me that even Ray, who played guitar for a living, sometimes got tired of it. I slid the hot gooey sandwich off the frying pan and served it to him on a plate. Ray put his nose to it with obvious pleasure.

"One last thing." He gestured toward the next room. "Could you feed the python?"

4

At this point, I had to consider that I might be a coward. No longer could I claim that I was unaware of what I wanted. The thrill of it had come twice. Once when I imagined myself as a clown and felt so weightless as to rise to the ceiling. A second time, as Ray envisaged my future, and a warm glow, like birthday candles, seized me. Granted, the path was obscure. I could not even see around the next bend. But to deny the markers at my feet, pointing the way, was no longer possible. Even so, I felt paralyzed, unwilling to surrender fourteen years of sustained commitment for a virtual pipe dream. Clients had looked me in the eye across my office desk and entrusted their cases to me. I'd promised them my best effort.

Leaving law would kill a paradigm I'd long carried with me. My great, great grandfather had been a smuggler, my great grandfather an immigrant baker, then came the post-war postman, and the me-generation teacher, and I was to be the golden shiner of this school of fish. It was a tale fraught with ego and family pride, and it was mine.

I had made the mistake of blabbing these ruminations, over the phone, to my mother. Alarmed, and aware that her influence over my life had diminished, she enlisted my brother to remind me of my place in the family evolution. Mom put David up to inviting me to the Orienta Yacht Club, and taking me out on his Boston Whaler. I understood David's allegiance to our mother. But he could have told her that I was old enough to screw up my *own* life.

I'd been to the Orienta Club before, situated on the Long Island Sound in Mamaroneck, with an imposing, three-chimneyed stone mansion as clubhouse. I drove up, parked the car in the lot, then headed to the Marleton House. The others were waiting at the entrance. David wore the club uniform: windbreaker, jean shorts, and topsiders. Felicia was on David's arm, her bathing suit a cutout one-piece with a skimpy cover-up. She was a prosecutor in the D.A.'s office. Clara stood to the side like a third wheel.

"You remember Clara," David said, after a quick brotherly hug.

Dark bangs, hazel eyes, a profile so perfect you held your breath. She was in a white crocheted beach dress, more bohemian than revealing. I was a fan of her very-local cable news show. When she improvised a joke for a human-interest story, I would laugh. Loud. Alone at my desk in the office. When she read the news, little glimmers of her humanity snuck through. Her eyes would pop if she found something absorbing. When reporting on something objectionable, she'd knit her brow, all her emotions plainly visible—including boredom at times. She had always rung my bell as a woman firmly out of my reach.

I met her eyes, nodded, mumbled unintelligibly. She smiled brilliantly—one of her many endearing expressions I knew from television. Not having any sisters, I didn't know if girls spent hours honing these looks or if they came naturally. But it worked. On me.

I stuck out with blue shorts and a Breton striped shirt like a French sailor. *Allons enfants de la Patrie. Le jour de gloire est arrivé!* What the hell was I thinking? When we all walked into the clubhouse together the manager's eyes lingered.

I lagged behind to avoid being studied—and to watch Clara. Her walk had a rhythm to it. Had she agreed to this because David's brother, Will, was going through a crisis and needed an excursion? Four is always more comfortable than three. Was it a mercy date?

A 15-foot skiff on the rough Sound is definitely a sit-down boat. David put Clara and me in the rear. I sensed her hesitation, as if she might be used to sitting up front. Felicia got the plum seat beside David. We backed out of the slip and navigated the cove toward the channel. Clara was sitting up straight, angling her neck, as if she didn't appreciate two heads bobbing between her and the horizon.

The inner harbor was uncrowded but even so, David scrupulously observed the 5 MPH speed limit. He had tackled maritime charts and outboard motors in the same elegant fashion that he'd mastered real estate transactions. David regularly flushed the Whaler's engine and disconnected the gas line so as to burn all the fuel in the carburetor. He liked systems. I railed against them. That's likely why he chose real estate and I landed in criminal law.

Clara gazed to her right at the unobstructed panorama of the Long Island Sound. She appeared to sense my attention, and glanced over. But then she fixed her eyes forward on David's bronzed fingers guiding the wheel.

Rejected ideas for small-talk overtures:

* We're approaching Bell Buoy 42.

* There's good fishing for blues here.

* Mamaroneck is the second largest small-boat harbor on the East Coast.

* Did you know I can name who won the World Series in every year since 1921?

We were far enough out so that most of the boats were cabin cruisers and yachts, no longer small crafts.

My brother frowned. "It's a little choppy for the Whaler," he said. "I'm going to head north of Turkey Rock."

He opened a cooler that contained Heinekens, club sodas, slices of Jarlsberg, and Triscuit crackers, bidding everyone to dig in, which they did, passing it around.

Felicia squinted into the sun. "You didn't take the Wilkes murder case," she called to me. "Word is you turned her down at the county jail."

I wondered how much David might have shared about my current career ambivalence.

Felicia twisted her body toward the stern, focusing intently on me. I'd always liked her professionally, she was one of the decent prosecutors.

"Maybe David has told you," I said. "I'm exploring various things."

Felicia opened her eyes wide. "Like what?"

I couldn't quite bring myself to talk about clowns or guitars. "Working with children."

"As a teacher? Are you going back to school?"

"No."

I steeled myself. "More like an entertainer. It's just fantasy at this point."

A half-smile froze on her face. Her eyes dropped to my fingers as if examining them for leprosy. "You can't mean that." Hair blew across her face and she captured it with an elastic and swept it back.

I glanced at David for support. He swiveled toward me, smiled grimly, and quipped, "Yeah—what she said," then mugged for the women.

Felicia raised a finger at me. "People would die to be in your position. No boss. No defined hours." She picked up a cheese-covered Triscuit, gesturing with it. "Everybody knows you. Think of the work it took to get you here."

Of course she was right—if I ignored all my feelings. I peeked over at Clara.

She came alive. "You're assessing Will from the outside." Her eyes brightened. "What about inside? What if he's *dying* inside?"

It took my breath away. How did this beautiful stranger have any conception of my private thoughts?

"Okay," conceded Felicia, nodding slowly. "Disaffection with law is an understandable reaction to the tragedy of that boy's death." She craned her neck, stretching her back. "But Will can recover. It's not worth throwing away his whole career."

No one spoke as four young women in uniform rowed past in a crew shell. Strands of hair escaped their blue visors as they labored in unison.

David grunted. "That's what we'll have to do if the motor craps out." He pointed to a hatch containing emergency paddles. From Turkey Rock, we had gradually drifted back into the open Sound, beyond the bell buoy. Not much a paddle or two could do in rough water.

Clara tilted her head toward Felicia. "Will is searching for his life," she said. "Not some idea of what his life should be, but his real life."

Her fervor seemed nonsensical given that we'd never said a word to each other. But strangely, I began to conceive of myself as the man she was describing.

Felicia restrained a mocking smile. "You see Will as doing what *you* need to do," she said, coolly inspecting her French manicure.

Clara's face crumpled. I struggled for a comeback to Felicia. But Clara pulled off her cover-up, stood on her seat, and performed an elegant dive into the roiling sound. She was gone for a few long moments under that cold gray turbulence. Long enough for me to start searching anxiously. When she emerged from the swell, the boat was a good thirty yards past her. We all stood and applauded, even David, poster child for nautical safety. Clara tucked her head and swam a few crisp strokes toward us.

Felicia started screaming, waving her in frantically. I spun to my right expecting a run-away jet ski. Instead, near our boat, a high dorsal fin dipped under the surface, still visible beneath, streaking toward Clara, the shark half as long as our skiff. Needles of terror pierced my gut. Clara glanced behind her, then swam madly toward the boat but made little ground. *Ka-shaw-ka-shaw-ka-shaw* thudded the blood in my temples. Clara flailed wildly, but the shark was gaining as if she were in a dead man's float, then it plunged beneath the dusky water. Mechanically, my hands emptied my pockets into the hull. An unfamiliar voice inside said, *here I go*. Belly first into the white caps, stroking and kicking. I felt a whoosh of current as the big fish sharply reversed course, its gill openings rending as if in shock.

"Hold on to me," I sputtered. She shook me off, clearly swimming much faster unassisted. David and Felicia crouched over the ladder at the stern and hoisted us up—first Clara, then me. Felicia wrapped her arms around Clara squeezing her so tight she soaked herself. A sun-glinted dorsal fin surfaced a football field away, heading out to sea.

"Oh my God!" shrieked Felicia. "You almost died."

Clara glowed. Once seated on deck, her teeth kept chattering, even in the strong sun, as if she were releasing shark energy. I re-lived the flash of jagged white scars and surge of flux as the shark had re-coiled.

Clara turned toward me, eyes of olive and gold. "Did you see him beneath us?"

I nodded taking her wet hand.

David called to me from the helm. "What got into you?"

I didn't know. It had something to do with what Clara had said she saw in me. But that bulletproof feeling proved to be temporary, only lasting for our time on the boat. Later, standing with Clara on the dock, I felt lonely, estranged, while David fit the flush muffs over the motor's intakes and ran water through the hose.

Risking death had scarcely bought me forty-five minutes of peace. Was that why people bungee-jumped from cliffs or leapt out of airplanes with parachutes? All for an hour or so of being enough? What was it that my clown client had said in the courthouse? "You can't change your insides with something on the outside." I wasn't really the man Clara had imagined, the guy who honored his inner calling, the one who'd jumped between her and the shark.

But now she was following me up the rickety dock stairs.

"What's wrong?" Clara asked, employing one of her myriad endearing expressions, a pursing of soft lips and widening of eyes.

"You are the woman I've waited for all my life," I said awkwardly. "I am totally infatuated," that wasn't quite right, "*in love* with you."

It was the kind of numbskull move that goes against every rule in the Real Man's Book of Seduction: admitting clunky, unwieldy feelings about a woman you don't even know. Nothing makes them run away faster. The mix of despair and inappropriate transparency is not what most females chase after in their Prince Charming.

"Let's have lunch sometime," she said.

"Really?"

"You tried to save my life." She smiled. "That's worth lunch."

Clara gave me her number, walked to her Honda Civic, and waved goodbye. I now had a problem. If I called her, I was obliged to be the man she'd projected—one searching, à la Diogenes, for an honest man, an honest me. How had she put it—looking for my *real* life?

Whether I'd actually become a different man in her presence, or merely posed as one, I needed to live up to that. Which put me in a predicament because I hadn't decided to leave law.

5

Sunday, July 12, 2009, Charlestown, RI

I had just a short time to remake myself before asking Clara to lunch. Time to get rid of some baggage:

* Valuing other people's opinions over my own instincts.
* Trusting that money and status would compensate for self-betrayal.
* Believing joy to be something for other people, mostly children.

Through circumstance or grace, I had a chance with Clara, but only if I detonated an incarnation's worth of limiting beliefs in a single day.

The antidote was coconuts. I bought five and drove up to my favorite beach on the Rhode Island shore. Charlestown Breachway Beach was where my mother, father, David, and I had spent a vacation week every summer until my parents' divorce.

The gravel crunched and spit from my tires. Rain on the windshield. Pink flowers rose from the dune beyond. I got out of the car with my Shoprite bag of coconuts. Lining the path to the beach were bushes of white blooms pressed against the rickety red-slatted fence. The tidal ponds along the Rhode Island coast have names like Winnapaug, Quonochontaug, Green Hill, and Ninigret. This craggy shoreline was where I intended to make things right with myself.

I headed across the ocean beach toward the breachway, a sliver of salt water connecting Ninigret Pond to the Atlantic. Granite boulders guarded the breachway, and they posed hard, unforgiving surfaces for cracking coconuts.

The two previous days had been scorchers but this evening was seventy degrees, raining lightly, getting dark. It appeared I was the only one there. The waves were fierce. Charlestown surf doesn't give a crap who you are. It's as wild and inhospitable as it wants to be.

Just as I was digging into the bag for the first coconut—"Hey, New York!" A lone fisherman, laden with rod and bucket, approached along the retaining wall. He must have spotted my license plate in the lot.

"I hope you're not going to make a mess out here." Jocular, mock-friendly tone. A slew of all-cash bids for Charlestown beach houses had run riot, squeezing out the locals. New Yorkers were an easy target.

Intending to litter, I waited, keeping my coconuts dry. Gorton Fish Sticks trudged out to the end of the jetty, thirty yards away.

Again I reached into the bag, poised to shatter my reliance on other people's opinions, cast off money as a salve, and re-acquaint myself with joy.

About the coconuts. The shell is the ego, the false self. The coconut milk, pure as gold, is the soul. I shielded myself from view against the wall of boulders. The guy wouldn't hear me over the roar of the surf. I hurled a coconut against the rocks, heard the cathartic burst as it fragmented into a million pieces. The sound was like connecting with a breaking ball and sending it over the fence. Throb went my arm, smash went another coconut—like stomping a ceremonial wine glass at a Jewish wedding. No subtlety about it. The decisive bang could alert a cadre of ghostly forefathers into blessing the ground with an age-old circle dance.

Two more coconuts exploded on the rocks, a festive demolition with shards flying. People smash cars, they smash marriages, hit their kids. But breaking coconuts was not an act of anger, but intimacy.

It was then I noticed Gorton Fish Sticks standing above me on the retaining wall, peeking into the crevice that held the broken carcasses. He used his free hand to simulate a pitching motion as his rod flailed and bucket swung, then flashed a sad little smile.

"Just go to a batting cage," he suggested. "You ever try that?"

The sky was darkening and waves broke into the shoreline at crazy angles. The last coconut in the bag I'd saved for Joshua. I wanted to tell the fisherman: *There was this boy. I helped his mother beat a child abuse conviction and later she killed him.* I almost said it plain like that. We stood staring at each other. My mouth felt dry. He had seen through my ritual.

The wind whipped and the rain flew. Still gripping the bag, I made it through the pebbled lot to my gold Malibu. On my way to Phil and Ann's Sunset Motel, my mother called. She had a way of knowing when I was trying to free myself from generations of conditioning.

"Not able to talk now," I told her, but agreed to a lunch date for later in the month.

With that last coconut festering in my bag, I tossed and turned in my motel bed, remembering the first time I'd met Norma Wilkes, and how she'd abandoned Joshua in my office. I had no idea she was a cabbie. On the phone, when we set up the consultation, she had cleaned up her borough accent and refined her diction as if she were a speech patholo-gist or a docent at the Met.

In person, she dropped her r's and let her broad a's rip. Norma had barely handed me the police report when her cab dispatcher rang her for an airport run. No one else available. I'd spilled coffee on my desk and was blotting my files with toilet paper, the only thing I could find. When I looked up she was gone.

I wasn't a damn child-care service. The kid, Joshua, nine years old, was gazing at me with raised eyebrows like I was his new babysitter. At first, I gave him a legal pad and pen. Maybe he'd like to draw a picture while I worked? But I saw his gray eyes gravitating toward an acoustic guitar I kept in the corner but hadn't played much since Bad Chemicals in high school. It was clear Joshua wanted to touch it so I told him to go ahead. He sat there, guitar in lap, his corn-silk hair feathered like the down of a baby chick, holding the instrument with the reverence of a prize eagerly sought, the newest Sony PlayStation or something.

I abandoned the pretense of work and showed him a few chord fingerings. It's hard at first, especially with steel strings. But he had tenacity. Have you ever seen a kid who's bent on whistling, or jumping rope, or snapping his fingers? He wouldn't give up. By the time Norma returned, his fingertips were swollen and red. He asked if I would give him guitar lessons, but I told him no.

A few weeks later I was home on a Saturday and Norma emailed that Joshua had taken off on a bicycle. His backpack was gone, she claimed, along with bread, cold cuts, soda. I gave her a call.

"Is he up at your house?" she asked.

"My house?"

"He wants guitar lessons."

"It's at least 25 miles," I said. "How would he even know where I live?"

Norma cleared her throat. "If it's on the internet, he knows."

I drove south on Route 22, guessing he wouldn't ride the Interstate. After a half hour of careful scrutiny, I spotted him laboring up a hill alongside opposing traffic.

I veered off the road, slipped out of the car, and ran toward him. He swerved by me, but I grabbed his handlebars and he fishtailed to a stop. Elbows over face, he covered up.

"I wouldn't hit you," I said.

"No?" he asked, stepping over the fallen bicycle. There was a bruise on his cheek.

I shook my head grimly, then loaded the bike into the back seat of my Malibu.

I almost didn't bring him home. But you can't just drop a kid off at Child Protective Services. You've got to call the hotline, file a report, and let the County deal with it. Defense lawyers are not mandated reporters. In fact, it's the opposite. Client confidentiality is sacrosanct. If I didn't return him to his mother, I'd be a kidnapper. We drove to my office. I gave him a short guitar lesson and told him to keep the guitar. Then I took him back to Norma's. Did I feel good about it? No.

6

"How about I make lunch for you at my place?" I asked Clara on the phone.

No reply.

"I live across the road from a lake—that's what the real estate agents call it. More like a large pond. I have two Adirondack chairs, a yellow canoe, and —"

"Stop already," she said, laughing. "I'll come."

My neighborhood, Lake Kitchawan, was a hilly, mixed-income hodgepodge. Some of the residents allowed old wrecks on cinderblocks to litter their driveways, others showed off their BMW's. I had roused myself into one of my rare cleaning catharses the day before, hiding the laundry, tidying up. I was pretty good at finding things to put in a frying pan: onions, peppers, mushrooms, tofu. Pesto Rosso in a jar gave it a fermented umami taste. It was waiting in a covered pan.

As a child and teen I'd been a fussy eater but those days were gone. I ate for pleasure, from nerves, to compensate for doing a job I hated. My errands were littered with treats—fresh-squeezed orange juice and dried mango at Trader Joe's, a peanut-butter-chocolate Rx bar at Stop & Shop. Whole Foods meant scoring some Lily dark chocolate sweetened with stevia. Emotional eating—all of it.

"Do you mind if I just lie down on the couch?" Clara asked as she stepped into the cottage.

I shot her a quizzical look.

"It's just that I'm not sleeping." She narrowed her eyes and dipped her head. I'd seen that expression, too. It was the snarky, faux-apologetic look she'd offer before delivering some cutesy human-interest piece.

Before I could ask for her insomnia story, she had beelined through the kitchen to the sofa in the living room, propped a pillow on the arm for her head, and kicked off her sandals.

"You're sleep-deprived?" I asked, sitting near her bare feet.

"Yeah," she agreed. "I've got this great opportunity, but it involves quitting my job, and I don't have the guts. Each night, I go over it again in my mind and end up where I started by morning. Maybe I sleep a little but I'm not aware of it."

"Do you want to tell me about the opportunity?" I asked, glancing at her toe nails—sky blue.

She gulped a breath. "If it's okay—*no*—because I get too nervous just thinking about it."

"Lie down," I said, as if she weren't already reclining. "Check your Snapchat. Relax."

I got up to warm our lunch.

"Wait." She reached for my hand and pulled me back. "I didn't mean we can't talk at all. Do you ever stay up all night worrying?"

"Uh no, I mean, yeah. I spent a night in a Rhode Island motel last weekend, and I don't think I got two hours the whole night."

"What were you thinking about?" she asked, widening her eyes.

"A bad decision." I blinked back tears, angered that I was getting emotional in front of her.

"Norma Wilkes?" she asked, surprising me. "Joshua?"

I glared at her.

"I'm a reporter," she explained.

Retreating to the kitchen, I opened the fridge. Murray's Whale Ale might lighten the mood. The waft of chilled air made me shiver. It all happened very fast—pounding heart, rush of blood to my face. I broke into a sweat, and my hands shook so violently that I dropped both bottles on the kitchen floor. Pure, unadulterated fear—the kind of chest palpitations that make you think you're having a coronary.

Clara rushed into the kitchen at the crash of the beers, mercifully unbroken. Involuntary tears were streaming down my face. My nervous system was unraveling.

"What is it, Will?"

"This happens sometimes," I stammered, short of breath.

She found a blanket in the living room and wrapped me in it, guiding me to sit. Then, applying a couple of sheets of paper towel to my face, she held me on the couch.

This was not exactly how I'd hoped our first hug would come to pass. Me shivering, taking gulps of air, tears saturating the paper towels. Needless to say, this was an absent chapter in the Real Man's Book of Seduction.

"What happened?" she asked.

When I could speak I told her. "Those nights I can't sleep," I said, "I think of all the ways it might have played out with Joshua. I drive him to Maine, or hide him in an attic, or track down a family member. Then I wake in a sweat and remember that I didn't do any of those things."

"It wasn't your job," she said flatly, as if that were the final word on the matter. "Wait here."

Clara went into the kitchen and brought back two plates of spicy tofu with vegetables, each with a fork. We ate silently, her company reassuring.

"What's this?" She was looking across the room at my altar, partially hidden by the TV. You had to sit in the corner chair to really see it, so she got up. There was a tree of life sheltering three figurines—meditating Jesus, a non-denominational Divine mother, and Ganesh, the Hindu elephant God. But what attracted her attention was a small brass pendant of Sekhmet hanging from the tree. Sekhmet had wings, breasts, long legs, and a lion head. Her miniature size did not blunt her formidability.

"I can't believe I've met a man with Sekhmet on his altar!"

I didn't feel like a man, more like a little animal in a blankie burrito.

"How do you know her?" I asked, as if talking about a mutual friend.

Sekhmet was not exactly Mother Mary. We're talking about a goddess who breathed fire, triggered plagues, and once, on a bad day, destroyed almost all of humanity before she drank a beer as big as a lake and dozed off.

How had my date, a nice, local newscaster, developed a relationship with this blood-thirsty deity? My own excuse was that she was the goddess of destruction and regeneration and I needed a stout dose of both.

"I don't know you well enough to tell you," she said, finally, folding her arms.

I would have pressed further but it was hard to keep my eyes open. My body had expended a massive amount of energy only minutes before and I crashed on the couch.

When I woke, Clara was dozing beside me; I spread the blanket over her, then went to lie down on my own bed. But now there was something else to worry about. What if I sleepwalked tonight and Clara witnessed it? I didn't want to mar my perfect record. I'd already admitted my massive crush on her. If that didn't endear her to me, the panic attack, complete with saliva and tears, surely had. But the *pièce de résistance* would be lumbering around the house with a glazed look, breaking things, as I sometimes did. And, of course, if she was the kind of girl who adored overly confessional moments and didn't flinch at the split-second explosion of a man's nervous system, never mind zombie night walks, and somehow through the grace of God, seduction transpired, how could she object to a less-than-hard penis?

So, no surprise that when Clara woke to pee in the wee hours and crossed through my bedroom to the only bathroom, she saw me lying in bed eyes-wide-open on high alert. Ostensibly reading.

"Can't you sleep?" she asked, gripping her own shoulders with crossed arms.

"I'm worried," I admitted.

"About what?" She leaned forward and focused in on me.

"Sleepwalking." I paused a beat. "With you here."

Her mouth fell open. "You do that?"

"I've started again."

"You think it's going to freak me out?" She placed a hand on her hip.

I shifted under the covers. "Wouldn't it?"

"What do you do? Traipse around like Frankenstein? Wait, I've got to pee." A strained smile.

Moments later, she walked out of the bathroom decisively as if she'd come to a vital conclusion.

"You're too fucked up to get involved with, but you're vulnerable and something moves me about that." She smiled puckishly. "Have you ever done *this* while sleepwalking?"

She kissed me. The book fell to the floor. I ignored it.

There was a luxuriousness to her kissing. It wasn't only that her lips were soft and tongue pliant. I felt like a wayward spacecraft docking to the mother ship. Our mouths sealed together. Time and place swirled down a black hole. I went dizzy, weightless. Her inner terrain was my world, urgent, warm, and wet. Everything fit, even her overbite. The pressure felt good, juiced up by her scent, her aura. The woman who I'd observed for years on TV was now suction-locked to me, her saliva anointing me as king. This was no means to an end. It was the most intimate act I could imagine. When, finally, our mouths parted, she asked if she could sleep next to me, just sleep, and I agreed.

Over breakfast in my kitchen, she teased me good-naturedly in a sisterly sort of way. If I were directing the scene, it would have been the morning after the hero lays down with the girl of his dreams. Soft gauzy filters. Warm pastels. Diffused orange/yellow light. Eye-level shots enhancing emotional impact. Tightly framed close-ups showing every detail of reaction.

But Clara was directing a sort of comedy. There was emphasis on things like the frying pan—*Yeah, I took you for a cast-iron guy*—and my morning hair—*You might use a capful of conditioner on that*—and how to remedy the hopelessly stained condition of my coffee mugs—*Brillo and elbow grease?*

Peck on the cheek. Not at all clear whether we had become anything to each other.

Before she ducked into her car, she turned and said, "Don't stick with law, Will. Experiment. Follow your bliss."

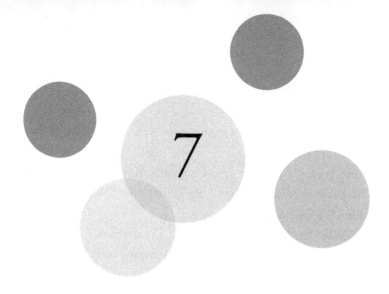

7

Saturday, July 25, 2009 Manhattan, Lower East Side

The clown meeting was in the basement of a building on Avenue D. Have I told you that I don't like to be in confined places? The ceilings were low. Chairs crammed together.

By the time I arrived, most of the recruits had already purchased their $85 clown kits and laid claim to folding chairs. The remaining seats looked like tiny islands in a sea of humanity. There was one available end stool, and I did not think I could sit through the presentation unless I scored that seat. I flashed my credit card to the man in charge of the kits, a short guy in his fifties with iron-gray hair and a pock-marked face.

The man frowned. "Cash or check," he said business-like.

I shrugged. "No credit cards?"

The man looked down at his own shoes. "Not here."

My party-clown yearnings were sufficiently embarrassing without this further indignity. It was summer, so I had no sweater or jacket to place over the stool. The requirement of cash was suggestive of a street vendor selling knock-off Gucci's. What was most distressing was the prospect of having to sit pressed against these others in a cramped basement. Just thinking about it gave me the jitters. I chanted to myself *relax and release,* walked up to the ground floor, and located a cash machine a block away. When I returned to buy the kit, sure enough, that end stool had been taken and I was left to choose between seats that were already half-impinged by hips, legs, elbows, and hands.

More people than I'd anticipated aspired to be fools. They were men and women, young and old. I slipped into a folding chair, collapsing my frame and sucking in air. The woman beside me wore a nose ring, pink lips, cartoon-penciled eyes, and hoop earrings. I avoided eye contact. Fumbling for some leg room, my knee brushed up against a codger with hair dyed blonde, sporting rouged cheeks and crayoned eyebrows.

"Sorry," I muttered, clacking my knees together. I felt squeamish, out of place. My desire to find life inside had thrown me in with society's cast-offs. *Chill,* I told myself. *God takes you out of your comfort zone.* I consoled myself by summoning up the two-inch-tall statue of the Divine Mother on my altar at home.

The instructor could not have been more casual. Like his partner selling the kits, he was in his fifties. He sat on a folding chair facing his audience, wearing jeans and a T-shirt, speaking in a Queens accent. His face was angular, voice deep, a city-stoop thespian.

"This is a change handkerchief." He reached into the sheer plastic kit bag and produced a red silk.

"Inside is a yellow tip hidden by my hand, which I produce just like this." He pulled, changing the color of the handkerchief from red to yellow. "Take it out of the bag and practice. None of these gags are hard. The important part is your story. You can sneeze into it—ah-ah-ah-ah choo! Yuck! Then get upset about making a mess. Desperate for a clean one, you pull on the hidden tip and *voila*! You've got a trick and a story to match. Notice how my story includes an emotion. I was upset." He smiled.

"Try to work that into your gags. It's more entertaining if you're scared or sad or mad or if something makes you happy. Just don't frighten the kids. Anything that puts them high and you low is good." He gestured with the handkerchief. "They want you to make a mess because they make messes."

This guy was not exactly Mister Rogers but he made sense. There was something here for me amidst the unwelcome closeness and shlock-shop vibe.

I could imagine acting scared so the kids felt brave, playing dumb so they got to be smart. A clown was a bundle of insecurities and so was I. After being trapped for so long in the frontal lobe of my brain, clowning seemed primitively emotional, thrilling even.

The instructor leaned forward. "You can repeat a gag once or twice but never more than twice." He waved a finger. "Even if the kids beg you to do it again all night, their parents will feel cheated." His forehead puckered. "And they're signing the checks. Actually, no checks." He frowned. "We insist on cash. You will take your fee out of the cash they give you and deliver the rest to us. Any tips are yours."

It was an interesting business model. There were obviously hordes of people like me, dying for a creative outlet, willing to perform for $45 a show plus tips. This brilliant scoundrel gave people a chance to express themselves in a society where such opportunities were scarce.

He proceeded to demonstrate all the tricks in the bag, but left us aspiring clowns free to construct our own stories around them, which I liked. I already had an idea for the drooping flower. Tugging on a ring around your pinkie pulled a cord that made the flower bend. I would profess my love for the flower and pucker my lips for a big kiss. The flower would bend abruptly avoiding the kiss and then I would immediately begin wooing it again with similar results.

"What about face makeup?" someone asked.

"It's all in the kit. You've got red, white, and blue." He shrugged. "Anything more you'll have to add yourself. There's also a red sponge nose, an orange fright wig, and plastic shoe covers."

They were going to book gigs and unleash us on children's parties without any testing. Was that ethical? I looked down at my bag. Enormous green clown shoes obscured the rest of the items. The thing was—I'd felt like a clown, a misfit, all my life, and this was my chance to actually be one, to act out how I *felt*.

As the workshop was wrapping up, the man with the Queens accent switched on a boom box and let loose some salsa rhythms.

"If all else fails," he said, "there's always the clown boogie." Palms down, he pumped his hands toward us like an amateur wizard. Just by that gesture I sensed that no full demonstration was imminent. "This dance," he continued, "should be totally uninhibited—flailing elbows, gyrating hips. Does anybody want to try?"

This should have been low-hanging fruit for a group of eccentrics. I expected to see them vying with each other to be called up front. No one lifted a hand. Instead, I felt mine rising.

After I hurt my knee in college, I developed a way of remaining stationary but thrusting my arms and hips to make it look like I was dancing. It was, I admit, somewhat bizarre. One of my old girlfriends had flat-out refused to dance with me. While adults shunned my twists and whirls, children greeted them with great amusement. So I got up, squeezed past the nose-ring lady, and moved to the front of the gathering.

I let my hips sway, shoulders circle, and elbows swing dangerously, something akin to boarding a rush-hour subway in Manhattan. I felt my creative impulse coalescing with pent-up fury and a sense of divine possibility. Despite the racket of sixty or so folding chairs being displaced, I didn't notice the congregation rising to their feet and adopting my style of popping hips and flying elbows. They were smiling at me as if I'd out-freaked them all. Part of me wanted to explain that no, I was actually a lawyer. But the warmth in my gut told me that I'd met my people—folks who refused to bend themselves to fit into the world.

8

Mom and I met at a brewery restaurant for lunch, although neither of us was likely to order a beer. She occasionally had a glass of wine with dinner, never with lunch. Sometimes I drank when I was stressed. Mostly I avoided it. To keep my anger under wraps I needed my wits about me.

My mother leveled her raptor eyes on me from across the table. Her red hair was cut and coifed, chin-level, in the style that she and her beauty shop in Harrison had settled on years ago. She picked at her ragged nails between sips of coffee. The familiar discomfort of being the focus of her anxiety weighed on me. I'd been the second child out of her womb. All the while she'd worried that I, too, could be born with Riley-Day syndrome, the congenital disease that killed my older brother at thirteen months.

Just to be silly, I pulled the trick handkerchief out of my pocket and changed it from red to yellow. I knew Mom wouldn't like it. Even my goofiness cloaked hostility. See why I don't drink? Passive-aggressive is better than aggressive-aggressive.

She narrowed her eyes. "What kind of grown man does tricks like that?"

I smiled. "A clown."

Mom swept a wing of red hair from her eyes. "I don't see you as a clown."

I'd spent my life trying to prevent others from thinking of me that way. "Too late," I said, "I bought the shoes."

"Oh that's funny." Mom forced a smile. "You're going to quit law and become a clown."

I steepled my fingers and maintained a gaze just below her chin.

She swallowed. "You're not really done with law?"

I took the cloth napkin off the table, spread it on my lap, and brushed off imaginary crumbs. "I don't know."

I watched the blood surge to her face. "You're ruining your life," she said.

When it was apparent that I had no rejoinder, she added, "Do you know what it's like to be poor?"

The waiter brought our entrees, salmon with spinach and mashed potatoes for me, a Mediterranean salad with shrimp and avocado for my mother. Mom was counting on my admitted peniaphobia, fear of poverty, to hobble me.

Throughout my early thirties, my mother or father had sometimes sent me money in a pinch. I glanced at my privileged little hands on the table. It was also true that I'd declared bankruptcy after law school because I couldn't pay back the student loans. The result was credit hell. No plastic for seven years. I'd never known poverty, but I was no trust fund baby either.

"*I* know what it's like to be poor," Mom said. "After my father died, my mother went to work in New Rochelle as a civil servant. We shaved it very close." She pointed a finger. "Being poor isn't as romantic as you may think."

I knew in Mamaroneck how the proximity of one's house to the railroad tracks and the Boston Post Road, and finally the Long Island Sound, defined class and position. My great grandparents, the immigrants, had been uneducated, battling to make ends meet. My grandparents found government jobs—fireman, postman. Mom and Dad were college-educated teachers who bought a house on the Sound side of the Boston Post Road.

I was their hope to attain a higher level of wealth and prestige. David had already done so, but I was the eldest and that meant something.

It wasn't that my parents needed the money. Their portfolios were adequate. It was the gospel of *Don't Fall*. Each of my male ancestors had metaphorically risen above his father. The fireman killed the baker. The teacher slayed the fireman. David and I were to murder the teacher. And Heaven knows, if I persevered as an attorney, what it might take to kill *me*.

Mom sighed. "I've made an appointment for you to see my psychologist." Her eyes flitted to her salad then back at me. "And you're going." Her upper lip pulled toward her nose when she made a pronouncement.

Have you ever noticed that when someone else takes you to a psychologist it's because they want to convince you of something?

I decided to wait until the end of lunch, and tell my mother, in no uncertain terms, that I would not see her psychologist. But after she stuck her credit card into the mini-clipboard over my protest, a feeble remonstration, I had no choice but to go.

9

It was a stroke of luck that before any disciple of Freud tried to talk me down from my clown fantasy, I actually received a call from the rogue gonifs of Avenue D. I had my first gig.

I drove down Central Avenue to Duo Pizzeria in Yonkers, a popular place for children's parties. I was scared but nothing like a jury trial. The host-mom had called and asked my clown name. "Willy," I'd told her.

"Not Buttons?" the mom asked. The birthday boy, Paul, liked a clown named Buttons who appeared on Wednesdays at Pico Fresco.

"You want Buttons?" I offered. That's me—willing to give up my identity at the drop of a hat. There was dead air on the phone while she decided.

"No, Willy is fine. Buttons sounds more like a cat."

My transformation from lawyer to clown took place in the shelter of my car at the Duo Pizzeria parking lot. I stretched on the orange wig, then opened the driver's door and struggled to fit the green-plastic covers over my furry shoes. Plain stupid to wear Hushpuppies. I applied white make-up and the red nose.

A young child getting out of an adjacent car pointed at me and said, "Look Mommy, a scary clown."

Scary? I restrained myself from howling a sullen "Boo!" My insides felt like a whirring blender. Scary was the last thing I wanted to be.

The restaurant parking lot wasn't particularly busy. Too late for lunch—not quite dinner time. They probably scheduled these parties so regular patrons wouldn't be irritated by creepy clowns. Tentatively I opened the driver's door then pulled it shut—not ready to be seen.

Tapping into meditating Jesus or faceless Divine Mother was futile. I wasn't on their wavelength. I reached into the center console for a mint and nicked my hand on a disposable razor. It was there in case I'd forgotten to shave. Blood stained my fingers. Scary wasn't the word—menacing more like it. After cleaning and clotting the blood with a tissue, I grabbed my puppets, slammed the door behind me, and silly-walked through the parking lot.

Truckin' up the stairs, in my get-up, with puppet bag in tow, I got a smile from a lady who held open the front door of the restaurant. The world was making room for me.

There was an aisle leading from the entrance into the main dining area where speakeasy-style lamps and fans hung from the ceiling. Adorning the brick walls were vintage photographs.

A woman with a frantic smile was waving from a checkerboard table of three mothers and a crew of seven-year-olds. When I signaled, her face relaxed. No doubt she had been contemplating the prospect of winging it without me. Shifting her jaw, she mouthed something to her friend beside her.

"Willy," a boy called. Must be Paul the birthday boy.

"Hello!" I hurried to the table, swiping off my glasses. The room went blurry.

"You've got to help me!" I said to Paul, sitting at the head of the table. "I'm supposed to be at the party of a boy named . . . Paul . . . who's turning seven. But I got lost and can't find it. I've been looking everywhere! Can you tell me where the party is?"

I fell to my knees. "Please, you've got to help me. I'm going to be late for the party."

I caught sight of the mothers and each had some version of a thin smile.

"Uh, Willy," Paul said.

"Yes?"

"It's my party. I'm the birthday boy."

"Oh, congratulations Paul! I feel so embarrassed. Let me come in all over again."

The host mother cast a conspiratorial glance at her friends. I wiped a bead of blood against my red trick flower, scurried out, and returned silly-walking. Now all the seven-year-olds at the table were watching.

"Willy," Paul asked, "are you a real clown?"

I almost said yes but the funnier answer was *no.*

"No, I'm not, and I'm so scared because I think you were expecting a real one. Paul, please don't tell anyone." I nodded toward the other kids, ignoring the adults.

"I think they already heard you."

"Ohhh, I feel embarrassed. I'm scared to do my first puppet."

"What is it?"

"You really want to know?"

"Yes," said Paul.

"Do you want to know, too?" I ran back and forth from one side of the table to the other. The mothers' faces were alert, eyes peeled.

"Yes!" The kids cried.

They were buying my act. They liked the nervous guy who wasn't a real clown and didn't even know he was at the right party.

Then one of them shouted, "No!" Light blue eyes, manic smile. The wise guy.

I swooped into a prone position and covered my head.

"Yes!" the others cried. I jumped up happy like a puppy and reached into my bag.

"No!" the one kid insisted. I dropped to the floor again.

"Willy, show us your trick," Paul said.

I sidled up to Paul. The wise guy said *no* again and again but I sprung a puppet from the bag anyway.

My back shielded it from everyone but Paul. "I'll just show *you*," I said.

"We want to see too!"

The kids got up from the seats and crowded around, all eyes, not saying a word. The mothers were blocked out. I'd found my sea legs. Not knowing exactly what I'd do next didn't bother me.

The puppet I produced looked like Joe Camel. It felt sticky inside.

My cut finger. One mother stood up and groaned.

"This is Monty," I said to the kids. "Monty likes to say *no*."

"Monty, is it a beautiful day outside?" I asked. It had been a perfect summer day.

"No!" Monty replied emphatically with a growling Bronx accent.

The kids laughed.

"Monty," I purred in a saccharine voice, "are you happy today?"

"No!" Monty bellowed.

The know-it-all kid was laughing so hard he almost fell off his chair.

"Monty," I dropped further into cloying pretense, "why aren't you happy today, sweetheart?"

Monty didn't answer immediately. "I," he began "got" slight pause "boo-boo!"

Some kids looked quizzically at each other, but the bigmouth went into hysterics, slipping onto the tile floor. Once the others saw him writhing at their feet they giggled too.

"Is your boo-boo on your nose?" I poked Joe Camel's nose.

"No!"

Laughter.

"Is it on your belly?" I tickled the puppet.

"No!"

More laughter.

I had them now.

At the end of the performance, Paul said, "Willy, I love you." His mother, a dimpled blonde, was all smiles handing me the envelope.

Safe in the car, I rested my head on the steering wheel. An unexpected feeling surfaced: happiness. A sign of inner life. That it had required wearing face paint in a Duo Pizzeria seemed trivial for the moment. Maybe you *can* change your insides with something outside! When I checked the envelope there was no tip. Zilcho. I'd made $45 for the afternoon. Tomorrow my mother would accompany me to her therapist and slip him a check for at least four times that amount.

10

Monday, August 3, 2009 Scarsdale, NY

I admit it was weird for my mother and me to share a therapy session as if we were a couple in a bad marriage. Driving down Old White Plains Road, Mom began naming every field of law in hope that one would resonate and bring me back to my senses. Couldn't I squeeze myself into one of these fine vessels?

I steadied myself. "Mom, I want to be an entertainer." Even in my own head it was as if I had said, *I want to be the pay-pig of a dominatrix.*

She let out a protracted moan like a humpback whale. "Over my dead body."

Mom didn't much care if she sowed disharmony. As far as she was concerned disharmony better watch out for *her.*

We entered a seven-gabled Tudor building in Scarsdale where her analyst had his suite. Ten minutes later he fetched us from the waiting room.

The doctor's office was a reassuring blend of mahogany woodwork and a classic Persian rug. He was a slight, bespectacled man with thinning dark hair and a beard. My mother's collaborator. A diploma on the wall showed that he was a Columbia PhD with a Jewish name. It was telling that my mother sought counsel with a man so much younger, as if all the years she'd amassed genuflected to his diploma.

"Doctor," Mom said before we even sat down, "this is Will. I'm afraid he's going to live on the street soon." She slipped him the check.

I wondered if she would be this agitated if she and Dad were still together. He lived in Fort Lauderdale now. Mom held onto her job, teaching remedial reading, in White Plains for the full pension. They were trying to get rid of her—making her teach in the cold modular classrooms hastily built on an old soccer field. But she was not so easy to defeat, even on two new artificial knees.

The doctor smiled and shook my hand. He motioned for us to sit. "Your mother believes that if you leave law you won't be able to support yourself."

"He'll end up living with me," Mom said, raising her chin.

The analyst steepled his fingers. "Is she right?"

I felt my temples grow uncomfortably hot and the office walls close around me. The drop ceiling seemed oppressively low. I hadn't made it big as an attorney. A lot of lawyers didn't despite the pervasive myth that all of us did. This doctor, I was certain, invited his mom to a fancy brunch on Mother's Day, and whisked her off to Belize with his family on Spring Break. Indeed, the man's forehead was tanned. But was he really cut out to be a psychologist? Maybe he didn't care.

I closed my eyes. "I want to love my work," I said quietly. Not a manly thing to say. Men weren't supposed to worry about that. They shut up and did their duty. Women would reward us by making nice to our anesthetized selves.

"What work do you think you might love?" the psychologist asked.

"I don't know." I shrugged. "So far working as a clown at parties." I tried to check the perverse smile creeping over my lips.

"He's very convincing," Mom said, as if this were part of my disease. "A wife and a baby would set you straight." She glared at me then glanced expectantly at the doctor who shifted in his seat.

"I wouldn't recommend marriage and children as a way to resolve a life crisis," he said. Nervously, he rotated his gold wedding ring.

The doctor and I were about the same age. He was the answer to his parents' prayers. Mom had told me in the car that psycho-analysts like him were big on frequent sessions. But she only consulted him at critical junctures in her life—like today. I guess he didn't mind taking her occasional checks even if she flouted the analytic design.

Mom made her eyes as big as she could. "So you think Will is having a life crisis?"

The doctor grimaced. Just when he probably thought he'd settled one issue, she'd opened another using his phrase. Always a mistake to sell her short.

He ran his tongue against his upper teeth. "I suppose so," he said, "but it's not my place to diagnose your son, Mrs. Ross."

She knitted her eyebrows. "You think I was foolish to bring him in?"

"I didn't say that." He offered a weak smile.

"But it puts you in a difficult situation." Her face went hangdog. She stared at him.

Now the analyst was the beleaguered party. He slouched forward. "Mrs. Ross, what is it that you really want?"

She perked up. "I want my son happy being a lawyer."

I imagined that was true, and sweet, though misguided. She was a great believer that square pegs could be hammered into round holes— and be tickled about it.

The doctor sighed. "That's not your choice. It's his."

Mom's shrink had sided with me. I smelled victory.

Her shoulders shrunk and face narrowed. I swear her chair was swallowing her.

The doctor glanced at his watch then rubbed his hands together briskly.

"Doctor," Mom said, her voice raspy, "he's sleepwalking again."

That launched a discussion around somnambulation even more cringeworthy than my admission that I liked working as a clown. Mercifully, I was able to keep my cool until the session timed out.

By this time, you may be asking yourself: Was being a lawyer really as bad as I insist? Settle a few cases, file a motion or two, occasionally go to trial. I could come and go as I pleased. Cash business. No boss or supervisor. Not exactly breaking rocks on a chain gang.

Yeah, except my inability to organize my environment was alarming, somewhere between Sherlock Holmes and Oscar the Grouch. Some methodology for order is essential to keep track of voluminous files, daily court dates, and frequent deadlines. My only hope was The Enforcer. That's what I called him. I would merrily let folders pile up on my desk until they heightened into gravity-defying twin towers. At some point, following a metamorphosis that I can only call Hulk-like, The Enforcer appeared.

He was a tough guy like David Fury and he was furious at me. What the fuck is this? No one around here does shit. So now we're doing it my way. We're going to classify and file every stinking paper on this desk before anyone sleeps tonight. I don't want to hear a whimper out of you, understand? This is your shit show. There's a motion due tomorrow. You still haven't prepared for the cross-examination of the police officer next week. I do all the goddamn work around here. You take off midday and sit in the hot tub at the recreation center. Don't test me! Skinning a cat wouldn't take the fizz off my rage. That's it— pick up the first paper. File it. Now the second. Don't even think about food. There's not going to be any. And so on. By the end of this I was exhausted, my nerves frazzled, but the work was up to date. Cue Mr. Ineffectual. He would return craving book-store espressos and frequent massages to soothe his transit through the world. Even with all this, it had taken a boy's death to make me seriously contemplate quitting.

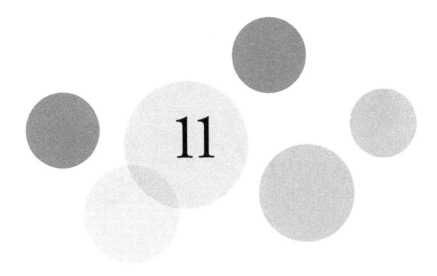

11

Over two weeks had gone by since my date with Clara. That parting peck on the cheek meant tepid interest. No other way to read it. When I'd called to give her an account of my clown meeting, her vibe was friendly—nothing more. So, when her name flashed on my iPhone, I interrupted a call with a client's probation officer to take it, and stood up from my law-office desk to clear my head.

"Clara!"

"I'm calling from work." She sounded distracted.

"What's up?" I asked.

"I want to do a feature on you."

"Oh, you do? How come?"

"You're trading in your wingtips for clown shoes. That's a catchy hook."

A warning pumped through my gut, but I was too high on her call to pay it much heed.

"Knock yourself out," I said with more nonchalance than I felt.

"So you're okay with it?" There was a tinge of reporterly verification in her tone.

"Yeah, that's fine."

12

Wednesday, August 5, 2009 White Plains, NY

The next morning I tuned into her morning news show on my office desktop. There was a story of a lawyer who decided he'd chosen the wrong gig and would rather be a clown. Me.

An afternoon text: *Check out the story!*

A few minutes later: *Would u drive me home from a gas station near the studio? The Civic is making strange noises.*

She could probably tell something was wrong the moment she got into the car. I didn't smile or greet her. Instead, I turned slowly and offered a half nod.

"Hey!" she said, but I didn't meet her gaze.

Sliding a finger inside my glasses, I rubbed an eye. "I saw the piece," I said.

"Yes," she nodded, "the one on you." She pursed her lips, trying to read me.

I put the car into drive and started down Central Avenue past City Limits Diner toward the Bronx River Parkway.

"I didn't mind the part about the Wilkes child abuse case," I said. "But the ending insinuated I didn't have the temperament for law. Who wants to hire a lawyer like that?"

I expelled a sudden noisy breath through my nose—a snort.

"You said you were fine with it." Her voice broke, and rose an octave. "I thought you were quitting law."

"Yeah, I thought so too," I admitted. "Now I don't know."

Clara frowned. "I'm this close to leaving the station and doing contract work filming a documentary. You've inspired me." I glanced over. Her face was flushed.

I changed lanes and got on the parkway. "I guess I didn't realize that I was taking down my shingle on live cable TV," I said.

The intensity of feeling surprised me. On the one hand I wanted to quit, and on the other, you'd have to pry my law career out of my death-gnarled digits with a crowbar. It had taken a good deal of work to mutate an eccentric screwball into an honest-to-God lawyer, and damned if I was going reverse the metamorphosis, my one accomplishment of a lifetime.

Clara's face was now beet red. Maybe it was dawning on her that, despite my consent, she might have thought twice. More precisely, I'd been a total idiot for agreeing to it.

"I'm sorry," she said, gazing down at her folded hands. "I see what you mean."

We were driving on the Bronx River Parkway, the granddaddy of landscaped thoroughfares in Westchester County. Traffic lights, hairpin turns, but still the best way to get to the Bronx.

The tension in the car came down a notch. The sun shone through the passenger window emblazoning that beautiful profile. She blocked the rays with her hand.

"You get off at East 233rd Street," she said. "Go up McLean Avenue and take a left on Vireo."

I vaguely knew of Woodlawn, a celebrated destination of the Irish throughout the world. The Gaelic kingdom. Bars lining McLean Avenue were legend, although I'd never been to one.

"That's McKeon's and that's the Heritage," she said, as if pointing out the Colosseum and the Trevi Fountain.

She directed me to park in front of the building. Instead, I pulled into the driveway.

Clara paused. "Well thanks," she said.

"How are you going to pick up your car?" I asked, stalling.

"I'll take the train up to White Plains tomorrow morning," she said.

I decided to press it. "You're not going to invite me in?"

She hesitated. Could it be because she lived with her parents? That fact had come out the morning after she stayed over. They were Irish immigrants. Maybe she didn't share her private life with them. It was clear that she would prefer not allowing me up. But guilt seemed to be working in my favor. I'd chauffeured her home and it was rude to not have me in.

She squirmed in the passenger seat. "You're welcome to come," she said curtly.

She buzzed her parents from the lobby, although a key was in her hand.

"Yes," I heard through the tinny speaker.

"I'm bringing up a friend," she said, screwing her mouth to the side, apparently regretting it already.

That just made me more curious. This was, after all, not only a woman I'd kissed, but Clara McLaughlin of "Live at Nine." Now I was going to meet her parents and see where she lived.

Clara's mom, having just rung us in, was already returning to her knitting on the living room couch. She waved. Her dad was splayed out on a recliner and simply nodded. They were a couple in their sixties watching "Beachfront Bargain Hunt." I'd caught it once or twice on lonely late afternoons, a show that demonstrated how inexpensively people could buy beach houses in Crystal Beach, Texas, or Lincoln City, Oregon, or Fripp Island, South Carolina. It culminated with the family celebrating their new abode by frolicking in the waves or picnicking on the sand.

Watching Clara's parents sunk deep in their cushions, I remembered the appeal of the show—its spell—as a numbingly-comfortable travelogue.

This paradox may surprise you: Along with being an anxiety-ridden sleepwalker, I was also a snob with a lengthy list of what I deemed déclassé. It definitely covered watching television in the daytime. In fact, it was comprised of everything I observed around Clara's parents' apartment: the Hummel figurines, Thomas Kinkade prints, the faux hearth in the living room. All of it rankled, especially the exaggerated luminance of those humble Kinkade abodes. But of course, these were the parents of Clara McLaughlin, so instantly an internal war commenced, as the love-sick puppy argued that maybe my taste was questionable, and the arrogant intellectual scoffed at the thought.

These forces clashed inside me consuming the lion's share of my attention, but no matter, the parents offered no further greeting. Even when I sat between Clara and her mother on the couch, no one said a word.

Why, I wondered, did what they hung on their wall matter? My hollow superiority astounded me. Why should I care about the peculiarity of their taste? But then it hit me. Since the kiss, I'd already begun to see Clara as compensation, or at least a cushion, for my imminent fall in rank should I leave law. I was depending on her to keep my stock from dipping too low. And as such, Hummel, Kinkade, and daytime TV didn't bode well. They destroyed the illusion.

So immediately, I decided that they were *not* her parents, just as on "The Munsters," blonde Marilyn could not be Herman's daughter. Once I'd made this mental adjustment I felt better and started enjoying "Beachfront Bargain Hunt."

When the commercial came on, the woman posing as mother, a short redhead, swiveled toward me and deadpanned, "Are you two dating? She tells us nothing."

I glanced at Clara for guidance. She gave no sign. "I'm the one your daughter profiled on her show today," I said, rolling my eyes. "The one that didn't have the right temperament for the law."

Dad frowned. "Well, do you?" he asked gruffly. He was long-legged and trim with cropped gray hair.

"No," I admitted.

"So, she was telling the truth." He let out a throaty chortle.

My cheeks felt hot. I glanced toward the window and looked longingly across the street to the shops on McLean Avenue.

"We don't get 'Live at Nine' here," the mother explained. "It's a local show in White Plains."

Amusement played on Dad's lips. "What will you do if not law?" he asked.

I hesitated.

His face reddened. "*You* must be the one telling Clara to leave the station, eh?"

Clara shot her father a withering glance. "No, Dad. That's Joe from work. Not Will. Although, I do have another job offer."

He stood up from his easy chair, bent to open a cabinet below the television, and removed a bottle of Jameson whiskey. He poured two glasses and handed one to me.

There was a devilish pucker to his lips as he offered a toast. Again, I looked to Clara for help. She chuckled and showed interest in an ocean vista in Destin, Florida, letting me fend for myself.

I raised the glass and took a swallow. Clara's father slammed down his empty tumbler.

"Arm wrestling!" he cried.

He retreated to the foyer table. Tilting his chair back on two legs, he stretched his long body. Then he placed the crook of his elbow square on the tabletop, and motioned for me to join him. It was a sucker's offer. I could see that. On the table were the pink, bouncy Spaldeens he used for strengthening his grip with the insignia of Woodlawn Gorilla Arm-Wrestling. I'd noticed a pull-up bar in the bedroom doorway. Clara sputtered out a word or two, perhaps intending to intervene, but then seemed to think better of it.

I assumed a seat at the table, placed my elbow, and clasped hands with Clara's father, feeling my cheeks grow progressively warmer as I strained against him. He lent me a whiff of false confidence by allowing me to gain superior position—the old man's wrist bending backwards toward the table. Abruptly with violent force, he jerked his wrist and slammed me down. I pulled my hand away and gazed incredulously as blood filtered to my skin through micro-abrasions.

"Stick with law," he barked. "And don't be giving my girl ideas about leaving her job."

I glanced at each of them briefly, one by one, the whole asylum, then rose, passed through the foyer, opened the door with my left hand, and fled.

The shame felt like bees swarming and stinging around my chest and throat. I couldn't catch my breath. It occurred to me that I might not be able to survive without the professional identity I'd nurtured all these years.

13

Saturday, August 15, South Salem, NY

I called her.

"Hi—you know I was really humiliated when your father slammed my hand against the table."

Silence on the other end.

"Failing like that in front of you was excruciating."

Nothing.

"Like in sixth grade, when I ran for classroom president, and this one girl, Wendy Barsotti, made posters for me. It turned out she was my only vote. I couldn't face her after that."

"Don't mind my father," Clara said, finally. "Truth is, he doesn't want me to leave home so he tries to scare men away. That's why I preferred you didn't come up, but I had no choice because you drove me home, and I ran that story you didn't like." She paused. "Any more clown gigs?"

"No," I said, drawing breath as if I'd surfaced from five fathoms. "My friend, Ray, told me that you can't lose a duel with the father of your—well, what are we anyway?" I waited in vain for her to define us. Again, no response. "Then I dreamed about visiting my own grave."

"You could at least visit *his* grave," she said.

I knew who she meant. She was right. Still, I wasn't so keen on it. "I don't even know where it is," I grumbled.

I could feel the eye roll on the other end of the line.

"Meet me at the White Plains Library. Bring your laptop."

This wasn't what I'd call a date, yet I felt a surge in the pit of my stomach, snaking up to my heart. Clara McLaughlin still wanted to spend time with me.

The library study room was a glass cell with table and chairs and a view of the courthouse across the street. Clara sat waiting for me, her long dark hair hiding one eye, and it reminded me of years ago when I would meet my college girlfriend in the library to cram. After we broke up, I burned every gift she'd given me in a makeshift funeral pyre. Studious girls had always appealed to me.

Clara wore a white embroidered shirt with butterfly sleeves and a V-neck. Her green jeans were slashed from thigh to shin, hippie-style, with tanned knees showing through. She already had her laptop out and I could tell that she was on to something, her eyes flashing from the screen to me, then back again. I peeked over her shoulder but she waved me off and motioned to a chair across the rectangular table.

"What are you so revved about?" I asked.

She ignored me, tucking a shock of hair behind her ear. Then with a burst of nervous energy, she produced a lipstick from a sling across her shoulder and began applying it, sucking in her lips for an even spread, checking the result on her cell phone camera. I paid close attention.

"Do you know what closure is?" she asked, putting away the lipstick. I nodded.

She leaned forward. "That's what you need. Closure." She focused on the screen and tapped some keys. "Did it ever occur to you where Joshua might be buried?"

"Of course," I said, touching my throat.

"Where do you think?" she asked—like we were playing twenty questions—animal, mineral, or vegetable?

My shoulders twitched. What would happen to the son of a poor, incarcerated mother? "Maybe their church stepped in?" That would be plausible.

Clara exhaled a small, disappointed puff of air. "Not in Westchester County. Here it's a government function."

Okay. I didn't like thinking about dead bodies. Just as I preferred to ignore bills I'd stuck in the desk drawer or pictures of my college girlfriend tucked-away in a photo album. There were a lot of damn things I chose to dodge, and Clara had already demonstrated a talent for sticking them in my face. I was afraid of death and she'd led me into close proximity with a shark. For years, I'd avoided quitting a profession I hated and she announced my departure on cable TV. Damn it Clara, I'd taken pains to make my life as carnage-free as possible—no wife, no kids. There was no way I wanted to, in any way, exhume Joshua.

I had one more guess. "The county coroner?"

"Right," said Clara, grinning like the fabled cat, engrossed in whatever misguided zeal was rousing her quest. "I called the coroner."

"And?"

"She told me virtually nothing—except they have an arrangement with the New York City Coroner's Office involving indigents."

My MacBook was up and running. I googled. A page surfaced.

"City burial," I read. "Cemetery on Hart Island serves as New York City's public cemetery and is maintained by the New York City Department of Corrections."

"Go on." Clara's eyes lit up.

"Hart Island gravesite visits. Family members and their invited guests can visit those interred at Hart Island by making arrangements in advance with the New York City Department of Correction (DOC), the agency responsible for maintaining the Island."

Clara lowered her head, staring over my shoulder as if she saw something there.

"We're not family members," I cautioned. "It was a good thought but —"

She ignored me. "Do you have power of attorney?"

I remembered Norma handing me a folded proxy in the county jail. There'd been no time to return it. Slowly I nodded, wondering if candor was the right move.

"Then you have authority to act on her behalf. *We*," she repeated the word, "*we* could step into her shoes and visit Joshua at Hart Island."

My college girlfriend had once taken me to task for never using the word *we*. "With you it's *I this and I that,* never we." "We" was a signifying word to women and yes, I wanted me and Clara to be a *we*. But instinctively I shrank from visiting a pauper's island grave—even if, in fact, Joshua was there. Stepping in as parents of a child, even a dead one, implied a frightening level of commitment. Also, Clara's motivations weren't clear, and I suspected she was writing a story. Or maybe, my college girlfriend had been on the mark—I was not a *we*.

"Are we a *we*?" I asked.

She shrugged. "Let's see."

14

Saturday, August 22, 2009 Bronx, Hart Island

We sat on the big orange ferry to Hart Island along with twenty-odd family members of interred indigents. City Island was fading away amidst the morning fog. It was comforting to have Clara there with me, her hair still damp and glistening. It gave off drifts of rosemary and thyme as the wind kicked up on deck.

Before our research, I'd never heard of Hart Island where New York City buried its anonymous or needy dead. Joshua had been "unclaimed." That meant neither Norma Wilkes nor any family members hired a private funeral director.

When Norma had forced a Power-of-Attorney into my hands, it never occurred to me that I would use it to visit her son's grave on her behalf. There were strict rules of access to Hart Island but the document allowed us to finagle our way onto the ferry. Clara's idea. Why was she so interested in my closure or lack of it?

The Long Island Sound, off City Island, glinted a cobalt blue under the shining sun. If you overlooked the orange ferry, resembling a mid-century tug, you might delude yourself into imagining a more carefree locale, shuttling off to Martha's Vineyard. But that fiction would be quickly belied by even a momentary review of the passengers. They were young women with dour faces, looking nothing like holiday seekers.

Clara seemed comfortable talking to strangers, something I usually avoided.

"Who are you visiting?" she asked a curly-haired girl with large, sorrowful eyes.

"My baby," the girl replied. "They buried him before I woke from anesthesia."

Without provocation, other women sitting near us murmured, "my baby."

It sent a chill through my sternum and Clara must have caught my look of dread.

"Stillbirths or neonatal deaths that occurred in New York City hospitals," she whispered.

"How 'bout you, boss?" the brown-eyed girl asked, eying me.

I felt like an imposter at a funeral—just there for the hors d'oeuvres. I wasn't like these women who had gone through the harrowing experience of giving birth and losing the baby. My parents had gone through that too, and it was the type of thing that destroyed marriages, haunted people for the rest of their lives. How was I going to explain my presence on this ferry to this hollow-eyed girl?

I said nothing, and she must have taken it as grief beyond words because she started to cry. This ushered me into the community of mourners. It was as if they'd enveloped me, had laid hands on my shoulders, my chest and abdomen, my temples and cheeks. Not one so much as moved but I felt it. And of course I didn't deserve it. I stood up and literally shook myself like a duck. Clara followed me to the bow where I found a seat away from the others.

I remembered my speech to the jury at the child abuse trial: *Norma Wilkes had the courage to do what was required that night. It was not a pleasant task but it was her duty as a parent. This is a case of a mother trying to take charge of an uncontrollable boy. Joshua Wilkes needed to be disciplined.*

I had objected to the admission of police photos showing multiple bruises on his arms, legs, back and buttocks, because the cop who witnessed the injuries couldn't testify. A technicality. I won the case. Joshua lost his life. As I looked over the bow into the waters of Pelham Bay Lagoon, my shame was overwhelming. These women, who I was trying to avoid, were innocent. I was guilty.

"What's wrong?" asked Clara.

"Nothing," I said.

She wasn't buying it. Front teeth dug into her plump bottom lip, she shook her head.

"You're in hell, aren't you?"

The question hung in the air. My first instinct was to defend myself. Then I looked at her. No attitude. She really wanted to know.

I nodded and closed my eyes against the tears.

"Don't you want *you* back?" she asked.

I put a hand over my eyes and shivered from shoulders to knees.

"Then you've got to face it."

I peeked through my fingers at her. "Why are you doing this? For a story?"

"No."

"Fun and games?"

She shook her head.

"An experiment?"

She gave me the bad eye.

Then what?"

She shrugged.

"I'd rather not sit with those women," I said.

She smiled. "You're scared."

"Isn't everybody scared of death?"

"You're scared of women." Her eyes glowed with an unnerving intensity. And yes, she frightened me, too.

"What do they do when they reach the island?" I said, thinking out loud.

"We all synchronize our menstrual cycles," quipped Clara. "Then, male sacrifice."

"No, really. What are all of these baby-less women going to do there?"

Clara stared me down. "Have you ever considered that your fears are really a way to avoid feeling anything? Have you ever just quieted down and let yourself have an emotion? That's the way we scary women do it—we just sit down and make a little space for it."

I sat on the bow away from all the women and closed my eyes. I felt pain and panic—and watched it—like observing dark angry clouds in the sky. The sense of failure was overwhelming and it would have been easier to sound an alarm and jump into some kind of frenetic action. Instead, I scrutinized the cavernous loss. It was almost intolerable. If the space I inhabited was a hotel, I would have berated the manager.

Me: How dare you put me in this room! It's bleak and gloomy. There's no floor and a sense of falling forever. No door, lights, or running water. And there's a little child screaming his head off.

Manager: That child is yours, sir.

Me: But I abandoned him thirty-odd years ago. Why the hell did you give me his room?

Manager: That room has been waiting for you since you deposited him here. You made the reservation. Would you like me to defer the booking for an additional thirty? That would make you sixty-seven. Would you prefer to deal with him then, sir?

Me: Yes, of course I would prefer to deal with him then. But who knows what kind of havoc that little devil is going to wreak with my heart, intestines, or white blood cells during that time. What the hell does he want?

Manager: He wants you to pay him attention.

Me: But there's so much pain.

Manager: That will happen when a guest leaves his little guy in a room for thirty years. Not recommended. We can't take responsibility.

Me: Do you have a senior manager? Can I speak to him or her?

Manager: Of course, but you've got to place your call from the inside.

Me: From inside that room?

Manager: Yes exactly, sir.

Me: Can you give me any guidance at all?

Manager: Just relax, that's the best way. Relax and make yourself at home.

As the ferry drew closer to the island, my soul sank further and further into a vortex of hopelessness and futility. If this was the way women dealt with their feelings, it seemed like a good advertisement for running away from the little buggers your entire life. It was just too damn heartbreaking. As if this weren't enough, I could see ruins of brick buildings ahead, windows missing, roofs crumpled. Finally, we squeezed closely between two gates, making firm contact with the ferry slip.

The women rose, very respectful of each other, no one jostling for position. Clara and I let them all pass and took up the rear. I reached for the paper in my pocket with its six-digit number.

The passengers filed off the ferry. They ambled together, chatting in groups of four or five, making their way onto dry land.

From the ferry, I could see the ruin of a Victorian-style building with a double exterior staircase and steeply-pitched roof. One of the corrections officers was ushering passengers onto the dock. I asked her about the old brick relic.

"That's the Pavilion," she said. "It used to be a women's insane asylum. Later, a jail."

"When?" I asked.

"Oh, like the late eighteen hundreds."

"And what about that church?" I pointed to a Gothic chapel with a circular rose window missing all its stained glass—obviously abandoned.

"That goes back to the 1930s," she said, "designed by a famous architect but I forget his name."

Clara gave a lopsided grin, admiring the corrections officer's grasp of island history. I considered all the prayers uttered in that church for the multitude of souls buried here.

We followed the women down the path to the cemetery portion of Hart Island. Once they were a safe distance from the officers manning the boat and ferry slip, the women began removing pieces of firewood from satchels or tote bags that I'd not really noticed on the ferry. They split off into groups, doused the wood with small vials of lighter fluid, and lit modest fires on the ground. This was illegal certainly. They'd all come armed with wood, matches, and fuel.

I don't have to tell you how this accorded with my most agitated misgivings about these mourners. Their fires implied to me some kind of biblical sacrifice like Abraham binding his son on an altar at Mount Moriah.

Clara exchanged glances with me. God knows what dread was filtering through my attempts to disguise it. She ventured over to a four-women clan that already had flames crackling in the shadow of a concrete, rectangular monument that said *Peace*. Hadn't her mother warned her about talking to strangers?

"How do you know each other?" she asked.

One of them, a young woman with a ring on each finger, said, "We carpool to the ferry." Her flat American vowels broke the spell and alleviated some of my anxiety.

Was I the only one who had a burial number from the Corrections Department? None of them seemed to have a clue where their babies might be interred. As Clara and I made our way past the cluster of small fires, the mourners seemed arbitrarily positioned, not fixed to any marker. I glanced back and noticed that some of the women were showing keen interest as to where we might be heading.

"Please don't let them follow us," I muttered through my teeth.

Clara rolled her eyes. "You're unhinged. You know that?"

We came upon a bulldozed field marring the verdant landscape. Here, markers with numbers littered the damp, brown earth.

Even before we found the correct location, I saw them approaching. Some of the women had doused and abandoned their fires, and were trailing us to the leveled grave site. Others still carried their firewood, not yet having set it aflame.

Would it unnerve you to have a horde of would-be mothers tracking you through the ruins of an island that hid the bodies of untold indigents buried and reburied since the Civil War? When my older brother died as an infant, my parents, like any respectable couple of their generation, never again said a word about it. I found his photos in a drawer when I was ten. So why did these women parade through this island of death on monthly ferry expeditions? I knew it amounted to a healthy demonstration of grief. But my parents would find it distressing, and I wasn't all that comfortable with it either.

Number 675926, Joshua's grave, was just one white plastic marker among many, strewn across a newly-created interment site. Clara and I sat down in the moist, roiled dirt. Several women followed and settled in about ten yards away. At least they allowed us that much room. More ferry women were coming. Maybe the stillborn and neonatal corpses were buried in mass graves and that's why none of the women had location numbers. Something about a definite spot must have attracted them.

A few who'd assembled around the grave were crying, and it was a surprise to me that my own cheeks were damp. I wasn't even aware of feeling anything. How does that work? Clara held my hand to comfort me.

The women who had not yet burned their firewood, stacked their sticks and small logs, splashed on some lighter fluid, and lit a blaze. The flames rose, fanned by the wind, greedily consuming the wood. Some of the mourners got up and foraged for sticks, feeding the hunger of the bonfire. That ravenousness seemed to portray the earth's unquenchable appetite for human bodies—all of them forever and ever. What might be left when the body was gone?

After some time, with the fire exhausted, and fuel spent, the women left me and Clara alone at the site.

"I wish I could ask him for forgiveness," I said.

Clara took a breath. "Try."

"No, I mean—and he could talk back."

Clara bit her lower lip. There were beads of sweat above the upper one. She shrugged, implying stranger things had happened.

"You know how to do this?" I asked. There was a trace of willingness, a feeling of pressure below my rib cage.

She nodded. "It's simple, especially when you've been lowered down a peg. The humility helps. Just ask him and listen. Really listen."

It started to thunder then, a low rolling rumble across the Long Island Sound, the kind that brings a dog to his master's feet whimpering.

"Close your eyes," instructed Clara.

I did.

"Find Joshua. He might be a sensation in your heart or throat, or even a light you can sense just above your crown."

I focused. Below my rib cage I felt something.

Raindrops splatted on the dry dirt around us. I peeked to see if that would deter Clara, but it didn't, so I remained motionless. The rumble was a vibration not only audible but palpable. I felt it in my body. A keen awareness in my solar plexus buzzed while the thunder clattered like herds of horses galloping across the Sound.

"Tell him something," prompted Clara.

"I'm sorry I put winning the trial over you," I muttered.

"Ask him something," said Clara.

"What do you mean?"

"Ask for forgiveness."

I complied.

"Just wait and breathe," she said. "Sometimes we treat dead people like we treat animals. We assume they can't talk back. We feel superior. Let that go. Focus on where you feel him. See what happens."

I felt him like a spinning top, wildly whirling in my solar plexus. My first thought was that such untamed gyrations were blatantly unspiritual. But I reminded myself that I knew nothing about this. Refocusing on the sensation, I again asked Joshua for forgiveness. An unmistakable *yes* exploded like a mushroom cloud below my ribs.

The rain was coming down hard now, quickly drenching us. We ran the path to the ferry whooping like kids playing cowboys and Indians.

When we took our seats in the sheltered part of the ferry, the women applauded. It had something to do with acceptance, a salute. I bowed to them. Had they somehow sensed something emerging within me? This felt like the real thing.

Clara's hair was sopped, shirt sticking to her breasts. She was beautiful. This angel had introduced a strange element into my existence, one I couldn't put in any cubbyhole. Even with my altar, my meditation, my daily prayers, there lurked a doubter underneath. Clara was a believer.

One long horn blast preceded three shorter ones. I could hear the propellers of the ferry begin to rotate, bringing bubbles to the surface which broke with staccato pops. We lurched forward.

The corrections officer, who'd offered tidbits of Hart Island history, came our way. She paused, shaking her head sadly. "It's going to be demolished. Orders from the City."

She was referring to the structures on the island but she might as well have meant my doubting heart.

15

Saturday, August 22, 2009 Bronx, City Island

An hour or so later, Clara and I were walking through the streets of City Island. On the horizon, I could see the Sound's gray offing shot-through with shards of pink. The light was fading. It hit me how hungry I was—ravenous.

Clara looked tired. She probably hadn't realized how much time the Hart Island pilgrimage would take.

"I feel like curling up with a good book in my room," she said, stretching her arms toward the sky.

"Aren't you hungry?" I was hoping to extend the evening.

She pouted. "I'd grab some take-out if I had the choice, but I made a date with two old friends."

I was a new friend. Old friends pulled rank. I was curious but didn't want to push it.

"Maybe —" She tested the word in her mouth, squinting as if to calculate exactly how my presence might impact the evening.

"No," I protested. "They don't know me. I'll cramp your style."

Clara waved that off. "They'll scold me for *not* bringing you. They're not easily inhibited. It takes more than a new face." An upward tug at the corners of her mouth exposed that one dimple, a charming asymmetry, suggesting a bond of intimacy between us. But I had a thing about meeting new people, especially when there were stakes involved.

"Who are they exactly?" I asked. She searched my face, narrowing her eyes. Did she sense my people phobia? It wasn't that I couldn't put on a performance. That's what it would be, though.

She clamped her lips and trained her eyes thoughtfully on an awning above us. "They're the sort of friends who will drink heavily and reveal my secrets," she said dryly. "We all worked together in Beijing and Bangkok."

I knew from David that Clara had been a teenage model. Nothing like perfect women to put me on edge. Did they become more dangerous when they fluttered in swarms? I imagined Clara's friends singling out my imperfections like buzzards picking at roadkill. It might be worth it if I were to discover things that only old friends could know. I wanted to learn everything about Clara.

"You have secrets?" I asked casually.

"Yes, I only look this young." She shot me a saccharine smile. "I'm really one-hundred and two."

We met her friends at a place named JP's located on a narrow spit of land that reached out into the Sound. Inside was nothing fancy, diner ambience, but every booth looked directly over the water.

I spotted two women around Clara's age sitting across from each other, a blonde and a redhead. Glasses of wine sat half-spent before them. They were laughing noisily. Even from this distance the glint of their cheekbones marked them.

"I brought Will," Clara announced.

They examined me as if I were one of the lobsters in the glass tank near the kitchen. Ava, the redhead, had aquamarine eyes that looked photoshopped. When Clara introduced her, she said, "Nice to meet you," in a Russian accent. The other was Jane, who I learned had roomed with Clara in both Beijing and Bangkok. "Are you sure you're ready for us?" Jane asked. She beamed brilliantly—a light show of eyes, lips, and teeth that, no doubt, she'd employed to her advantage a thousand times. I was not in the least ready for her or Ava.

"We were talking about Klaus," Ava explained.

Clara filled me in. "Klaus was a male model in Beijing. Sometimes we'd bring him his morning coffee because he did the same for us. No surprise if he was in bed with three Chinese girls. He had stories, lots of good stories."

Ava chimed in. "Remember when he snorted dust from the pinky nail of that Brazilian night-clubber. He woke up in a hot tub surrounded by fat, Japanese men. Didn't bother him a bit. He shrugged his shoulders, borrowed a towel, and hailed a taxi."

"I love the visual," said Jane. "Klaus wearing nothing but white terrycloth whistling for a cab."

The waiter came and I knew enough to order a round of drinks. These women had a sheen. They'd ventured out on their own as teenagers. The equivalent for me would have been if, instead of going to college, I'd toured with Ray and Bad Chemicals, something he'd asked me to do at the time.

I sat up a little straighter, settled my shoulders, and wondered where I'd be now if I'd had even a pinch of their chutzpah.

"Do we shock you?" Jane asked me, narrowing her eyes as if she were holding a dagger under the table. "I love jolting people a little. Did you know that Ava used to have a sugar daddy in the Russian mafia?"

Ava rolled her eyes and shrugged coyly. Sure thing they'd trotted out this act countless times.

Jane continued. "He bought her an Audi TT convertible and a lot of nice things. When they broke up, all he wanted back was the iPad. Ava refused, locked her windows and door and took a nap. When she awoke, everything in the apartment was ransacked. Silently. Gone was the iPad along with both sets of keys to the Audi TT."

"Loved that car," quipped Ava. "Still looking for another 1996 Audi TT roadster."

"What do you drive now?" I asked.

Ava snorted. "A Camry. But it *is* fire-engine red."

"Ava's a middle manager at a pharmaceutical company," Clara explained. "Jane is still a model."

"Not for long I fear," said Jane. "Soon I can move on to what I've always wanted."

"What's that?" asked Ava with the finesse of a straight-man.

"Night-club singer. You know the kind that stands on a bar table in a mini-skirt?"

Jane's brand of gall was what I needed now. Even just to borrow.

"How have you lasted so long?" Ava asked.

Jane laughed. "My dancing background helped. But I wasn't like you. I didn't troll the clubs all night, get an hour of sleep, and arrive at castings hungover. The only thing that saved you were those eyes." Jane turned to me. "I know you think they're contact lenses, but *no*. That's the color."

All of us crowded in for a good look. They were the blue-green of a mermaid.

"Clara has the *best* story," Ava said, deflecting attention across the table.

Jane's face lit up. "Clara, tell your story."

"No, I don't want to." Clara seemed to retreat inward, her eyes lit like two protective beacons. This, I assumed, was one of the secrets Clara didn't want revealed.

Her refusal to tell acted as a disruption in the energy of the gathering, as though Clara were breaching a private sacrament. Ritual plainly decreed that she should damn well tell her story or else she wasn't Clara—their Clara. I leaned forward in my chair.

The waitress interrupted to bring drinks and take food orders.

As soon as she left, Ava clinked her glass with a fork. "The evening cannot go on," she announced, "without Clara recounting the famous assault and how she kicked ass."

Clara winced. "I'd like to put that behind me."

Ava ignored her. "After thirteen years you're going to erase it from the record? This is one of the holy tales of the round table." Ava did a comic double take at the decidedly square table beneath us.

I didn't understand why she was pushing this, but Jane, too, observed Clara with grave urgency. Sure, I wanted to hear the story but no way was I going to add to what almost seemed like bullying.

"Okay," said Clara. "I will tell it but not the way you want it. No sweeping things under the rug. No blushing giggles. I'll tell it the way I really feel it, have always felt it."

Ava took a long swallow of wine. Jane crossed her arms against her chest.

Clara glanced at me as if to say, sorry, you didn't bargain for this.

"In Bangkok," she started, "when I was seventeen, I tried to hail a cab home from a night club at four in the morning but couldn't get one. I was always very restless in those days."

"In those days?" quipped Jane.

Clara gave her a look. "The model compound was maybe a mile or two. I started walking through the nightclub district. A man grabbed me by the neck and pulled me into an alley. He slit my pants with a knife. I had been raised on take-downs and escapes. My father was a high school wrestler and performing such moves was the only way to get his attention. I reached down to grab the guy's ankle—they call it an ankle pick. He fell hard on his coccyx and let out a scream, at the same time kicking out and catching my elbow. A radial head fracture, they told me later. With my arm hanging limp, I sprinted all the way home. Jane will remember that I waited until the afternoon to get the bone set, not knowing if that man was waiting outside.

"Bangkok summer *over*. I flew home, put on some weight. For some reason, I couldn't bring my hips down to 35 inches. I never modeled again. We've laughed about it and I've played along. We like to say that I kicked ass. But it's never been funny to me. One thing I always left out. He was about to rape me."

Her voice trailed off as she waited for her friends' reaction. She met my eyes, then Ava's and Jane's. No one spoke. Clara steadied herself in the chair and raised her chin a notch.

Then Jane lifted her glass and said simply, "To Clara."

Ava shrugged, smiled, and said, "But you did fight him off, right?

"Yeah," Clara said weakly.

Ava offered a toast. Jane joined it, as did I, and we waited for Clara. Reluctantly, Clara hoisted her glass.

"I'm not blaming you," she said, "for thinking it was funny. I see the humor. Kung Fu Clara." She wiped away a tear. "My elbow healed fine. It's just that I stopped taking chances, stopped forging my own path. It's Will who's inspired me—giving up his law career and every-thing."

Ava leaned forward. "Inspired you?"

Clara straightened her back. "I'm accepting a nine-month con-tract to make a documentary film at an elementary school in the South Bronx. The New York City Department of Education wants me to tell the story of one classroom for a school year."

Ava ran her tongue against her upper teeth. "What happens after nine months?" she asked.

Clara shrugged and smiled.

Nervously, I proposed a toast. "To taking chances."

Clara and Jane raised glasses, then Ava, squinting warily, picked up hers.

"To taking chances," she echoed, with a rising inflection, convert-ing it to a question.

"I couldn't have done it without Will," Clara reiterated.

Both friends leaned over and looked at me keenly, as if speculating whether I was destined to become a permanent fixture in their circle.

Later that evening, I dropped Clara home. She surprised me with a long, tongue-probing goodbye kiss, then purred, "You give me cour-age."

I knew myself to be one of the most fearful men on the planet, but damn I was going to finesse the role she gave me. The problem was that making Clara my *raison d'être*, the new inducement for my transforma-tion, put me back to step one. Once again, I was changing myself to fit the world, or in this case, Clara McLaughlin. It worried me that maybe my inner transformation on Hart Island might have just been adaptive behavior aimed at ingratiating myself with her.

16

Monday, August 24, 2009 White Plains, NY

In my law office, large bookcases behind the desk held a set of McKinney's Consolidated Laws of New York Annotated. Pure affectation, as I typically researched statutes online. But McKinney's, along with a handsome set of New York Supplement, were much-cherished props in a business where mastery and solidity were prime selling points.

The books on the shelves, the files in the cabinets, my iPhone contacts, were bricks confining me to an identity I'd created to protect myself from the world. Einstein said the only important question was whether the Universe was a friendly place. I'd voted no.

But this was not why I'd finally made my decision. It was that Clara had left her job and was taking a chance, and I couldn't let her be the braver one. In the end, it was not my desire for an artistic life, or the feeling that law trapped me in an oppressive square inch of rational gray matter. It was not the shame of Joshua's death or my return to sleepwalking. With Clara now in my life, I couldn't bide her being the only hero.

At four years old, when my nursery school friend, Madeleine, got new sneakers, I had to have them too. It was like those red Keds.

I drafted an email to all my clients: As of October First, I will be closing my law practice. I will be unable to continue representing you on your pending legal matters or take on any new ones. I recommend that you immediately retain another lawyer to handle your legal concerns. You may contact the Westchester County Bar Association Lawyer Referral Service, etc.

I pressed Send. Already, I was sweating, depleted. It was morning but it felt like I'd worked a full day. Kicking off my wing-tips, I hoisted my feet onto the desk. My cell phone rang.

"Is this Will Ross?" The caller ID said WPHosp.

"Yes, this is *he*." My imitation Dad voice, *basso profundo*.

"Mr. Ross, this is White Plains Hospital. We've got your mother in the emergency room. She's had a stroke. Can you come down immediately?"

My first thought was that I'd actually triggered the stroke by pressing Send. The second was: *Not my mother!* Was David already on his way? How could I beat him there? What with traffic and parking, walking might prove faster than his motorcycle. I put on my shoes and broke into a run. Breathing hard, my soles flapped against the sidewalk, then slip-slided over the tile of the hospital lobby.

When I entered the room, Mom sat propped up in bed with David beside her. There was a pink ID bracelet on her thin wrist. She wore a hospital gown of pastel green with blue polka dots. A clown costume. It seemed cruel that she'd succumbed to that in sickness. There was a breathing tube strapped to her face like a single-bar, football facemask. The IV in her arm looked like either a nutrition tube or an intravenous trickle of anti-clotting drugs.

"Mom!" I cried.

"I know," she croaked, "I look terrible, don't I?" It was jarring to see her hooked up to the hospital machines.

"No." I shook my head vigorously then paused to take account of her black eye and a bruise on her right temple.

"I fell and hit my head on a kitchen chair." Her pronunciation was thick as if her tongue had grown fat and dry.

This was all wrong. It was not supposed to happen to Mom. She cared so much about her appearance and now her red hair was sticking out zanily and her eyebrows seemed frozen in an expression of surprise. Why her? She was sixty-seven, exercised, ate lean meats, fruits, vegetables, never smoked, and rarely exceeded one glass of wine.

"Mom, can you walk?" I asked.

She squirmed as if she were going to get up and see.

David put a gentle hand on her shoulder restraining her.

"She's temporarily paralyzed on the left side," he said softly. "They want one of us to act as her medical proxy."

"Mom," I asked, "who could best decide what you would want if you're not able to make a choice?"

Her wide-open eyes scanned David, then me, but she said nothing. It struck me that she didn't want to contemplate a world in which she would not be able to make her own decisions.

A nurse was eavesdropping by the door. As I tried to re-phrase the question, she interrupted me.

"Why don't you two go out in the hall and I'll ask her outside of your presence," she suggested. Ah, perhaps that was it—Mom didn't want to voice preference of one over the other.

"We'll be right back," David said. He nodded toward me and I retreated, noting my mother's visible annoyance in our having to leave the room.

Backpedaling, I barely avoided a collision with an older woman guiding her walker down the hallway. I apologized, and she glared at me.

"How long will Mom be like this?" I asked David. Heat-sealed into his red and black leather jacket, he dangled the helmet by its strap.

"I talked to the doctor," he said, scratching his neck with his free hand. "I think it could be a while."

Our eyes met and David took a deep breath. "She can't live alone," he said.

I shook my head. "Maybe not."

David shifted his jaw.

"Even with care?" I asked.

He considered it. "No, I don't think so."

I wandered a few paces down the hall then circled back. "You know, I just sent a shut-down letter to all my clients. My life is going to change."

Everything around me went slow-mo, the way it does when you're at the plate discerning the trajectory of a pitch. My awareness heightened. It would be death living with my mother. My dreams, even my will to live, hung in the balance. Avoiding that possibility was a matter of survival. "I was wondering —"

David cut me off. "How do you feel about *me* taking her in?" he asked. "I have two extra bedrooms, enough for her and a caretaker when we hire one."

I felt a stab of guilt mingled with great relief. David was going to save me. All for naught was the adrenalin coursing through my veins.

"David, I appreciate this. I really do."

The nurse interrupted us. "Your mother wants to speak to Will."

I shot David a look and he followed me in. Mom was adjusting herself to sit taller but she couldn't get traction against the bed and kept sliding down.

"Mom, the bed can do that. Let me." I found the controls dangling on one side, and slowly raised her into more of a sitting position.

"I chose you," Mom said. "You're my *prossy.*

David and I exchanged glances. Slurred speech—or did she no longer know the word?

"That's fine," I said, wondering how David was taking this. He was more devoted to her and yet she had chosen me.

"I want *you* to move into my house."

Her words were slurred but her intent was clear. It was a pronouncement. My mother was asking for an indulgence during the most difficult challenge she'd ever faced.

"We talked in the hallway," I told her. "David has two extra bedrooms. My cottage is so small."

"I want *you* to move into *my* house," she repeated. This time her hands shook a bit but her tone was firm.

"Why me, Mom, when David has volunteered? He has more living space and lives closer to the hospital."

"I want to see if you will do it." She stared hard at me.

David retreated back into the hallway. Whether he deemed this to be my gunfight, or his feelings were hurt, I didn't know.

"Of course I would do it," I said. "But David's makes more sense."

Mom sneered at that.

I was not going to move in with my mother now that I was finally free of the life she'd dreamed up for me. *Was I a horrible person?*

The horrible person question had been weed-whacking through my psyche since, I don't know, diapers? My mother doubted me enough that she was putting me to a test. For years she'd said that I was a dirty rotten kid and now it was as if she wanted to confirm the truth of it. One thing was clear: I could not live with my mother and embark on this new road. I harbored enough of her voice in my psyche without also getting it in my ear.

"You're staying at David's," I said curtly.

Mom summoned her reserves. "No," she said sharply. "*You* will live with me. You're not going to give your responsibility to David."

The word "responsibility" felt like a jab to the throat. Why *couldn't* I just move in with my mother and defer my dream? She was right. I never put myself out for anyone. Just like I hadn't bothered to make sure Joshua was safe. How was Clara supposed to love someone like me? No wonder David was so attractive to women. There was an intrinsic goodness in him. Or was his generosity a finesse to show, once and for all, who was the better brother?

My mother peered up at me, her mouth crooked like a hooked fish.

"Mom," I said. "It's just temporary. Move in with David. Maybe, after a while, I'll move home with you."

"I am very disappointed," she said. "I thought you would be more than you are."

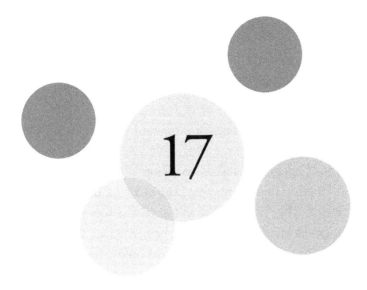

17

A week later, David had already bought a hospital bed and set Mom up in one of his spare bedrooms. In the other, resided her young Russian aide, Tiana, who spoke little English, and was on call 24 hours a day—with just two days of vacation per month. Much cheaper than having three different women serve daily shifts. Money mattered. It wasn't clear how long Mom would need this level of care.

Sunday, I came checking on her en route to Clara's Manhattan Spiritualist Church, letting myself in with a key.

"David?" It was her voice.

"No, it's me, Mom."

She was flat on her back in bed staring up at the ceiling.

"Oh, Will, can you get me out of bed? I need to walk to the bathroom. My aide was up half the night with me. She's sleeping." In a whisper, "She's not much good anyway."

A quick glance into David's bedroom revealed that he wasn't home.

I helped Mom sit upright and shifted her legs over the side of the bed. Her blue walker had to be close enough so that she could grab the handles. She hoisted herself to a standing position and staggered forward. I trailed her, hands ready should she fall. She made it just in time, not even able to close the door behind her, the jet of urine spattering the toilet bowl. When she finished, I helped her back and propped her up with pillows. Her face relaxed as I covered her with the bedding.

An uneasy feeling crept up my spine. She needed me, and my time was limited this morning.

"The visiting nurse is coming tomorrow for your physical therapy," I said.

Mom cupped her good hand to her mouth. "I don't like Tiana. She doesn't speak English. I need someone I can talk to. Could you get me a new aide? Please?" The old authority was gone. She was lonely, pleading with me, hunger in her eyes. Of course, she needed an aide who could talk to her. The care was almost secondary to simply having a companion.

"Mom, I'm going to get you an English-speaking aide—I promise."

People recovered from strokes. I knew that. But it wasn't the disability. Mom was lacking something that she'd always possessed. Gone was the tenaciousness that had propelled her through an often-difficult life. In its place, a frightening despondency.

I retreated into the kitchen and started preparing a breakfast of eggs, toast, orange juice, and herbal tea. Halfway through, Tiana got up and pitched in. She was thin and intense, mid-twenties. Well-meaning as far as I could tell. She spoke only words in English, not sentences. I served Mom breakfast on a tray and kissed her forehead. She looked lost as I backed out of her bedroom, apologizing my way through the apartment.

How would I tell Tiana to pack up and leave? Go ahead and laugh—I was a lawyer who hated confrontation just like my old friend, Ferdinand, the bull, who shunned conflict.

I had begun to make cold calls to libraries as Ray had suggested. The librarians wanted references. Clara solved this problem by hooking me up with her Spiritualist Church. She arranged a regular gig in which I played guitar for the children while adults attended the Sunday service. This appealed to me—not only seeing Clara on Sundays, but writing songs for kids, and getting immediate feedback.

Clara was already out of her old job—placed in a Bronx elementary school classroom to film a documentary.

I wheeled down Central Park West hunting for legal parking, finding a spot near the church. Divine Providence. Or maybe just Sunday suspended alternate-side-parking rules.

This was my second visit with the kids. Last time, I'd introduced *Bossa nova Boo-boo*—my call and response song. I'd had no luck in getting them to reply *ouch, ouch, ouch!* So I'd dismissed the song as a dud.

This time, even before I reached the second-floor classroom, I caught the sound of children yelling the refrain. When I came to the doorway, they crowded in with expectant faces chanting *ouch, ouch, ouch*. It was like the mantra of some secret society.

The other teacher chimed in, an older woman with a half-tamed afro, who smiled a lot and appeared immune to almost any racket the kids made.

"They're mad for that boo-boo song," she said.

The kids were crowding me, shouting from too close, taking swipes at the strings—they were hungry to tell me something: that they had boo-boos too.

I raised my instrument above their sticky fingers.

Bossa nova boo-boo! Ouch, ouch, ouch!
Bossa nova boo-boo! Ouch, ouch, ouch!

They were all over it. My words echoing from their mouths lifted me briefly above the constraints of earthly existence. I was seen. And heard. My chronic numbness cleared like fog before the sun. These Upper West Side savages fed my feral soul.

"That one's a keeper," the teacher said.

While I had them, I introduced an original song about a train that sneezes and misses its stop at each station.

Don't sneeze, don't sneeze, choo-choo train
Don't sneeze, don't sneeze, choo-choo train
AHHHHHHHHHH – CHOOOOOOOO!

The kids immediately fixated on the *ah-choo*, couldn't get enough of it. I had to remind them that it came only at the end of each verse—as the train sneezed through stops in Buffalo, Albany, and the like.

After the singing we played Duck, Duck, Goose, and I spotted Clara peering through the cracked door of the classroom. I was cross-legged on the floor with a small group of kids, the ones who couldn't sit long enough to paste a collage.

A girl of five or six with ash-blonde hair walked around the circle of children tapping each on the head, saying "duck, duck, duck, duck, duck —"

"Goose!" she cried fleeing with a boy in pursuit. Her glossy Mary-Jane's slipped on the slick floor and she fell, tearing her white stockings. Little hands reached toward me, and as I lifted her, she nuzzled against my shoulder digging in her head. Clara told me later that she witnessed the most sublime expression on my face as if I'd discovered, like Copernicus, that the sun was actually at the center of the solar system. That must have been when Clara approached and asked if she could wash the girl's scrapes and affix Band-Aids. But I wouldn't surrender her. I felt like I was holding my own soul in my arms.

Afterward, in the church basement, Clara joined me on the couch with her coffee, peering at me with one eye, the other hidden by a shock of hair. I was picking a Travis pattern on my guitar.

"You glared at me," she said.

"I did?"

"Yes, when I asked to take the girl, you glared at me."

"I wasn't aware," I said.

She narrowed her one visible eye. "You're funny."

"How's that?"

"Well," she mused. "Most men I've met are hard on the outside but soft on the inside. You're soft on the outside and hard on the inside. I'm not used to that."

"That's blunt," I said.

She yielded a thin smile. "Holding back isn't my specialty."

I was picking a little hillbilly thing on the guitar.

She asked, "Do you know that song 'Smooth'?"

"What key do you want to sing it in?" I slid a capo down the fretted neck.

She frowned. "I used to sing," her voice dropped to a murmur, "but not in public."

"This isn't really public." I reached out and tucked her hair behind her ears so I could see both her eyes.

She let out a soft groan that I took for acquiescence. It pleased me that I could change her mind.

I sang the first line. Tentatively she came in by *midday sun*.

Our pacing didn't match so Clara was only on *melt* when I sang *cool*. She narrowed her eyes. "Come on, Mr. Guitar Guy. You're off key."

I shrugged like I didn't care. "Okay, sing it to me then."

She sang the opening couplet, nailing the pacing and pitch in her rich alto.

"I tend to take liberties with melody," I explained.

"You could say that," she laughed through her nose—donkey snorts.

"How about I follow you?" I said. "Sing with the guitar. I'll listen and come in."

But I wasn't a good follower. I drowned her out and she made a face.

"Okay. Let me try again."

This time I sang softly behind her, matching her cadence. Her voice grew fuller and rounder. The rich tone pulsed in my chest as I watched her puckered lips form the vowels. A few stubborn strands of dark hair slipped from behind her ear and obscured one eye again.

After we finished there was a lull. Then cheers and a smattering of applause rose from the coffee-klatch of forgotten congregants. Clara blushed and lowered her head.

18

Saturday, October 3, 2009 South Salem, NY

I was out of my law office already, but still only performing for the church kids. I'd made some progress in contracting with libraries for a summer tour. Clara was forging ahead on her classroom documentary, getting what she needed—conflict. The second-grade teacher who served as her subject had run into almost immediate trouble with a hard-ass principal. Clara blithely filmed it all.

Where I wobbled, she glided, and never did the rift seem so flagrant as the weekend after I wrapped up my law practice. We had started spending the night together but not having sex. I was willing to take it slow if that's how she wanted it. She lay next to me in bed, eyes half open. Something seemed funny about the shading of the room, as if the two of us were encapsulated in a 1930's movie. I was about to mention this to her but then there was a blip like someone had edited the scene, and I was recounting my gigs for next summer's tour.

I knew that in real life people talked back, but I seemed to be encased in a bubble containing only my own thoughts and words, not hers. Clara's eyes had closed. Was that why she wasn't talking? A spider about the size of a hand crawled leisurely along her pillow. It didn't seem a big deal somehow. I thought I might casually mention it. Never did it occur to me that my dream state was being superimposed on reality.

I said to Clara, "There's a wolf spider near your nose." She jumped up screaming, threw the pillow across the room, and pulled all the bedding off. That woke me.

She was dressed in one of my long T-shirts.

"What are you doing?" I asked.

"You saw a wolf spider!"

The tarantula from my dream came back to me. "Ah, I think I know what happened."

This was a byproduct of my sleepwalking, I explained to her.

"Not so much sleepwalking as sleep talking, right?" she asked.

"Yeah, they're both related. Parasomnias they're called." We were both standing now. I shook out the top sheet and spread it over the bed.

"Is it a mental health condition do you think?" she asked, her brow creased with concern.

I retrieved the blanket from the floor and lengthened it over the top sheet.

"Sometimes it's a symptom of depression," I admitted.

She leaned toward me. "Do you have depression?"

I unfurled the coverlet more violently than was strictly necessary. It snapped up and folded over on itself. Clara took a step back.

"Oh, I don't know," I said. "I have this feeling that my happiness is hidden away somewhere and I just can't remember where I left it." I watched her for any indication of judgment.

"I remember where I left mine," she said thoughtfully, as if remembering some long-ago mislaying of it.

Her hands were shaking as they gravitated toward her cell phone like a nicotine addict reaching for a cigarette. I picked up the pillows from the floor and laid them on the bed.

She evened out the coverlet, which was skewed to my side. "I want to tell you about my principal."

I nodded.

"*Mrs. Rodriquez.*" she said the name through gritted teeth, making every syllable count.

"That bad?" I asked.

Clara raised one palm, then snapped her fingers. "You be me," she said. "This is your camera." She looped a belt around my neck.

Clara, as the principal, glared imperiously at my camera. "You will turn that off or you will leave my office," she snarled, grinning self-consciously.

"I put the camera on wide-angle," she whispered, "and filmed her reprimanding my teacher."

Assuming the squat stance of Ms. Rodriquez, Clara glowered and addressed my guitar in the corner of the room. "Ms. Pano, I was deeply hurt by what you said. That *I* would desecrate a child's work!" She gripped the edge of the bed as if to steady herself. "Your comment stayed with me, and ate away at me, and the more I thought about it, the more injured I felt." Her voice trailed off. "Children have been the love and motivating force of my life and for you to think that I would put black exes on a child's bulletin board work." Clara grunted, then dropped character and laughed.

"Doesn't she sound like an old bullfrog?" she asked gleefully.

I nodded. "You just kept on filming?"

"Yes," she said.

I shook my head in admiration.

"She's such a perfect antagonist," Clara gushed. "She's brilliant, committed, a force of nature!"

"What would she have done if she knew you were filming?" I asked.

Clara smiled mischievously. "She'd lop off my head and impale it as a feast for Bronx flies!" She focused again on the guitar in the corner.

"I will cease treating you with kid gloves." Her teeth flashed like a matinee villain. "Every mistake will be documented. No more friendly talks. I did not appreciate your diarrhea of the mouth. Your teaching career is in jeopardy, Ms. Pano."

Clara danced around and squealed like a twelve-year-old on a sleepover. "I got the whole scene," she cried.

"Are you really as cool as you seem to be?" I asked.

Her eyes shut and fat tears welled beneath pink lids. She went limp in my arms. *What the hell?* I sat her on the bed and sheltered her like a second skin.

She dug her head into my chest. "Do you love me?"

I nodded and told her I did. Our bodies pressed together in undefended openness and I began to respond, awakening, swelling, engaging. As we held each other, a deep corridor opened, as if appearing from behind a hidden door. It was a space of intense connection, rarely visited, but in excellent order as if someone had kept it ready. It was impervious to thoughts, good or bad, that I had entertained about her and there was something about our joining that was real in the way a thought could never be. I told her she was my darling. She said that she loved this new sensation of my stomach against hers. I felt her tears and rather than try to make anything happen, I just let it unfold. On top of her, I suddenly felt very hot, so took off my shirt. This was enough to soften the physical manifestation of my ardor and once it flagged, these days, it wasn't reviving. But I put that aside and focused on expressing what I felt, lance or lance-less. And Clara responded. It was very dear—passion unsupported by form, but we didn't care. We were expressing it from the inside. Lo and behold, form followed like Lazarus rising from the tomb. I cried, I wailed. It was a high-pitched, feminine sound but I let it out.

In the afterglow, seeing the tarantula near her nose seemed unbearably hysterical. I laughed, and when I explained why, we both succumbed to giggle fits. All one of us had to do was sing a few words of Itsy Bitsy Spider or stroll our fingers in a creepy crawl and we'd shriek until we collapsed—only to erupt again when she pretended to brush one off my arm, or I slammed a pillow against the wall.

"I never told you how I know Sekhmet," she said in a solemn tone.

I had regressed to about six years old. It would take a double shot of maturity to focus on serious subject matter. Pain might help. I bit my lower lip hard.

"Ever heard of the Temple of Karnak?" she asked.

I knew it was in Egypt and told her so.

"There's this side enclosure of the temple. A small cell with a dirt floor. Just a black statue near a clay-colored wall. For such a tiny room, the ceiling is extremely high. It has a skylight, a square opening."

She glanced at me to see if I followed.

"So I walked in there," she continued. "Sekhmet—but I didn't know. A pitch-black woman with what looked like a large halo above her head. Her nose was broad and there were two short, horn-like things protruding from her head. The light from the skylight reflected as a small square on the floor in front of the statue."

Her stare was solemn. I nodded meekly.

"I walked toward it. A huge lioness, life-sized, living color, rolled out of the black quartz. I was surprised but not frightened. The power of it was amazing. Sekhmet revealed herself to me. My legs continued to move slowly toward her, approaching the patch of light on the dirt floor. An inner voice told me, 'Stand here, but you are not to cross.' I wasn't scared so I asked why. 'Speak to her but do not cross that light,' the voice said."

Clara paused.

"What did *you* say?" I asked.

She wiped away a little moisture from her temples, sweeping her hair back.

"I wanted to know if communication was possible."

I looked at her, not understanding.

"With the dead," she explained. "My grandmother had died and I wanted to know if I could talk to her. Sekhmet said yes." Clara widened her eyes.

"What do you think would have happened if you crossed the light?" I asked.

"I would have joined my grandmother," she said assuredly. "But it didn't seem like a big deal. In that room only a thin veil separated the worlds."

19

Sunday, October 4, 2009 South Salem, NY

My summer tour was slowly taking shape. I'd settled on the price of $100 per show, twice what I'd planned to ask but not the $150 that Ray suggested. By the end of October, I had 25 gigs marked with push pins perforating the map of Connecticut on my bedroom wall. This was thanks to an enthusiastic letter written by my fellow teacher at the Spiritualist Church. Now all I had to do was develop the content.

Producing good material for kids required extensive testing—something I hadn't really understood. There was no substitute for sharing the material with various groups of children over and over again.

My only audience, thus far, were the kids at the church. Sometimes a song I'd fussed over for hours would bomb and another I'd dashed off in minutes would catch on. There was no way to evaluate an idea until my infatuation with it had worn off, and I could tell whether the composition itself, or my eagerness, was provoking the children's response. My new obsession, a musical story about a princess, seemed to be playing well with my test audience.

I was going to give it a shot for a small group of librarians in East Hartford, Connecticut. What if all five booked me? I'd have 30 shows—not bad. And if they block-booked maybe I could do all five in two days. Plus, if they spread the word around, I might conceivably spend a week in the Hartford area.

I envisioned myself camping out with a pup tent, retreating to the

Chevy Malibu if it rained. No staying in hotels on $100 a show. I'd find campsites with lakes—Connecticut had more than a thousand lakes—and take refreshing morning dips before my gigs.

It was a mistake to tell Clara about it. Almost imperceptibly I began riding the tingle of pleasing her—shaking down her approval. It's toxic to lean on someone like that. Down deep I knew this. The purpose behind my altar, of meditating Jesus, Sekhmet the destroyer, Ganesh remover of obstacles, and faceless holy mother, was to aim high and avoid people-pleasing. But the temptation of discarding divinity for a flesh-and-blood woman is deep-rooted. Don't all of us, at birth or shortly after, relinquish the entire cosmos for the promise of a mother's love?

The East Hartford librarian who had organized this intimate showcase was all smiles the day I made the trip. "Nice Hawaiian shirt," she said.

I'd bought seven of them at a thrift shop in New Canaan. The clerk told me they'd been made to order in Hawaii. Some rich guy must have died.

"I'm a little nervous," I admitted.

She dismissed that with a toss of her hand. "Oh, they'll love you."

The time had been set for 5:30 pm so that the visiting librarians could duck out of their jobs, catch my act, and then go home. They arrived one by one, all prompt and friendly.

It was time to begin. Gripping my guitar, I ascended the few steps to a small stage while the librarians sat in wooden chairs.

I did a rapid fingerpicking intro and began chanting the story.

"Once upon a time, a long, long time ago, the sun was looking down through the clouds, through the treetops, and as he was looking, he saw something in the forest. Was it a wily coyote?"

It required a simple yes or no. The librarians squinted at each other, baffled. One threw up her hands. Another eyed the floor.

"A howling wolf?" I asked.

"No?" one said tentatively.

"A laughing hyena?"

Again, they exchanged uncomfortable glances.

"It was a little princess," I continued. "She was dancing in the forest, and the sun had never seen such a beautiful dancer. The sun fell in love with her."

At this point in the story, at the Spiritualist Church, the kids laughed, or shouted "Ooooooh!" in disgust. But the librarians just sat listening. There was no one to play off.

"The sun followed the princess everywhere she went and she became known as Princess Sun. She had a father—and her father was the what?"

They offered blank looks. I tried again: "The father of the princess would be the …"

"King," said the East Hartford librarian.

"The princess was playing with the forest animals when the king said, 'Princess Sun come home this instant!'" This was a tag line that I encouraged the children to repeat but I decided not to burden the librarians with it.

"Usually she would come home but this time she raised a finger and said, 'No, no, I don't want to go. Can't you see I'm busy?'" This was another tag. I solicited faint responses.

My heart was sinking and it affected my grasp of the material.

"When Princess Sun played, she didn't just talk to the people or the animals but she talked to the sun – and the sun talked back to her." A third catch phrase that I just repeated myself. The librarians looked bewildered.

Now I was hesitant to engage them. The presentation dragged—my confidence shot.

The women stole quizzical glances at their host. She'd stuck out her neck, invited them over, and now she'd lost face—because of me. Mercifully, I came to the end. They all graciously thanked me.

It was the loneliest distance from the makeshift stage to my car in the parking lot. I'd been having some trouble with my battery, but thankfully, the engine turned. I could only imagine the embarrassment of having to go back and ask for a jump.

Once on Interstate 84, I fell into the slow lane, not up to driving fast. The cars whizzed by me. Some were trapped behind, unable to change lanes. I didn't care. The dream of making a living with my voice and guitar was as intangible as moonlight and fairy dust. How to explain this to Clara? I'd built this up to see the excitement in her eyes. Now she'd know the truth.

The reason most folks didn't do what they really want was that they weren't good enough at it. What if my true talent lay in law? Where did that leave me? I'd been unhappy as a lawyer. What if my genius was being unhappy?

I took a deep breath, slowed even more, switched to the right access, and veered off the exit. A McDonald's chocolate shake would make everything right or at least shift my attention to digestion.

Near the McDonald's in the shopping center was a store called Jolly Bean Magic. It made me think of fairy-tale Jack who trades his mother's cow for a handful of magic beans. That's what I'd done with my law career, right?

Through the display window, an image caught my eye. A black-stone statue of the goddess, Sekhmet, a foot-and-a-half tall, painted with silver hieroglyphics, holding an ancient rattle. Mouth clenched, eyes bulging, as if holding back laughter.

Laughing at me, right? But then I got it. How to move on from my failure. The crude power of the statue reminded me of Clara's principal—what's-her-name.

Sekhmet was the tough-love queen of celestial beings, a doppelganger of the moody, temperamental principal. The more I thought about it, the more I believed that Clara needed something to align her with the force of this door-kicker goddess.

To bring her this figurine would prove me a good listener. It would show how tuned in I was. Making the parallel between Sekhmet and, ah yes, Ms. Rodriquez, would be a tour de force. It would take all the attention off of my lack of talent, my ineptitude.

No one appeared to be in the store. I walked in and examined the stone figure. It was engraved with a large ankh, which I knew as the sign of everlasting life. I could feel its power. The price tag read $450. Too much, given that I'd stopped earning anything.

I counted the reasons why I should take it and run. The polar icecaps were melting. I was a talentless fraud. We were losing 150 species of plants and animals every day. A dream tarantula had creeped into my waking life. There were five trillion pieces of plastic waste in the ocean. At 37 years old, I had no idea who I was. Me and the world—both on the verge of shut down.

That Ms. Rodriquez was Sekhmet in human form had been my one exceptional insight—and I needed to bring that home.

I grabbed the figure and skipped out the door. Immediately an alarm sounded. I ran through the shopping center toward the McDonald's. Glimpsing back, store workers buzzed out of their outlets and chased me on foot.

Running faster, I widened the gap. My pursuers seemed older, sedentary. I tucked the figurine like a football and leapt over a curb. Posse in hot pursuit. One of them was getting into a car. I couldn't elude him through yards of open asphalt.

I jumped the fence into the outdoor McDonald's Play Place. A painful tug in my groin as I straddled it. Fear shot up my spine. Kids climbing the slide ladder screamed as I dashed through, brushing some, side-stepping others, dodging insect-spring-riders on my way into the restaurant.

"What the hell—?" blurted a man in line. I skirted him, headed for the street-side door. Out to the six-lane highway feeding Interstate 84. I stopped short as a motorcycle nearly grazed me, then lunged for the thin concrete divider.

From the shopping center, a flat-bed truck hooked right, and then slowed, opening a window. He knew me—one of the vigilantes. By the time I reached the opposing sidewalk, my pursuer had reeled through a no U-turn intersection and come up right alongside me, just behind a short-box truck hauling extra-long lumber. As the light changed, I hoisted myself atop the two-by-fours and lay flat, gripping the statue. I'd copped myself a ride. But to where?

Probably the Interstate. I hopped off and scurried head-down toward the shopping center, not daring a backwards glance.

My car was parked near McDonald's. I stayed low and slipped into my Malibu, hidden on the far side of the Play Place. The onyx statue twinkled on the passenger seat. Precious as all hell. But I would have liked a chocolate shake, too.

Afterwards, driving down the highway, my stomach was in my throat. At 37 years old, I thought I'd progressed beyond depravity, that my ethics had hardened into a code that I was no longer capable of breaking. Apparently that wasn't true. I glanced at the stone figurine on the passenger seat. It was one thing to steal, but another to be in criminal cahoots with the goddess of destruction. That made me smile. You know those romantic songs—I'll jump off a cliff for you. Intercept a speeding train. Wasn't this the same? I *had* stolen for Clara, right?

20

Wednesday, November 4, 2009 South Salem, NY

Kissing her in bed that night I was especially obsessive. Occasionally she'd push me away then flash a smile that could light an underground cave. She was in a playful mood withholding her tongue and then shooting it into my mouth.

My senses felt heightened. I could hear the gurgling of the brook that weaved just below my bedroom window, a sound that hadn't penetrated since the first week I'd moved here.

Every so often she allowed me a calculated view of her tongue skimming her lips as if she herself was picturing how it might appear. I felt turned on but also wondered what kind of person grew more stimulated by imagining how she might look, rather than really engaging with me. But I was like that too. My own erection was more of a thrill than anything my partner might do.

We rubbed against each other through our jeans, shifting positions, her on top, then me. Our shirts came off and then our pants. I explored her body with my fingers then lowered myself on top of her even though I wasn't truly hard. When she told me she didn't want that, I felt more relieved than anything. She'd saved me embarrassment. Making love had once been the most comfortable thing in the world. Now talking was easier.

"Are you angry with me?" she asked, sweeping a hand through her hair. "It's not that I don't want you. I'm just distracted by something that happened today. It's running through my mind like a video loop."

"Tell me," I said. I lifted off her and lay back against my pillow on the headboard. My neighbor, or really the live-in caretaker of the cottage next door, was reviewing the troops outside our window. Neighborhood cats comprised the platoon and they congregated near his porch because he put out food for them.

"About face," he called. "Eyes right, ready front. Look sharp soldier. Parade *rest*. Legs straight. Heels in line. You, soldier, I did not say fall out. Disperse, except Short Tail. You are the worst fucking soldier I've ever set eyes on. Short Tail to the rear march!"

"Is he dangerous?" asked Clara.

"No," I said. "He gets drunk and plays drill sergeant to the cats. In the summer I put the fan on high. I'll close the window."

I got up and peered out beyond the glow of my neighbor's cigarette to the darkening lake and surrounding hills barely discernible after sunset.

"Sorry," I said. "You were talking about a thought you're having, like a video loop, over and over."

She nodded gravely. "It's her again." There was only one *her*. "She came into our classroom today and called Ms. Pano into the hallway. Shut me in so I couldn't film. I went out the back door to the playground and returned into the building through the cafeteria."

Clara sprung out of bed and growled like a she-bear. She stomped her feet in frustration. "That woman makes me scream." Her eyes widened as if to gauge whether I truly understood.

Not quite game for another Rodriquez story, I felt my powers of empathy waning. But to show solidarity, I jumped out of bed and stood beside her.

Clara stood up straighter. Her shoulders relaxed back, opening up the front of her body. Her arms fell to the side. She made focused eye contact with me from a seat of authority, wielding a new level of personal power. She was now Rodriquez.

"My detractors within the school call me a bitch." Clara mimicked in a gravelly voice, infringing on my space. "And yet they're not the one who is up 'til midnight putting out fires and they're not the one who is responsible for every child in this school. They're not the one who saves jobs each year there is a cut in the budget!" Her voice escalated to a chant. "Those who are doing their jobs I leave alone. But even they don't speak up for me!"

Clara bore in, breathing too close. She jabbed a finger precariously close to my eye. "This school is my beloved garden and you—you are a weed."

Her laugh sounded more than ever like horse snorts. Manically, she skipped around the room. "Now you're me," she directed. "Sneak up behind."

As I did, Clara, or Ms. Rodriquez, pivoted with disarming speed, her gaze startled and simultaneously fierce. She lurched toward me and I bounded back to get out of the way.

"Are you going to catch me?" I asked.

She reached out abruptly and gripped my arms.

"Who behaves like that?" she asked. "I'm terrified to go to school tomorrow."

She withdrew her hand, cast me a frozen stare, then shook her head uneasily. "Did you know she hired her daughter, a former heroin addict, as one of the teacher's aides?"

I shrugged, not knowing what to say, then got up from the bed and put on my shorts. Her eyes darted rapidly as if I were about to abandon her.

"Where are you going?"

"I've got something that's going to help," I said.

I walked out of the room, through the living room and kitchen, out the front door, and to my car where Sekhmet still lay partially wrapped in newspaper.

When I laid the black figure on the bed, Clara frowned.

"You bought me a statue of Sekhmet?"

"Yes," I said. "I thought it might help at work."

"So, correct me if I'm wrong. You get the cold shoulder from not one, but five female librarians, then you hypothesize that *I'm* the one being plagued by an incarnation of the destructive feminine?"

"Aren't you?" I asked, settling on the bed next to the statue.

"No." She crossed her arms.

Folding my legs into lotus, elbows on knees, I rested a heavy head on my hands.

"Will," she said. "I'm not with you so you can fix my life or show me the way."

"So why are you with me?" I asked without looking up. Now there were three of us in bed, Clara, me, and Sekhmet.

"Because you're tall."

"You're with me because I'm tall," I repeated.

"Yeah," she said.

"But there are plenty of tall guys," I pointed out.

"Not like you."

"But—" I stopped myself.

"Next time," she said, switching off the night-table light, "bring me flowers."

She turned away from me on her side, pulled up the covers, and I thought she was done.

When I'd almost fallen asleep, she whispered, "Don't pay any mind to those librarians. They know nothing."

Her words penetrated my heart as if I were three years old—the age of the part of me that loves.

I listened to the crickets singing outside. They would die with the first hard frost and that frost could come tomorrow or the next. For the moment they still chirped brightly enough to rival the muted cursing of my neighbor and the stiff crunch of tires spitting gravel by his feet. The woman of the house had just arrived home and that usually put an end to all military exercises. In a week or two, she'd be off to a Florida winter house and her caretaker, perhaps part-time lover, would be free to swear at the cats until his beer and smokes were gone or the night grew too cold.

For now, I had something to latch onto—the final sounds of summer, a warm body within reach, and best of all, Clara's staunch decree that those librarians knew nothing.

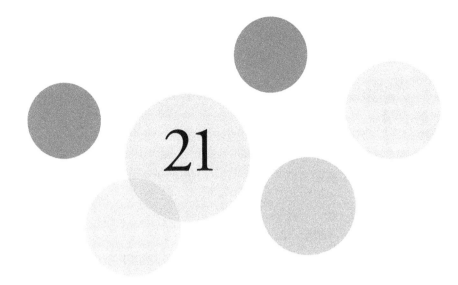

21

Sunday, November 8, 2009 White Plains, NY

"*David* is putting Mom up?" Dad asked when I met him at the airport. He smiled and his cheeks crinkled.

He had lost weight in the last few years. A good sign. No longer was his face round and open. His cheeks had narrowed and his nose, always fleshy, claimed new prominence.

I reached for his suitcase but he held on tight, dragging it through the terminal, across the parking lot, and depositing it in the trunk of my Chevy. I was surprised that he didn't insist on taking the wheel on the short drive to David's.

Once there, Dad and I crowded around a dozing Mom in the bedroom as David prepared lunch in the kitchen. Without opening her eyes, Mom, from under the covers, growled, "The chickens have come home to roost." She didn't even crack her eyelids.

Were we the chickens coming home to her, the mother hen? Or was it a reference to our bad deeds—my father having divorced her and me not taking her in? Neither of us asked.

"How are you?" Dad said, bending over to kiss her cheek, which was half-buried in the sheet and blanket. With his terse expression in the dim light, he resembled a bear rummaging.

"I'm ruined." Mom pulled the cover over her face. "Ruined," she repeated as if we hadn't gotten it.

"Can you eat?" Dad asked. "David is almost finished making lunch." Eating had always been critically important in our household.

"First Naya has to help me with my exercises," Mom said. "Get Naya."

I'd kept my promise and replaced Tiana with an older woman named Naya. Naya spoke good English and had a talent for asking my mother questions about herself. She wasn't much of a cook and barely had the strength to lift my mother out of bed. But she was the *one*. I could tell by the way Mom cooperated with her. Naya had a track record with stroke victims. She'd assembled a series of exercises, not only what the doctor ordered, but others gleaned from previous experiences. The sequence took about sixty minutes.

Naya disappeared into the bathroom in her nightgown promising to start Mom's morning routine soon. We retreated to the kitchen as the door buzzer sounded.

When Clara walked in, resplendent in a black shirt and gray form-fitting yoga pants, I felt a shot of guilt. Why had I asked her to come? To show off for my father and David? And what about *her* motives? Who arrives to meet her boyfriend's parents showing, in full delineation, the longitude and latitude of her gluteus maximus? I led her into the kitchen. David's neck turned so fast it was like Winnie-the-Pooh smelling honey. Then he called, "Naya!" as if he had been searching out Mom's aide.

"You are *David's* girlfriend?" Dad asked. It wasn't a reasonless guess because we were in his apartment. My father had an excellent people sense and I wondered if he also felt something between them.

I put my arms around her, claiming Clara in the most inelegant way possible short of roping her with a lasso.

Dad smiled broadly, picked up a football resting on a magazine rack near the kitchen table, and said, "I can still throw this thing." He was always competitive with us about everything—even our girlfriends. And he could pull it off because there was no question that we were his beloved boys.

"Oh," Clara said. "David once told me you were the quarterback at Hofstra." One of the adorable little lies he'd told us in our youth. I was surprised David had passed it on.

"Not exactly," he admitted. "But something like that." He looked at his watch. "We have an hour." David and I both knew what he meant.

It was unseasonably warm, in the sixties, as we entered a park nearby. A game of tackle football had been my favorite thing in the world until the recovery of my body started taking a few months rather than a few days. Still, I found assault-and-battery cathartic—often happiest when bleeding. Clara, striking a pose like she was Scarlett Johansson in a Black Widow costume, promised to make the game a virtual war.

At the park, Dad chanted, "hup, hup, hike."

I sprinted down the boggy field, sloshing as I went, waving for a lofty pass to exploit my height advantage over David. Dad heaved the football, a wobbly lob, but on target. I pulled it in and David tripped me up. No two-hand touch for the boys.

As a child, I'd learned to fall right. My body still knew. The moment I lost balance, it curled fetus-like and rolled, soaking up water from the grass like a sponge. Wickedly, my eyes immediately found Clara on the sidelines. The war was on.

Cutting wasn't possible on this field so I cupped my hand to Dad's ear and told him to throw the same pass. This time David was all over it. He jutted ahead of me, grabbed the frail toss, then sprinted untouched to the water bottle that marked the goal line. He was in better shape, thinner and faster. Clara watched from near a chain-link fence, the bleakness of that background accentuating her long-legged magnificence. To prove my worthiness, I would need to counter David's speed and conditioning with physical aggressiveness.

On the next play, I blocked David hard, knocking him to the side, and plowed ahead for another completion.

David rubbed his hands. "It's going to be like that, eh?"

This time, he hit low, spilling me into a patch of mud, his body falling hard on top of me. We both got up and I persisted with my pattern, bumping David, who pushed back forcibly. Dad drilled one in my gut. The constant tussle was already beginning to irritate my knees. But there was no going back. The blueprint for these games had been set long ago. The urgency of impressing Clara masked any pain. Maybe, in an unguarded moment, I might detect who she genuinely wanted to win.

My father liked to play hard. It was a religion for a man who had no religion, and it had gotten him through two minor strokes and a difficult marriage. I didn't know whose approval I craved more—his or Clara's. I could not shake my childhood compulsion to please the man. But Clara's presence spiked the punch.

As we played on, our tackles turned hostile, then brutal, and later still, devolved into brotherly embraces. There's no bonding like rolling in the mud, but this wasn't about fraternal love. My twenty or so extra pounds didn't allow me to keep pace with him. I'd let myself go too long. It didn't help that at each turn I was glancing over at Clara, trying to read where her allegiance lay. Was she cheering David's pass reception or just stretching? My obsessive peeks and glimpses obliterated my concentration.

Even so, I tried to grind it out. I clipped, elbowed, juked, straight-armed, hacked, bull-rushed, and razzled whatever dazzle I could muster. Sadly, I didn't have the speed or wind, most of all, the single-mindedness. David won, seven touchdowns to five, and I was left lying in a pit of saturated soil. The defeat fed my whirling eddy of doubt. Maybe I should have bucked up and stayed in law.

I tried to read Clara's face from the low angle of the mud puddle. Then, I got up and charged David, nailing him, grappling his body to the ground. My extra pounds now served as an advantage. I slithered on top then lost my hold as he rolled both of us into another sea of glop. He freed an arm and plunged a handful of mud into my face. I sprung to my feet, then leaped on him with the full brunt of my girth. Pinning him, I lathered his face and neck with brown muck until I was so tired I could hardly lift an arm.

"I give up," he gasped.

Peering up at Clara through one unobscured eye, I sought some kind of payoff.

"This is beyond stupid," she said, standing over us.

Maybe so. Maybe not. I got up and staggered toward my father. David hoisted himself up and attempted to brush himself off.

"David won the game." Dad shook his head disapprovingly, then focused his attention on Clara. "This is just the way we play," he explained apologetically. "It's been going on thirty years."

My attention strayed to Clara. Was I mistaken or did her lips wear the hint of a smile? As an only daughter, boy culture might bode mystifying, but you couldn't convince me that beneath the façade, in the recesses of her conceit, there didn't lurk a kernel of gratification. Helen of Troy had launched a thousand ships but she, Clara, had inspired the mud puddle war. And I'd retained a scintilla of pride.

Caked in muck, Dad and I trudged toward the apartment. My eyes flitted back to Clara and David, walking behind us.

Dad asked me, "Was it that boy's death? Is that why you left law?

I rubbed the back of my grimy neck and nodded.

"Your mother told me you were sleepwalking again," he said. He was smiling, but his eyes showed worry.

I glanced back to Clara and David again.

Speaking softly I said, "Last night, I peed in the kitchen. No memory. Just a yellow puddle near the stove."

My father's brow creased with concern. "Do you have any idea why?"

No, I didn't. Couldn't put my finger on it. I felt angry about these nocturnal misdeeds but somehow resigned to them. There was nothing to be done. Just as nothing could change Joshua's death or Mom's stroke. When I returned home that evening I found a solid dent in the sound box of my guitar that I hadn't noticed before. I loved that guitar. But all I did was shrug my shoulders and go to bed.

22

Monday, November 9, Bronx, Tremont neighborhood

The next morning, Clara and I were on our way to her school, the Bronx classroom she chronicled as if she were a photo-journalist embedded with a military unit during wartime. And wartime was an apt analogy. There was something karmic going on between Clara and her principal, even if Ms. Rodriquez wasn't literally Sekhmet in the flesh. As I watched from the passenger seat of Clara's Honda Civic, the sun played hide-and-seek, poking between buildings to the east then ducking behind us as we headed west to the entrance ramp of the Bronx River Parkway.

It was Clara who had suggested that I work with one of the students in her classroom to atone for Joshua. That never would have occurred to me. Atonement reeked of sacrifice and I'd never bought the notion—from Abraham's binding of Isaac to Jesus offering his own mortal existence. Would a good deed really clear me of a cosmic offense? Could you really heal the inside with something on the outside? I didn't know. So when Clara proposed that I teach guitar to one of her students, I thought it couldn't hurt to try.

We stopped at a light. No modern parkway has traffic signals, but the Bronx River dates back to 1907 and for context, the Model T came out in 1908.

"The boy's name is Charley." Clara tapped on her steering wheel for emphasis. "He fights in school—mostly with Jorge. He has little patience for anything he doesn't want to do but he's crazy about music. No dad. At least not one he ever sees. Remember I told you that Ms. Rodriquez hired her ex-junkie daughter as a teacher's aide? Charley is her son."

Clara hadn't so much as glanced at me this morning, though only the armrest console separated our bucket seats. I wondered if yesterday's battle with David had anything to do with it. All my muscles hurt. Surely she'd detected my limp as we'd walked together to her car after I'd parked on Vireo. But she'd not said a word about it.

"Are you mad about my fight with David?"

"You are so lucky," she laughed, "because if I were a sane woman, I'd have a rational point of view about what you did yesterday, which would be that people who resort to physical violence are ticking time bombs—anger-management catastrophes waiting to happen." She turned to me and pointed a finger. "Brute force may have been a distinguishing trait a million years ago when impaling a bison fed the family. But with ground chuck a few bucks a pound at Shoprite—not so much anymore. So yes, if I were a rational woman, sound of mind, I'd be repulsed. But my father was a high school wrestler who taught me to fight at an early age. I'm proud that I can defend myself. It's almost never let me down. Being raised by a wild man left me with a soft spot for combative guys. You know what they say about the opposite-sex parent."

"No," I replied. "What do they say?"

She pursed her lips and closed one eye to remember. "The observed features of the opposite-sex parent are used as a model for mate selection."

"But you don't even like your father, do you?"

"What makes you think that?" she asked. "I love him."

I didn't see any commonality between me and Clara's father, but apparently she did. That bothered me, so instead of thinking about it, I focused out the window on the reedy stream that gave the Parkway its name. Before the shoveling and blasting required to build the road, it might have been a proud waterway, reduced now to a tired trickle.

At the Moshulu exit, she swung over to Webster Avenue and then down to 180th Street.

We passed a gated storefront: *Live Market—Chickens, Goats, and*

Rabbits, replete with storybook pictures of the live animals housed behind the gate. Peter Rabbit for dinner.

"You said Charley's mother is a teacher's aide?" I asked.

"Paraprofessionals they're called. His mother is gorgeous." She gave me a knowing look as if physical beauty was the extent of my interest in any woman. It wasn't—thank you very much and besides—women who other women thought gorgeous usually weren't.

When Clara reached the school, she pulled into a small adjacent parking lot. A short man with gray wooly hair, anywhere from fifty to seventy-five, approached the car. His broad shoulders were covered by a checked flannel shirt as if he were fly-fishing in the Adirondacks rather than tending to a small plot of gravel in the Bronx. A woman stood next to him.

Clara rolled down the window. "George," she said, "this is Will."

George smiled. "Hello, Will." His voice had a game-show-host timbre.

"And Will, this is Ms. Pano, the star of our documentary." Clara gestured toward a young brunette in a print dress standing beside George. "I've been spending a lot of time with Ms. Pano recently." Clara brayed nervously.

"You doing okay, McLaughlin?" Ms. Pano asked.

Beneath her breath Clara said, "We all call each other by last names." She shrugged. "Doing fine!"

"You look like you could use a little more sleep," George said.

"No beds around though." Clara smiled.

"There's a lady I know in these apartments—she got a bed," George said.

"Oh?" Clara played along.

"She's keeping it warm for *me!*" George's face lit up, his eyes wandering out toward the housing project behind the lot. Clara grabbed her camera and knapsack. I slid two guitars out from the back seat, one was a Guild I kept in the basement.

We had arrived 45 minutes before the first period so there would be time for a lesson. I'd brought that spare guitar for Charley, but I didn't want him to take it home. After the lesson, I planned to ride Metro North back to my car.

First stop was the school office. Clara punched her card, a necessary ritual she said, even though she'd been hired by the DOE and not the school itself. The whirlwind of activity in the office kicked up my social anxiety, but Clara was in her element. She moved gracefully through the cubby-hole loiterers and time-card punchers. I held a guitar case in each hand, and people maneuvered around the bulky instruments, hemming me in. Feeling trapped, panic rose in my chest, and subsided as I edged my way into the hallway. Couldn't she hurry up in there?

Ms. Pano grabbed papers from her cubby and smiled over her shoulder. "Lunch today?"

Clara agreed with a smile. Then she led me down the hall toward the classroom.

We stopped to greet a woman with straight auburn hair and an enormous smile on her face.

"This is Charley's mother, Alessia Perez. Alessia, Will Ross." Gorgeous she was. "She's a paraprofessional for one of the kindergarten classes." I bent to shake her hand and she smiled even wider, her light body springing up on tippy toes. There was something either manic or electric about her, I couldn't decide which.

"Where's Charley?" Clara asked.

"Oh, he's in the bathroom," Alessia said. "A little nervous I think."

I had to go too. Back in high school, on the baseball team, I was notorious for ducking into the woods for a pee before each at-bat. Children passed through the hall before us in a blitz of glow sneakers, cornrows, and shaved temples, with the occasional hijab, hoodie, or flak jacket. Charley strolled out of the boy's room. His green eyes focused on his mother, then flitted to me.

Alessia took her son's hand and said, "This is Will. He's a guitar player."

Charley eyed the black cases in my hands and grinned. "That's my favorite thing."

I smiled back. "Do you have a guitar?" I asked.

"No, not yet," Alessia said, biting her lower lip.

Clara thought for a moment. "Maybe the school has one."

"I'll loan him this." The words just tumbled out. God knows, a pretty woman was exactly what it took to trigger my latent generosity. Clara shot me a questioning glance, then almost imperceptibly recoiled from my side.

The four of us squeezed into Ms. Pano's tiny classroom, a glorified closet. How it fit eight students and two paraprofessionals was hard to imagine.

"We'll leave the two of them alone or would you rather watch?" Clara asked Alessia, glancing at her cell phone.

"Maybe the first time I'll stay," she replied softly.

Clara yielded a thin grin, then continued down the corridor with her camera and briefcase. I followed her rhythmic gait until she blended with a throng of students. Her power to dislocate my heart, just by walking away, left me shaky. The only other woman to hold sway over me like that had been my college girlfriend. Had Clara accurately read my impulse in handing over the guitar? Yes, I was male, and erringly susceptible to beauty. But that didn't mean what she thought.

I put the guitars on tables and coaxed them out of their cases. The back-up Guild I handed to Charley. Now that I was parting with it, my Taylor just better stay in good repair.

Pulling a couple of chairs out from under a table, I offered one to Charley. Alessia remained standing.

"You don't want to sit?" I asked, digging out another.

"No, this is fine." Her smooth shoulder-length hair matched the color of her gingerbread dress. She had the stillness of a doe, watching from a safe distance.

The guitar was big for Charley so I told him to bend his right knee and sit on his calf to help balance it. Finger by finger, I molded his fret placement of a C chord, and then a G.

"You can play hundreds of songs with just those two," I said. "The tricky part is getting from one chord to another."

Charley tried transitioning from C to G. I'd seen other beginners, girlfriends mostly, test those rarely-used muscles for the first time. They invariably found the fingering awkward, struggling to withdraw from one chord and groping blindly for the next. But Charley switched without much fuss, fluently even.

I looked hard at him. "You've done this before."

"No, no," Alessia replied from the doorway. "He hasn't."

Within a short time, the boy was strumming, C to G and back to C, smoothly enough to play a song. You didn't have to be more than a hack guitarist like myself to see he had potential. It was simple math that a single-parent household headed by a teacher's aide didn't have the resources for guitar lessons. Rent, food, and utilities probably took most of her paycheck. Admittedly, I didn't have any great desire to teach him. But it wasn't hard to take a cue from circumstances, from the shape of things. God, or the Universe, or just four billion years of evolution, had placed me in this cramped classroom with a talented boy asking me to help.

"Okay," I said. "You play those two chords over and over and I'll sing a song. We'll get your mom involved too. Alessia, just echo what I sing—you ready?"

"Okay." She grinned nervously.

Charley had a steady beat going so I started in, "Lou, Lou, skip to my Lou."

I nodded to Alessia.

She smiled. "Lou, lou, skip to my lou!" No timidity.

"Lou, lou, skip to my lou."

"Skip to my lou, my darling." Alessia, on beat and with attitude. Charley's rhythm on the guitar flagged, then started up again.

"Lost my partner, what do I do?"

"Lost my partner, what do I do!"

"Lost my partner, what do I do?"

Alessia cried out, "Skip to my lou, my darling!" She burst into ripples of laughter. Charley stopped and shook his fingers.

"That's a good start," I said.

"Can we do it once a week?" asked Alessia.

I knew this wouldn't be the lone lesson, but once-a-week was a serious commitment. I thought of suggesting maybe once or twice a *month* when I heard myself say that would be fine. A chill crawled up my spine. I grinned foolishly.

Yes, Alessia was distracting. But something else was at play. It reminded me of lifting that young girl into my arms at church. Teaching Charley guitar seemed like part of the plan.

"How about that, Charley?" Alessia asked, smiling effervescently. "Yay!" shouted the boy. He looked at his sneakers, dimples carved into his cheeks.

"Thank you," said Alessia. Her eyes absorbed me as if I were the very protector of her beating mother's heart. "I'd better tell Clara that we're done here." She headed down the hall toward the teacher's room. I retreated to the bathroom to relieve my bladder.

When I returned, one of Charley's classmates had blocked the door to the classroom. He was a beefy kid with his head shaved bald.

"Who gave you that guitar?" he shouted to Charley. "Give it here!"

Charley hugged my Guild to his chest like he was shielding it from a fire. I ran over but the bald boy escaped my grasp, tripping over the leg of a chair, and plunging onto the guitar.

The instrument jounced from Charley's arms and the boys fell on it grabbing and pushing.

"Hey, hey, guys." I pried off Charley's attacker and helped both boys up. The Guild's neck was not damaged but there was a quarter-sized hole in the sound box.

"It's broken," Charley wailed. "It's broooooo-ken."

"Fuck," I cried, placing the guitar on the table, then looking away, not ready to take it in. Better sit down, I thought, before I hit the kid. The boys were staring at me, wondering what I was going to do.

"You," I said to the bald kid. "What's your name?"

"Jorge," he replied. His eyes darted one way then the other—looking to escape.

"Why did you want the guitar, Jorge?"

"Because Charley gets everything. I want something too."

I let out a wistful groan and the two boys eyed me warily. What could I give him? Money would be too crass. But a photo maybe? I could take a shot of him.

I produced my phone and met his eyes. "Say cheese."

He smiled. I snapped.

My phone recognized the classroom printer and in a few seconds a photo of Jorge rolled out. He swiped it and bolted into the hall.

"The guitar's okay," I told Charley, grabbing the Guild and demonstrating. I had once owned a 1954 Martin parlor guitar with a hole the size of a fist, and it played good as ever. "See?" The notes rang out clearly. "Take it home and practice those chords."

I heard the sound of Clara's heels approaching. Hoisting my Taylor, I headed her off at the door and planted a kiss on her lips.

"Oooooh," cried Charley.

Fearing reprisal at my indelicacy, I skipped down the hall.

"Wait a minute," Clara said, placing a hand on her hip. "How'd it go?"

She stood in the doorway and beckoned me back.

"It went . . . great," I said. "The kid's got talent."

She met my eyes. "Jorge showed me the photo you took of him."

"Yeah that," I said. "There was a little—uh."

She nodded. "That happens here."

I bounded down the hall with my guitar, hopping four tiles at a time. These kids were raw, but they connected with something fresh and unsmoothed in me.

23

Saturday, November 14, Larchmont, NY

The Bronx neighborhood where PS 463 resided had once been dubbed the Alamo. Only twenty miles northeast was the posh bedroom community of Larchmont, New York. I was familiar with its coastal enclave known as The Manor. The jewel of The Manor was a gracious private park on the Long Island Sound with manicured walkways, quaint wooden gazebos, and peaceful views of the sea. If not for this park, only mansions would crowd the shoreline. The woman who wrote the book *Please Don't Eat the Daisies* once lived in one of these, and her home was the model for the house that appeared in the movie and TV show. What did these country houses just a-hop-and-a-jump from Manhattan cost now? Enough so that a five percent Realtor's commission amounted to a healthy six figures.

I parked my Chevy outside a Spanish Tudor with six stone angels, five gargoyles, four copper wolf heads, and three lions. I counted them. This wasn't my first birthday gig. I'd done one for the daughter of a Spiritualist Church regular, which gave me the courage to place an ad in a parenting magazine. The marketing lady had asked what name I used as a performer. "Willy the Guitar Guy," I told her. My new identity.

So, here I was, carrying an oversized backpack full of shakers, bells, and puppets, armed with "Bossa nova Boo-boo," "Mr. Train," and an assortment of other songs. I rang the mansion's doorbell—an eight-gong chime. "The Yellow Rose of Texas." The birthday boy's mother came to the door. I knew by our phone conversation that she spoke with a French accent. Maybe the Texan was her husband. Here she was—pretty, petite, businesslike. I could swear I'd seen her before. And remembering faces was my specialty, whether last week or ten years ago. Never names.

Her pupils flared. "What, no costume?"

I couldn't imagine why she'd expected me to dress up. It might have been her way of accentuating our status gap. Since those initial clown shows, I'd never appeared in costume and my ad pictured me in a Breton striped shirt. It was too bad because I had been disposed to like her—what with this being my second party. But now my antennae were up.

She ushered me through the Tudor-top door. Around the corner to the right was a spacious living room sprinkled with guests on couches and chairs. Servers in white shirts, bow-ties, and black vests circulated with hors d'oeuvres.

The lady of the house pursed her lips and waved a finger. "You must not let the adult guests see you," she said, leading me down a corridor to the left. "Your place is in the basement with the children." She frowned. "Please, if you must go to the toilet, use the one downstairs."

It had come to this. From an officer of the court, privileged to participate in making critical decisions about people's lives in the sanctity of a judge's chambers, I'd descended to basement-level hired help. Below, the children were at war. Their shrieks and hysterical laughter were punctuated by the low guttural grunts one might associate with trying to capture a greased pig. The hostess closed the door against the noise. Temporarily, I was on the adult side.

Who was this lady? I shut my eyes trying to place her. The answer came like bubbles rising to the surface of a lake. I saw her in my office, hair worn up, dour expression, contrite bearing. More bubbles emerged, and I remembered the plea bargain, a wet reckless charge dropped from driving while intoxicated. She'd blown a 1.5 on the Breathalyzer. Anything less than admission-as-charged was a gift from the gods, and she was savvy enough to know it. I recalled her gratefulness, how she'd poured on the charm. But now, the great lady clearly didn't remember me. Her charisma would not be wasted on a party musician. Where was the costume indeed?

I shook my head. "I can't both supervise the kids and perform the show. I need other adults down there with me for liability concerns if nothing else."

The corners of her mouth drooped to signal that she was not amused. She pushed a button on the wall and presently two young women in matching aprons, like servants from the Gilded Age, appeared. Ah, this explained her notion of the help wearing costumes.

"They will supervise," she said without emotion, then slipped me an envelope. "Remember to use the toilet on the lower level and then exit through the garage."

For a moment, I was tempted to show her that I knew an intimate fact about her life, her guilty plea to an alcohol-related reckless driving charge. My dignity was screaming for me to traverse the chasm between us with this privileged information. I warned myself not to do it. I'd chosen to leave that other life, and freely exchange status to play the Fool. That was not her affair. The final details of the case came to mind—the judge had sentenced her to attend AA meetings as an alternative to jail time. It took all my will, but I restrained myself from asking how the court-ordered meetings had gone. Willy the Guitar Guy had work to do.

I survived the show in the swarming basement, pride intact. There was someone in me now who knew how to sail in these waters.

On the way home, I mused over my downwardly-mobile trajectory.

Maybe this loss of status connected me with all the people who wanted something good in their lives but couldn't manifest it. I was thirty-seven now and still did not know my way forward. That bound me to the seventy-year-old guy bagging groceries at the supermarket. It forced me to empathize with a man up the road from my cottage who couldn't work full time because he was bipolar but somehow managed to keep his house. It joined me to the mom next-door, divorced with two kids, who changed jobs regularly and now was in default with her mortgage. It affiliated me with various neighbors who worked various jobs or didn't and drank a lot in their spare time. I didn't drink much but I understood. This experience was bulldozing the wall between the winners and the losers. Failure was an important part of life, not just a sorry heap of rubble. If nothing else, it stripped away the false self, brought you to your knees.

Could that be what it meant to be willing? Willing for life to have its way with you. Was being broken what it took? Light getting in through the cracks.

"There is a crack in everything God has made," wrote Emerson 150 years earlier than Leonard Cohen. The nursery rhyme says Humpty Dumpty can't be put back together again. But I suspected that wholeness was a different thing from the soul's point of view.

24

Sunday, November 29, 2009 Bronx, Woodlawn neighborhood

Speaking of soul, I was still working with the kids at the Spiritual Church on Sundays and since Clara preferred to take the express bus to Manhattan, I usually drove her back to the Bronx.

I had vowed that I would never again invite myself into her parents' Vireo Street apartment and risk bruised knuckles. But when I pulled up one Sunday afternoon, she said, "You're coming in—aren't you?" Glancing up at my face, she laughed, or really brayed, and told me her parents weren't home.

We got out of the car and I studied the building doubtfully. "How do you know?"

"That window there," she pointed up two floors, "looks into our living room. See the upper corner of the wall TV? It's dark. That means they're out."

I remembered her parents watching television with their deadpan faces. Their brows heavy and lips terse like the heads on Easter Island. How could they be so dead and Clara so alive?

She took my hand but I hesitated. "What other shows do they like beside 'Beachfront Bargain Hunt'?" I asked.

She raised her eyebrows as if to say—you really want to know?

I nodded and yawned simultaneously—a mixed message. She eyed me warily.

"My mom loves a show called 'Home Town.' It's this couple in

Laurel, Mississippi. They're wizards at fixing up houses. You can get a mansion down there for about $100,000." Clara lowered her voice and made her face expressionless. "Mom wants to go to Laurel, buy one of those houses, and sit on her porch with some of the nice people she sees on the show."

"What does your dad say?" I asked.

"Dad leave McLean Avenue?" Clara rolled her eyes.

"Do you think she'll really do it?" I asked.

"For her sake, I hope she does." Clara raised her chin. "What Dad doesn't know is, he'd follow her."

She was probably right. Men were so pitifully unaware of how dependent they were on their women. I gave ground and trailed Clara upstairs to the foyer. There was the table I'd bled on. Set with floral placemats it looked innocent enough.

She led me into her room and closed the door, then sat on the bed and motioned me to do the same. I plunked down beside her. She slid out the first drawer of her night table revealing the Sekhmet statue I'd stolen along with a red diary: the first one reminiscent of my secret crime, and the other boding a new level of intimacy. She reached for the diary. Blood rushed to my face. My hands tingled.

Clara's eyes burned. "This may look like a book, but it's my Nana."

I leaned forward, studied the photo of Clara's grandmother pasted on the cover, but stopped short of examining the pages.

There was a constellation of freckles on Clara's nose and cheeks, not unlike The Pleiades, rendering her familiar and unique. Love surged up my chest sending a shiver through my shoulders.

"Are you okay?" she asked.

I wasn't—in that love opened me up to a sense of vulnerability that made me uncomfortable.

"Tell me about her—your grandmother," I said. It was crucial that my unblinking gaze evince sincerity. Not that my interest was counterfeit. But it was hard to relax in this apartment.

Clara's eyes flicked toward me then retreated to an inner place. "Nana spent a lot of time with me. Took me to Ireland most summers. Just the two of us." She smiled remembering. "Made me feel special. I was closer to her than my own mother. She really knew me."

"Hard to lose someone like that," I said. My knees were shaking, so I stilled them with my hands. Why was I so jittery? It was as if I could smell her father in the foyer.

Clara winced. She examined me, perhaps to ferret out any signs of pretense. I stifled a fidgety yawn.

"Would you like a beer?" she asked, already heading to the kitchen. Was she seeking out an anodyne for my vibrating knees?

"What do you have?" I called.

"There's Miller Lite and Miller Lite," she said, snorting drolly. "Also Manischewitz. My mother likes her wine sweet."

"I guess Miller Lite then."

She brought in two bottles and we twisted off the tops.

"Cheers," she said. We clinked them together. I surprised myself by drinking half the bottle in a few glugs.

"Here's to—" but before I could get the words out she kissed me hard on the lips. We moved closer and reclined. The curve of her nose, a sweep of hair against the pillow, the vulnerability of her eyes from two inches. I trusted her. My body followed. There was no place I'd rather be.

We were under the sheets, naked, when the bedroom door sprung open. Clara's mother appeared in church clothes. She screamed. A soprano tremolo.

I dove under the bedding. My penis shriveled. Clara sat bolt upright, sheets pulled to her neck. I peeked out from the side.

Grabbing a robe from the closet, Clara's mom started laughing, a cowboy yodel which degenerated into donkey snorts. Ah, that was where Clara got it.

As her mother's snorts abated into snuffles, Clara pivoted out of bed into the proffered bathrobe, grasped her mother's arm and steered her to the living room, leaving me alone in bed.

Snippets of their conversation soared and dipped like a remote-controlled micro-plane piloted by a preschooler.

"Big strong man like yours—of course that was what he wanted." The older woman made a tsk-tsk sound.

Unintelligible whispering.

"I'm so mad at your father! He *could* spend one Sunday with *me*, you know. Put myself between him and the 34 bus—me in my heels. The neighbor took my side and your father threw him into the street! The bus knocked him five yards. An officer put him in handcuffs. Your father needs a lawyer."

Clearly, something big. I understood that. And I wasn't so self-centered as to be mourning my erection. It was the abrupt loss of *her*. The scent of freshly-aroused sweat and Herbal Essence lingered where Clara's skin had pressed against mine. The absence of her leg urgently pinned against my pelvis. Our intimacy so handily severed by a mother's high-pitched yelp. That was the unique power a mother wielded over her daughter's life. Of course, Clara had to attend to her in a time of crisis. No doubt in my mind that Clara wasn't coming back to bed. I slid on my underpants and jeans.

Scuffling in the next room. More whispering. "Oh no. Nuh-uh!"

"Mom," Clara snapped, "go ask him yourself."

"I will not." A sharp rap against the table.

Clara scurried through the door in a red-and-white striped robe. "She wants you to represent my father in court. He's charged with misdemeanor assault. Is that serious?"

"Up to a year in jail," I said. "Depending."

"On what?" Clara asked.

"Severity of injury. Degree of intent."

Clara's mother stood behind her daughter in the doorway, peeking around her shoulder. A panda bear hiding behind a barber pole.

From across the apartment came knocking. Mom jumped. "Would it be the police?" she asked aloud.

No one seemed keen on answering the door. Another jarring series of concussive thwacks.

Bare-chested, I slipped past the women and pulled the door open.

In walked a fiftyish matron dressed entirely in black as if in mourning. She eyed my torso disdainfully, then swept by me like Special Forces making a hostage rescue.

"Máiréad!" Clara's mother exclaimed.

"Don't Máiréad me. Your husband put my PJ in hospital."

"That man!" Clara's mother mimed pulling out her hair. "How is Patrick Joseph?"

"Broken tibia—that's how he is. Won't be able to work for two months. Thank God for union benefits."

"Liam didn't know the bus was pulling out," said Clara's mother.

"There's a lot Liam doesn't know, Mary."

"Will here," Mary glanced at me, "is going to defend him on the assault charges." Her eyes ripened with expectancy.

"He'd better put on some clothes then," said Máiréad.

All three of them examined me.

"So," I added things up, "Liam threw Patrick in front of a bus."

The three nodded.

"Where was Liam going when he tried to get on that bus?"

"Hurling," Clara and her mother said in unison.

"It's an Irish sport," Clara explained. "He was going to Gaelic Park to watch the hurling match."

"Did the police try to cite him instead of arresting him?" I asked.

"They did," said Mary. "The officer knew him, but Liam wouldn't accept the citation. So he got arrested."

The drawbacks of the case were obvious. Given that the assault had occurred at a bus stop in the Bronx, there were certainly witnesses. Clara's father had thrown PJ in front of a bus. It would be hard to argue that his conduct was what an ordinary prudent man would have done under similar circumstances, even if PJ had been trying to prevent him from boarding. The hospitalization of PJ with a broken leg virtually ensured jail time. If I took it to trial, the complete progression of the case would take three months, at minimum, when I'd promised myself that I was done with law forever.

I tried heading back to Clara's room, hoping to curl back under the covers. Máiréad fled through the foyer, out the door, but Clara and her mother trailed me, standing over the bed.

They did not need to speak. Their faces registered suggestions of a telepathic tête-à-tête. I began to imagine what it would mean to be the bearer of bad news, that Clara's father was going to jail—even for a few months. I'd be tarnished with the stench of it. It wouldn't matter if I procured a relatively good result. And yet, to say *no* seemed impossible. Clara had been my biggest supporter in leaving law. That was history. The situation was obscenely concrete: her father was being held by police. Only a lawyer could help him. I was the lawyer they knew—the one who wouldn't charge. They didn't know it, but $20,000 was what any other lawyer would bill for the case.

As if synchronized by some control tower in the sky, their eyes latched on me simultaneously.

"Please help us!" Their voices indistinguishable.

"Listen to me," I said, using my lowest, gruffest register, "I will represent him up to trial. If he won't accept a plea bargain, I'll ask for a continuance for the purpose of selecting new counsel."

They looked at me blankly. Eyes innocent as rain.

"Is he the type of guy who might accept a deal?" I asked hesitantly.

They shook their heads. The answer I'd anticipated.

"So you'll be hiring a new lawyer in a couple of months. You get that, right?"

Angelic faces. Guileless gazes.

I waited.

Clara nodded tentatively.

No surprise that the law had risen from the coffin and sunk its sharp teeth into my neck. It was a profession not so easily renounced. This wouldn't turn out favorably. Not for her father. Not for me. Meanwhile, I was about to perform my first real kiddie concert—at a Pottery Barn Kids store in New Jersey.

25

Saturday, December 5, 2009 Princeton, NJ

The plan was for Alessia to accompany me to a children's concert she had arranged. In gaudy, road-trip mode, she wore curlers of every color tangled in her long chestnut hair. A fashion statement. I told her to hop in and she handed me one of two large containers of deli coffee. The other she drained quickly and it made her talkative. A friend of hers had volunteered to bring Charley to Saturday morning soccer and feed him afterwards. Alessia launched into a comic description of this soccer mom who, like a chameleon, changed her political views according to the environment. With progressives, her friend was high on President Obama but smiled and nodded when her Cubans friends deemed Barack Hussein a rabid socialist. Alessia asked how I felt about that. Understandable, I said, remembering an instance when my father, an inveterate liberal, had conformed his rhetoric as his reactionary barber shaved the skin above his throat with a straight razor.

There was a lane closed on the Alexander Hamilton bridge which led, via the Cross Bronx Expressway, to the George Washington Bridge. Alessia had spotted a yellow crane beside the Alexander. Anyway, she said, the Cross Bronx was the worst highway known to man—or woman. She demonstrated a deft mastery of Bronx side streets: Valentine to Tremont to University, which spit us out on I-95 only a half mile from the George. I'd always admired my father's faultless sense of direction. That she shared this quality magnified my perception of her. My own was like an unmagnetized compass.

Clara and I had attended Alessia's "bringer" show at a comedy club in Yonkers in which she'd confessed to being a former heroin addict. She'd come on stage in black leggings, crimson blouse, a fake Puerto Rican accent, and hair shielding half her face. She had an uncanny knack for capturing attention, but scored only a few nervous laughs. "Heroin frees you from using the bathroom," she said at one point. "The urge just goes away. You stop getting mad or sad, but no shit or orgasm either." The subject matter was tense but I, who had watched my father address many assemblies, appreciated the drama of a hypnotic speaker.

In turn, she graciously asked to see me perform. I was playing a few nursery schools now but had no public shows scheduled until summer and told her so. She dreamed up a solution. There was a Pottery Barn Kids in Princeton, managed by an old user friend of hers, which staged regular kids shows. Alessia got me booked and we were on our way to Jersey.

Crossing the upper lane of the George, I glanced out at the blue expanse of the Hudson River. With the morning fog lifting, lights of factories and warehouses gleamed along the banks. As we touched down on the Fort Lee side, signs flashed by: New Jersey Turnpike Keep Right, and later, Vince Lombardi Service Area, Sports Complex Exit 16W.

Alessia mentioned that nearly two-hundred parents and children were expected for the show.

My shoulders crept up my neck. "How do they draw that kind of crowd?" I asked.

She hesitated. "Their usual performer is a children's music legend in Princeton."

"She's the one who flew to South America with her partner to adopt a child?"

Alessia had alluded to this on the phone.

"Yeah," she nodded.

I took a breath. "So these people are expecting a superstar?"

She brushed away a wing of hair. "It didn't make sense to change the advertising. What? You nervous?"

I sucked in some air. "Excuse me, parents and children, today playing the part of music legend is—"

"Oh, they're sick of her," she said.

I winced. "That's why she draws two hundred."

Alessia applied some lipstick in the sun visor mirror, eyebrows rising. "Sometimes David exaggerates the numbers," she added.

"Is he clean now?"

"I didn't ask." Small shrug. "Honestly, my addict friends or former addicts show more loyalty than my normies. David didn't even question hiring you."

I cleared my throat. "Does he know this is my first amplified show?"

She patted my right knee. "It's time. You've polished your repertoire."

I'd actually made that case to her before, but felt tempted to argue *against* it now.

When we arrived, I saw strollers lined up outside the store. Inside, it was standing-room-only all the way to the door. David, the manager, an emaciated rock-star type, cracked a relieved smile and greeted Alessia with a warm hug. He buzzed for a warehouse guy to bring me a hand truck for my forty-pound speaker, mixer, wires, and props. Yes, I'd invested in the whole set-up.

People kept flooding in. They sat wall-to-wall on the floor and stood in the back, babies in arms, toddlers sucking pacifiers. The crowd stretched beyond the cash registers, all the way to the entrance. It had only been a month or so since I'd auditioned for those five librarians in East Hartford, but since then, I'd ditched the princess story and worked hard on testing songs and puppet plays at the Spiritualist Church. Also—a couple of new schools had me coming regularly.

Once I wired up the mixer and powered speaker, David borrowed my headset mike and made a quick introduction. Meeting new people one-on-one often proved uncomfortable but somehow, like my father, I was at ease before a big crowd, safe and tethered when watched by many eyes.

I plucked two puppets from my hat rack and launched into a scene between a whale and a chameleon. I leaned toward the children, angling the puppets, inflecting my voice, luring them into my orbit. Then, I plucked a gentle *ostinato*, inviting the children to lie down as I sung a soft lullaby, only to rudely interrupt myself with a driving rhythm, and a raucous prompt to jump on "Mommy's bed." The kids leapt up, squealing with joy, bouncing on the farm-animal rug until, as "Daddy," I told them once again to lie down. One boy protested that he didn't want to go to sleep, and the other children joined in and refused. It all culminated smoothly into more jumping on the bed.

Song to song, I got them up, sat them down, flew them into a mania, floated them back to tranquility, got silly, then grounded them in something familiar. Finally, I'd put together a formula that was working.

At the end of the show, David handed me a check for $450.

Rolling my equipment back to the car on the hand truck, I showed it to Alessia.

"Didn't I tell you what they paid?" she asked. I didn't think she had. "This is almost five times the price I've been quoting," I said.

She helped me load my stuff into the trunk and back seat. When she got in the car, she gestured to me with a baseball cap she'd bought for Charley. "David's not complaining. He's got a store full of happy people. You were great." She laughed. "And I'm relieved. David and I go way back. He knew me *before*."

I programmed the GPS and started the car. Johanna, my name for the navigation voice, began barking out instructions.

"Before what?" I asked Alessia.

She sighed, eyed me warily, and continued. "Before Papi died. Before he left us." She took a breath. "He came here dirt poor from Venezuela and met my mother. When he got to New York, his first job was at a bowling alley. The owner took him to the men's room, stuck his hand in a pile of shit on the tile floor and told him to clean it. By the time I was ten, he owned a home security store in Brooklyn. When I was fourteen, he was installing security systems for nuclear plants in South America, traveling there regularly. He was my favorite person in the world. Of course, we didn't know about his second family in Venezuela. When my mother discovered the secret, he left us. A few months later, Papi died of a stroke. It was too much for me. That was when I started with percocet, then heroin. In time, I was living out of a hotel room, selling my body for money. David knew me when I was still Papi's girl."

Alessia's story frightened me—all the more reason to summon my authoritative lawyer's voice. "Fathers are very important to teenage girls," I said, like some kind of expert.

She nodded. "Yes, and we were very close. He'd wake up every morning with back pain and call for me. I'd snuggle against his lumbar in my pajamas. He said it was the only thing that allowed him to get out of bed. *La curandera* he called me, which is like a witch doctor."

I stretched my arms holding onto the steering wheel.

"I know he loved me," Alessia continued. "He left me trust money that I can draw from when I turn thirty."

I was afraid that if we talked any more about this I'd betray my discomfort. It wasn't that I hadn't represented heroin addicts, but I'd never had one as a friend.

I opened a window for oxygen. "Why did you come to the show with me today?" I asked.

"I enjoyed seeing David," she said. "And you went to see me in Yonkers with Clara. I wanted to return the favor." She touched my knee.

"I loved your show," I lied. "Just one question: why do you speak with a Puerto Rican accent on stage and not a trace of one otherwise?"

"I guess it's a way of distancing myself from the intimacy I'm sharing with the audience. Kind of like a writer using a pen name. I can be pretty intense, yes?"

"Oh no." I failed to hold back a nervous chuckle.

"Oh yes, you mean." She grinned. "Oh yes."

"Do you regret that part of your life—when you were on heroin?"

"Sure I do," she said, "but it got me *here*." She was quiet for a moment. "Do you regret the past?"

I felt a twitch beneath my eye. "Lots of regrets," I said, and left it at that.

She shot me a wry smile. "Who are *you* to think you should have it all figured out? Most of us don't even get close."

We were on the highway now so I buzzed up my window. There was something comforting about her words—that I was just fine where I was.

"How did you kick heroin?" I asked.

"I got pregnant with my son." She pressed her lips into a smile. "Charley coming into this world was the only thing that could have done it. He woke me up."

26

Clara came over that night. We were lying in bed clothed. Now that things had calmed down, and the police had released her father with an appearance notice, I tried to explain to her that I'd started a new life, and didn't want to return to law.

"I understand your career change," Clara said. "What I don't get is why you won't do one more trial. My father will pay you, and I know you need money."

"I don't want to turn back."

A hint of amusement played on her lips as if she found me ridiculous. I tried again. "You'll understand this. Sekhmet. She's working on me."

Clara knitted her brows. "My father's in real trouble and your excuse is that you're possessed by a three-thousand-year-old goddess?"

I looked helplessly at the ceiling. "She killed something I wasn't willing to kill myself."

Clara maintained an unblinking gaze. "Your law career."

I nodded. "Can you see why I can't go back, even a little bit?"

Her face muscles relaxed, she seemed to soften.

"I would have to assume my old identity," I said. "I'm done with that guy."

She angled her head to one side and eyed me with a smile. All of the energy went out of my body. It was a tremendous relief getting through to her, but it left me drained.

She leaned over and kissed me fully on the lips. I was pretty sure I couldn't perform. Not a speck of libido detectable. But somehow I didn't care. I sat up willingly.

My mind didn't rush ahead to whether or not I would get hard. It was content to stay in the present. I watched her disrobe and allow her blouse and bra to fall on the floor. She knelt, deft fingers unbuttoning my shirt, squeezing my nipples.

I don't know why my mind simply couldn't hang onto the thought that she was squeezing too hard, that a little subtlety, a more expert approach, would be appreciated. The idea registered but it couldn't stick. I surrendered to her grip. Couldn't believe it should be otherwise.

When Clara issued a terse directive to shut off the night-table lamp, I didn't see that as an interruption. Just rolled over and did it. What I remember is worshiping her. Everything about her. Buttocks, thighs, breasts, vagina. I experienced it as a prayer without words.

I smoothed the way, she put me in, and I was there half a minute. In and then out. The mast gave way. And surely at that point you might think my world caved in, and I cursed the gods and their fathers and forefathers, along with Prometheus who shaped humans out of clay and endowed them with a spark of life?

No, I just retreated to a lower place on Clara's body and adored. It was a fervent sort of reverence so that when she cried *yes* I slithered back up and the eel found its place and I was making love—so taken for granted when I was harder and prouder before my botched hernia surgery. And now—just as wonderful without the vanity or hydraulics of youth.

I yelled too loud at the end, back arched, elbows digging into the mattress. Our neighbor stopped commanding cats and berating Obama, which is how Clara knew he'd heard something. She scolded me, so I tried to soothe her by rubbing her head as appreciation for her uncompromising Clara-ness. When I finally lay beside her it was not as a hero—the dominance of the missionary position aside—but as pretty much, nobody. I could not find a sliver of pride in my being. Only gratefulness. Peace.

I was to need that bit of ease and humility for what was to come.

27

Tuesday December 29, 2009 White Plains, NY

My brother and I had been warned that my mother would be susceptible to a second stroke up to three months after the first. On a Sunday morning, after breakfast, David called me. He'd found her unconscious in front of "Face the Nation." By the time I arrived at White Plains Hospital, she'd slipped into a coma and was blocked off in a section of intensive care. Every so often they'd give her medication intended to elevate her vital signs. They rose temporarily and plateaued again. This happened repeatedly over many hours. The doctor grew discouraged that the elevated vital signs could neither be maintained nor restore consciousness.

At first, David and I tried talking to her. We told family stories and asked her questions as if we expected an answer. But there came a time when we had little to say anymore.

I sat by my mother's bed, fixated on her breathing, the intimacy of holding her hand. For some reason David and the doctor had left the unit. I was alone with her. Words came to me, "May you be at peace. May you feel supported. May you feel loved. May you go where you need to go. May angels greet you. May you experience yourself as the love that you are. Mom, I love you. My heart is bonded with your heart."

I felt as if, to the extent I could, I was taking a step of her journey with her. In this trance-like state, I was aware of my brother re-entering the room. My mother's breathing had become erratic. Along with weak inhalations, there was an extremely slight recurring spasm just below her eye that told me she was still alive. And then she didn't breathe again. I looked for the eye spasm. It had ceased. A nurse rushed into the room. She felt for a pulse, then fetched the doctor, who hurried in, detected no heartbeat, and pronounced my mother dead. After he closed her eyelids I felt a peace thicken the air, and I dwelled in it with my mother, and whatever invisible beings might be present.

28

After the new year, we sat Shiva. The Rosses were not observant enough to give a hoot about Shiva seats and David knew that, of course. Regardless, he rented a slew of low-to-the-ground chairs. There they stood in the living room of his apartment, black-cushioned, and lined up on either side of a rented buffet table. The guests were due to arrive.

My brother had his back to me, sorting out the caterer's delivery of various appetizers and entrees. I had just laid out the buffet ladles and serving spoons and followed him back into the kitchen. Without a glance at me, he crossed into the living room with a tray of mini-bagels and lox. I trailed with a large bowl of fruit salad.

"You broke Mom's heart," David said. "It won't say that on the death certificate, but that's what happened."

I let the heavy bowl down on the buffet with an intentional thud. "I caused both her strokes?"

David retreated to the kitchen. "You were the love of her life," he said.

I elbowed past him to claim a heavy tray of chicken cutlets. "I visited her three times a week," I howled.

David nodded. "Yes, she counted. Not two. Not four. Always three." He hoisted a large bowl of three-bean salad and brushed by me toward the buffet table.

I trailed with the cutlets. "What are you trying to say?" I let another tray clang to the table upsetting the breaded filets. The porcelain stayed intact.

"You've always had your limit," said David tersely. "God forbid you ever let yourself exceed your limit."

David answered the phone. "Oh Dad," he said. "I'm sorry. I'm coming now." He hurried to the coat closet and threw a jacket over his shoulder. "I forgot to pick him up. He took a shuttle to the Crown Plaza and he's at the bar."

"He asked *you* to pick him up!" I shouted. "Put down those keys. I'll get him."

I didn't see Clara standing in the doorway and caught her with my elbow as I turned.

"Sorry," I said. She opened her arms and we hugged briefly before I flew through the door to beat David, who was fumbling with an umbrella.

By the time I hurried back with Dad, the guests had arrived, some standing, others sprawled out in mourner's chairs. Dad had a drink or two in him, judging by his gait, and we were both wet from the drizzle. Clara reached up to take his raincoat and I stepped on her toe. She stifled a yelp.

"Sorry," I said. "So sorry."

Felicia showed up in a black mourning dress of heavy crepe. She barely returned David's weak smile. Something was up. She took her place on one of the low seats across from the long table. The girl had class coming tonight if there was trouble with David. Alessia appeared with Charley. She gave Clara a double-cheek kiss, lightly brushing each one. Charley, adorably and wetly, imitated the gesture. My guitar-playing friend, Ray, arrived from upstate. In rushing to greet him, David shaved past me, grazing my shoulder, and I glared at him.

"Remember," Felicia said kindly, "tonight is about your mother."

"You're right." I nodded and forced a smile.

David started recounting a memory of Sarah Ross to Ray and my father. "She was always there for me," he said. "I knew that I could call her at any time for any reason and she'd answer. I remember, as a kid, floating on a boogie board in the ocean and suddenly realizing that I didn't know how to get back. She plunged in and dragged me out even though she didn't swim."

"What I remember," I said, not to be outdone, "is being in the bathtub at five years old, Mom washing my hair with baby shampoo. As she massaged my scalp, she said, 'You are going to be a very smart man, a very smart and successful man.' Mom," I paused for effect. "You were wrong." There were a few titters and some clearing of throats. God, I was making a fool of myself.

Then, as if by silent decree, private conversations sprung up. People stood, took plates, and lined up for the buffet. I realized that I wasn't ready for prime time and retreated to David's guest bedroom, closing the door. David had already restored the room to its previous state. The hospital bed was gone, replaced by a twin. There was one of those European electric tea kettles on the dresser along with a tea cup and a few sealed pouches of Earl Grey. The kettle was heavy with water so I switched it on. The door behind me creaked open. Clara. She glanced at my face and must have detected my displeasure at being found.

"You don't look very happy to see me," she said. "First you elbow me on the way out to get your dad. On your way back, you step on my toe."

I began to cry, tears which hadn't come so far, and I thought might never. They poured out with moans and whimpers. Clara approached, first within comfortable talking distance, then arm's length, and finally the proximity of only mothers and lovers.

How radiant she was! She had a face which looked better from four inches than it did from farther away. No one who hadn't looked at her that close could know how lovely. She ushered me down under the covers of the twin. There was one angle, peering up at her nostrils from her throat, where she was exquisite, a chiseled symmetry revealed at close range.

I kissed her and felt as if I were spinning, losing my sense of place. I was blinded, dumb—unable to distinguish between me, her, the water boiling in the hot pot for tea. As we groped for each other, I broke into a sweat, sucking her tongue, seeing flashes of eye, tit, hair, nostril. And when she reached down for me, my dick lay prostrate, in awe.

She began to help me. It was if she were feeding me, creating me, little by little. Then I was coming back at her, surprised, elated by my own power, pinning her down, showing my strength. She guided me in. Slick and raw and hot.

"I'm going to turn you over," she said. She flipped me with surprising strength and thrust her chest above me. Her features clenched as if trying to remember the date of the Louisiana Purchase. Slowly she rocked her torso, allowing my penis to almost jerk free and then absorbing a full stroke. Mastering this, she increased the speed. A great furrow formed in the middle of her brow as her mouth spread into a crookedly intense smile and every ridge and valley of definition showed in her shoulders and arms. She was wild—grating pelvis, laboring arms, a passionate grimace, and now a cathartic *ahhhhhh*! My penis thrust, her center swallowed me up and, a thought surfaced—with my mother gone, I wanted to marry Clara.

"Would you?" I asked.

Would I what?" She was sliding off me now.

"Would you turn the tea kettle off?"

29

Saturday, April 23, 2010 Schenectady, NY

Clara and I were invited to Ray's engagement party. And you haven't really seen it done up right until you've attended a Hindu *mangni*.

It all took place in a giant, heated tent on the front lawn. There was a white canopy for the betrothed couple, pink balloons, and garlands of yellow and red flowers. Presiding was a long-winded Hindu priest in a gold paisley gown who sounded like a Top-40 DJ with a Guyanese Creole accent.

Colorfully-garbed musicians sat in a circle cross-legged on a wooden dance floor. One strummed a sitar, which looked like a pregnant banjo. Another beat on a barrel-shaped drum, cross-laced with twine, which he said was called a *dholak*. His son beside him tapped on a bowl-shaped *kanjira*. A man with legs splayed out to accommodate his sizable belly fingered an Indian harmonium, which folded out from a box. Women and children danced in glorious saris of orangey red, apricot, and sky blue.

Ray was marrying a Guyanese woman in Schenectady, and her parents were hosting the ring ceremony and engagement party in a tent replete with patio heaters. Later, there would be a long, vegetarian buffet. When I asked Ray's future father-in-law why the dishes looked and tasted so much like Indian food, he told me that the British had imprisoned Indians in colonial times and brought them to Guyana to work as slaves. Ray's parents and a gaggle of his friends were the only white people in attendance.

We got to approach Ray, sitting with his fiancé under the white canopy, when it was our turn to sprinkle them with rose petals. They played it stoically—sitting there like prince and princess while guests lined up to anoint them. She resembled depictions I'd seen of the goddess Kali. Not with four arms, and certainly no giant sickle or severed head, but long raven hair, groomed wild, a small jeweled tiara perched on top, and a gorgeous sari of indigo and gold. Her appearance was striking. I wouldn't have been surprised to see her dancing on a prostrate Lord Shiva. Or that might have been a teeny projection, because I had arrived at this engagement party bearing a ring of my own. Was I frightened? Oh yes, and it made me wonder how Ray felt now. He was a bland Presbyterian. No way were his parents zealous enough to assemble a collection of musicians, chanters, dancers, along with a priest, and congregation, for a ring ceremony on their trim Mamaroneck lawn. This was all courtesy of the bride's Schenectady clan. It was quite a scene and, if nothing else, might make Ray think twice about breaking the engagement, if Kali's wrath wasn't enough of a deterrence. But that noble goddess, like Sekhmet, transcended Western notions of good and evil, and it was childish of me to project otherness onto foreigners, or females, as the ring burned in my pocket.

Musicians played, exhorting the dancers to higher and higher intensity. The loopy *dandiya* beats and haunting harmonium riffs cut through my defenses, teleporting me into an almost trance-like state.

"What are you doing with your shoulders?" Clara asked.

I hadn't even been aware that they were moving. Just an extension of the rolling flow I was feeling from toes to crown.

"Are you alright?" she asked, genuinely concerned.

We were sitting right by a heater. But that didn't account for the beads of sweat rolling down my face. I felt that I couldn't keep it in any longer, that if I didn't get that ring out of my pocket, I'd experience a catastrophic melt down, like a nuclear reactor with stalactites hanging from my valves and tubes. I dug the jeweler's box from my slacks.

"Clara, will you marry me?"

When she caught sight of the diamond her eyes grew wide and cheeks flushed with color.

"Ooooh!" she cried, fanning her face as if it were hot to the touch.

"Well?" I asked eagerly.

She took a breath to calm herself and deadpanned, "I knew you'd ask me when your mother died."

Of course she was right, but I tossed that off with a backward flick of my fingers. "What does my mother have to do with it?"

She smiled puckishly and moved toward me. "That's the secret to landing an old bachelor like you."

My mouth went dry. "I'm only thirty-seven."

"The odds that a single man will marry after thirty-five are only five percent." She nuzzled my cheek.

"Really?" That gave me a chill, a quick spasm up my back, but yes, men did establish certain habits by my age.

"After forty, you're more likely to be killed by a terrorist," Clara teased, then kissed me.

"Does that mean yes?"

She took the ring, slipped it on her finger, and gave me a bashful nod.

"This isn't a mercy yes, I mean, given my odds?"

She assured me that it was not.

Energy shot through my body and I extended a hand to Clara, then got up to move with the sari-clad ladies to the beat of the *dholak* and *kanjira*.

Clara giggled, pink creeping into her cheeks. I was shaking off an old skin, finally making a life for myself. I let my body dance.

30

A few days later, arriving home in the late afternoon, I found Clara shivering on my front steps, elbows on knees, body slumped forward so that hair covered her face. It wasn't like her to show up unannounced on a work day. PS 463 was an hour and fifteen minutes south, assuming minimal traffic, and there was never minimal traffic.

"I'm the enemy." Her voice cracked.

"Not to me you're not," I said, approaching with two bags of Trader Joe's groceries. I rested them on the wooden porch.

"Here, have some dried mango," I said, flipping the bag to her. She let out a hoarse, nervous chuckle, and shook the bag as she spoke.

"My principal made a deal with my teacher, the star of the documentary, to disown me because I'm the enemy."

I cleared my throat. "Divide and conquer. It's the strategy Julius Caesar used to defeat Gaul over two-thousand years ago."

She waved a piece of dried mango in the air. "You're the one who thinks Ms. Rodriquez is Sekhmet. *Three-thousand* years old. She taught that tactic to Caesar."

I laughed. "That's it. Don't take it seriously. Wait for the game to come back to you."

I could almost hear her heart beating inside her chest. She was breathing fast. I pulled her close. Her shoulders felt tense, sinewy.

"All drama is good drama," I reminded her. "This is just another complication that will make your film more compelling."

Clara swayed a bit as if all the blood was leaving her head. She put down the sliver of mango and grabbed my shoulder to steady herself.

These power struggles with her principal were a daily occurrence. Something else was eating her. "What's wrong?" I asked, pressing my fingers against her spine.

"Nothing," she said quietly.

I'd interviewed a lot of defendants and could recognize a lie, a deflection. Her eyes said, *don't ask*. I should have asked anyway.

Instead, I turned and embraced her. Her breasts pressed against my ribs, her fingers light against my lower spine. We held each other. Each moment beat long and round, fragrant with fear, or a cold sweat that smelled like it. I put my ear against her warm head and heard my own pulse beating, so raw and stubborn that I pulled away. I was afraid she'd sense how much I needed her. Then I lowered my face, planted a kiss, and as I withdrew, she opened her mouth. She coaxed me down again to lips and tongue, feeling me, measuring her impact.

I got up, slipped the key into my front door, pushed it open, flicked on the light. The kitchen smelled like frying pan grease.

"We don't need the light," said Clara, behind me. She turned it off. We crossed the kitchen and plunked down on the couch in the living room.

"Mmmm," she purred as I cuddled up. Sweeping aside her hair, I kissed her on the side of the neck, then nibbled my way down to her collarbone. More hair flowed in and I fended it off. She wriggled out of her blouse and slacks. Watching my eyes, she allowed her breasts to round comfortably out of her bra. Her nipples were broad and puffy, pimpled with goose flesh. I moved my mouth from her throat down her jugular and finally to her breast. Closing her eyes, she moved her pelvis rhythmically.

Oh God, those moans. A whimper, a prayer, a chant—it seemed as if she were crying out in order to feel. I thought I'd make her come just sucking on her breasts. Each move of my mouth generated a shiver or shout, a celebration of sensation, as if something treacherous in the room needed to be forced back. She was no longer concerned about my neighbor with his platoon of cats.

Suddenly I was on my back with the elastic of my cottons raveled at my ankles. I kicked them off. My penis stood up as gamely as it could these days. Clara was about to put me in her mouth.

"Is this okay?"

"God yes."

She had never offered before, and the wonder of it made me stop breathing, stop feeling, until I realized that it was my time to feel, and tears came.

"You like this, Will?"

"Yes, oh God, yes."

I closed my eyes and let my head loll on the armrest. As I was about to let go, I thrust my hand triumphantly into the air and Clara wheeled back and cowered. She must have thought that I was going to hit her — like the guy in Bangkok. I felt crushed. I knew her reaction had nothing to do with me, but it felt like it did. We looked at each other in shock as my penis gurgled over. In the midst of that exposed moment, warm cum pooling on my belly, it came clear to me that Clara was hiding something.

I stood and made a pretense of remembering to collect my frozen Chicken Tandoori and other perishables from the front porch. *That I would hit her!* The thought was repellant to me. I carefully put away groceries. *That Clara would think I was unsafe!* With the food now stacked in the fridge and cupboard, I washed the dishes.

31

Tuesday, May 6, 2010 Bronx Criminal Courthouse

I feared the worst. Blood ties are stubborn no matter what Clara had said. If no plea bargain could be reached today, I would be forced to waive time on Liam McLaughlin's case and make good on my threat to step down as his lawyer.

I approached the Bronx courthouse fearing I'd lose Clara. Funny that I'd left law to rid myself of the daily fear. It wasn't working.

The Bronx Criminal Court House stood about a half mile from Yankee Stadium in the southernmost part of the borough, a huge, limestone building with wide corridors. Swinging open the heavy door, I caught a glimpse of the recognizable gait of a colleague of mine disappearing into the men's room. I followed. Familiarity was welcome here.

The heavy-set fellow, a Westchester attorney, stood at one of the urinals wiping the sweat off his brow with a handkerchief as he piddled. We weren't well acquainted, but he inhabited a place in my imagination because I knew him to live in an idyllic cabin on ten acres in Brewster. I pictured him playing his Gibson Les Paul full-blast unrestrained by any complaints from distant neighbors. A kindred soul.

The cloying sweet odor of para blocks rose from the bank of urinals to the right. A row of sinks were to the left, with stalls to the rear, across a black-and-white tiled floor. The man zipped up and turned around.

"Elliot!" I said.

He smiled broadly. "Will! I thought you were disbarred." His forehead creased. "That's the rumor around the White Plains courthouse."

Elliot had a tendency to say exactly what was on his mind. My stomach sank. Why were my colleagues so quick to believe that I was guilty of moral turpitude?

I dismissed it with a carefree toss of my hand. "No, just winding down my practice."

My mind started racing. If Elliot were to ask me what I was doing now and I answered "writing songs for children," he might infer that I was having a nervous breakdown. That would engender more gossip around the courthouse.

But Elliot just smiled and nodded. He was not overly curious.

Correspondingly, I held off inquiring about any specifics of his life. Instead I asked, "What brings you to the Bronx?"

He touched a finger to his temple and focused on me so earnestly that his eyes crossed. "Will, I've got something for you." Darting brows. "Easy money. Maybe you need it now."

I had begun to think about money. It wasn't coming in fast enough. I'd lived comfortably as a lawyer, but hadn't put much away.

I took a slow breath. "I'm listening."

Elliot dipped his head furtively. "You still got a bar license?"

I nodded, fidgeting with the keys in my pocket.

He took a step closer and lowered his voice. "How would you like to make $15,000 for what will probably amount to one court appearance?"

My ears popped as if adjusting to a higher altitude. To bank an extra $15,000 would make a difference, the added cushion affording much-needed time.

The pace of Elliot's speech accelerated. "My sister's husband clopped her. Black eye. Other injuries. When the police arrived, he was plastered. He's wealthy. If I accept the case, I'll take his $15,000, plead him to a lesser charge, and then have to return it when he sees it was an hour's work." Elliot leaned forward. "He's my brother-in-law. But if *you* take the case, he can't ask for his money back. That's what I want."

I was already beginning to think of myself as a misfit. Why not make easy money fast? Another thing—what if Elliot took Liam Mc-Laughlin's case in return? I'd be free. Though hard to explain to Clara.

There was only one thing I needed to know to say yes. "Is he an asshole?"

Elliot turned his palms up. "My sister has given *him* a couple of black eyes through the years." He emphasized her ferocity by furrowing his forehead. "No, he's not an asshole, but I want to teach him a lesson."

Ah well. It didn't feel right to take the guy's money. A real misfit would grab it. But maybe I wasn't quite there yet.

I shrugged. "It's not for me, but thanks."

Elliot nervously rubbed his thumb against his forefinger. "That's okay," he said flatly. "I guess we'll keep it in the family." He headed toward the men's room door then turned back. "What you got today, misdemeanor trial?"

"Yeah," I said. Tight-lipped smile. "Assault."

"Family member?" asked Elliot, joking.

A flush sounded from the one of the bays and I spotted the tips of black shoes under a stall door. A well-dressed man emerged, pausing at the sink.

Elliot mouthed, "Judge Goldberg."

I didn't say anything further.

As I staggered toward the courtroom, I was reeling from Elliot's news. The dope among Westchester lawyers was that I'd been exiled, disbarred. This hurt. My social conditioning ran stronger and deeper than I'd imagined. It didn't take a pillory or dunce cap for me to feel publicly humiliated—censured for a crime, real or imagined. I wondered whether the search for deep satisfaction and fulfillment ever really eclipsed the instinct to conform. Only in rare people I decided—probably not me. I didn't know what I'd do if push came to shove today, and Clara pressed me to represent her father at trial. Now I couldn't trade with Elliot.

In the courtroom, Mr. McLaughlin was sitting in the gallery, regaling a new acquaintance with a story.

"I was riding Metro North," he said. "A young woman claims that I'm sitting in her seat." He paused for effect. "Nothing was there, not an umbrella, a jacket, or nothing."

His listener, a man about the same age, nodded. Clara's mother sat to Liam's other side, staring straight ahead.

He pressed on. "I had a big bag of things, because I was visiting my sister at St. Patrick's Nursing Home. So I get up and move to the next seat, sliding my bag over. I felt nothing, but somehow my hand moves instinctively to my pants pocket and my wallet is gone." He pantomimed that discovery. "The thief sits down in my seat and I stand up and block her way out of the aisle. I say to her, 'Give it back.' And she says, in broken English, she don't know what I'm talking about."

Liam worked his lips a bit while checking his audience. "Two of her girlfriends come up behind me and demand I let their friend out of the row. I reach out and grab the girl like this." He grabbed Mrs. McLaughlin. "I grip her wrist and twist a little." She pulled away and dismissed her husband with a wave.

"The girl gets scared and the wallet pops onto the seat. Her friends point to it and say it's proof I've falsely accused her. I pick up the wallet and she snakes right out with her pickpocket cronies." He nodded at his companion. "Not so easy to fleece me they found out."

"That's the truth," said his new friend.

I drew close enough to draw both men's attention.

"Where's Clara?" I asked him.

"Don't know," he said with pursed lips. "She's never home anymore since that new job. Loves that job. Don't know what the hell she's doing, but she loves it."

Mrs. McLaughlin's blue eyes opened wide. "She's going to get fired by that principal."

Her husband frowned. "Oh, don't tell him that!" he snapped.

"I'm due in chambers with the judge and prosecutor," I said, excusing myself.

Every jurisdiction has a community of lawyers. If you're an insider, you know what to expect, including whose breath might smell of alcohol at nine in the morning. You can tell the lawyers who'd been born in their monkey suits from the poor souls like me who'd been badgered into the profession by their parents. Elliot, with his Fender Les Paul, was in my camp and I chose the seat beside him, a chair like you'd expect to find in a movie theater. With our shoulders practically touching, I smelled pipe tobacco and aftershave. Six other lawyers sat around the judge, and newcomers had begun standing in the back. Apart from Elliot, I didn't know the others in the room. My home turf was White Plains. The Bronx was a foreign land.

Judge Goldberg was speaking on the phone and rapping his fingers nervously on a mahogany desk. Panels on the top and sides were inlaid with patterns like those carved into a cowboy's saddle.

Elliot's office was just shy of the Bronx line so he knew the terrain down here. This judge, he whispered, was an avid Western film buff. He'd initially ordered the reclining seats for a home theater but they'd been banished to his chambers by his wife.

Across from us was a Chesterfield-style black velvet couch packed with three lawyers. Melissa Aiello, the deputy D.A., sat on a swivel chair by a name-plated desk loaded with her files.

There was a club-like feel to the cozy chambers. The judge and lawyers were insiders who dickered over the business of the outsiders in the gallery, each represented by a file. As locals, they all knew each other, and whispered amicably. I was aware that there was a limit on how vigorously I could negotiate a plea bargain, given my interloper status. The judge and prosecutor would tolerate polite debate, but a case too strenuously argued might tip the scales against me.

I did have a strategy. I would refuse to waive speedy trial on the assumption that the docket was too crowded for my case to be tried today. That might incentivize the prosecutor to sweeten the deal and get rid of me. Most misdemeanors had to be tried within ninety days, but in my case, one of the witnesses interviewed by police had been a child. This gave me an advantage.

Judge Goldberg put down the phone and cleared his throat. He was getting down to business.

"Your Honor," I said, "I'd like to invoke New York Criminal Procedure Section 190.30, which ensures a speedy trial for matters involving child witnesses. My case should take precedence." I rubbed the back of my neck nervously. This could backfire, I knew.

Judge Goldberg's left jowl hung a little lower than his right, tilting his mouth into a scowl. His broad hands seemed poised to grab a lapel or wring a chicken's neck.

"Mr. uh," he glanced down at the docket. "Mr. Ross, don't pull a one-ninety on me. That ought to be reserved for instances in which the child is a *victim*, not merely a witness. Do your client a favor and plead the case. I'm sure Ms. Aiello here," he gestured to the prosecutor, "will make an offer."

So far so good. This was the response I'd hoped for.

Ms. Aiello thought for a moment and said, "Misdemeanor conviction. Three months jail time." This was the offer proposed and rejected by Clara's father at the pre-trial conference.

I shook my head sadly.

Judge Goldberg shifted his jaw. "Are you kidding, Mr. Ross? Your client should take that deal and run. If the jury convicts, Mr. McLaughlin could get far more." He leaned toward me.

I straightened my back. "This was an accident. My client has no criminal record. We'll accept a fine, probation, weekend work detail, but not jail time."

"The victim's got a leg fractured in two places," the judge said. He waved a hand. "What am I going to tell his family?"

Strictly speaking, it was not a relevant question as I was sure he knew. The State had to prove the requisite state of mind for Clara's father to be convicted. But a jury could very well decide that Liam McLaughlin had been criminally negligent. And the legal system was, in essence, an alternative to aggrieved parties exacting their own vengeance. The judge wanted a result that provided an appearance of justice.

"Can we get creative?" I asked. "Can we fashion a penalty with strong deterrent effect but without jail time?"

Ms. Aiello cut in, "It would be easier to discuss a compromise if you were to withdraw your one-ninety request. That way at least we'd know what trial is going this morning."

Clogging up their busy docket was my only leverage. I hesitated, searching for a way to politely refuse.

"May I, Judge?" said a lawyer sitting on the Chesterfield. I spun around to look back. Deep lines were etched into his face. He reminded me of a wildcat oil driller or a crane operator.

"I'm sitting on a three-month-old, time-not-waived, spousal abuse case. It would take precedence except for your child witness who probably won't even be called. You may not know how good a deal you're getting," he said. "Take the three months and let *my* case go this morning." He looked at the judge expectantly.

Judge Goldberg raised his palms. "Whoa Jack," he said to the older lawyer, then turned to me. "Mr. Ross, I'm going to work with you." The judge peered over his half readers at Ms. Aiello. "Can you see clear to bringing this down to a month? The defendant's in his late sixties without a record. My guess is that you could prove criminal negligence under these facts but the equities here point to leniency." He flashed me a reassuring grin.

"No problem," answered Melissa Aiello, playing with her dangling earrings. "One month, Mr. Ross. You're new to this jurisdiction but that would be the best plea bargain I've ever offered on an assault case with this degree of injury." She dipped her head toward me.

I fiddled with the keys in my pocket through the cloth of my trousers.

The judge gave me a long, fixed stare. "I want a misdemeanor plea because the court needs some leverage over your client. But we're giving you everything else. He walks out of here with a month. In reality, that's about 15 days, two weeks. Pretty damn good for pushing a man under a bus."

I laughed nervously. "Thank you," I said. There was absolutely no doubt in my mind that this was the best possible result. Any further dissent could easily unravel it. I'd made such mistakes before.

The judge perked up. "Okay then. Case settled. Let's see who's going to trial today. Jack, I hope you're ready to try your spousal abuse case. We'll start picking a jury right after we negotiate and accept the other pleas."

Grumbles of disappointment rose from the club of attorneys. I tucked the file into my briefcase, stood up, and left the other lawyers to their plea bargains.

Returning to the courtroom, I saw Clara, wearing a knit business dress, huddling with her parents. Her face was pale. It didn't look as though she'd had time to apply make-up.

Her mother, Mary, was in a tea-length frock, light blue, and Liam in a handsome dark suit. They remained seated as I explained that with good time, Liam would serve 15 days in jail.

His brow furrowed. "What does that mean," he asked, "plea bargain?"

I'd already explained at the pre-trial conference, but I feigned patience. "It's an agreement. The charge is reduced in exchange for your plea."

"No deals," he snapped.

Clara winced. She leaned forward and stared at her father. "Dad, do you really want to go through a trial? Will showed me the police report." Her hazel eyes pulsed. "They have three witnesses who say you knocked that man in front of a moving bus."

Her father scowled. "Rubbish. I didn't know it was moving. He shouldn't have been interfering in my business." He waved his hands impatiently.

"But Dad, the jury might not see it that way." Clara aimed me a sly glance.

Liam set his jaw. "I can tell them myself."

This provoked a withering gaze from Clara.

"If Dad's convicted at trial, what's he facing?" She pointed at Liam as if to say, *you listen now.*

I tilted my head toward her. "Up to a year in jail and a substantial fine."

Liam let out a *humph.*

Clara shook her father's shoulder. "Did you hear that, Dad?"

Liam pressed his lips into a sarcastic leer. "They can put me on bread and water. I can handle myself if those inmates bother me." He was clearly enjoying it now. Putting on a reality show.

"I'll testify for him," Mary offered, but her frozen face revealed that was the last thing she wanted to do.

Clara's mouth fell open, as in *for that I'm going to kill you later.* She turned to me. "Honestly, is this a good plea deal?"

"It's a *great* plea deal," I said. "The victim has a compound fracture. He could have been killed."

Liam harrumphed. "I've got rights," he said. "Constitutional rights." The facts had ceased to matter. He was on a roll.

Clara glowered. "Dad, if you take this to trial, I'm *not* coming with you. You'll testify. Three witnesses will say otherwise. They'll put you into custody right then and there. Is that what you want?"

His face grew animated. "Bring it on! I won't go down without a fight!" A smile tugged at the corners of his lips. He was entertaining himself.

Clara gave me a look. "Will," she said, "let's talk privately."

We slipped out to the hallway and took cover in an alcove right by the gallery door.

She leveled a gaze at me. "Bring Dad's case to trial."

"That's crazy," I said. "It's reckless, by definition, to throw someone in front of a bus. He doesn't have a chance. If he pisses off the jury, they'll put him away for a year."

"He won't." She maintained an unblinking stare. "My father can be charming. Beneath it all, he has a heart of gold. You'd be surprised how many jobs he's finagled for poor families over the years. Taken men under his wing. Guided them into the union. He wants you to fight." She softened her tone. "*I* want you to fight."

"Clara, fifteen days. Two weeks and this can be over. The victim's still in a cast."

"You don't get it," Clara said. "The McLaughlin's want you to fight. Please. It's in our blood. It will mean everything, regardless of outcome."

We heard chairs creaking, feet scuffling, and we quickly re-entered the gallery.

A uniformed bailiff had announced the judge. The older man was making his ascent to the bench.

I felt dizzy. It was all I could do to maintain a standing position.

"The People v. Liam McLaughlin. Are both counsel present?"

Liam's face turned red. "I won't have it," he cried.

Mary shushed him but he stood anyway.

"You won't have what, Sir?" asked the judge.

He let out a hoarse, nervous chuckle. "I don't want a deal. I want to stand trial today."

The air in the courtroom was dense, dusty, unbreathable. The walls closing in.

"And your attorney is," the judge peered down at his notes, "Mr. Ross."

The judge flinched. "So Mr. McLaughlin, do I understand that you reject the plea bargain negotiated by your attorney?"

"Reject," he growled from deep in his throat.

The judge returned a weak smile. "That would be, 'Yes, Judge Goldberg.'"

Liam blinked twice. "Yes, Judge Goldberg."

I steadied myself against the defense table. Clara had begged me, but I was dead set against continuing with a doomed case and delaying my clean break with law.

Judge Goldberg turned to me.

"What do you have to say, Mr. Ross?"

I was shifting my feet from side to side as a poor substitute for what I really wanted to do—escape. "I can't conscientiously agree with the defendant turning down this plea bargain. I want the court to know that I've advised my client that he's making a huge mistake. I'd really rather not be party to it. This is my last case, your honor. I've sold my practice. I was appearing today as a favor to Mr. McLaughlin's daughter. "

Clara glared at me. Smoke burning from her eyes. The judge glanced toward her and then at the defendant.

"So, Mr. McLaughlin, you're not paying your attorney. Your daughter is his girlfriend?"

Liam raised his chin and looked squarely at the judge. "No, I'm not paying him."

"And I'm not—" Clara's voice trailed off.

I turned and looked back. Her attention was trained on her shiny black pumps. My anxiety rose like a tsunami. I'd been a fool to take the case.

Judge Goldberg ruminated, stroking his beard like Solomon.

"Mr. McLaughlin, you have a choice either to proceed as your own counsel or accept the plea bargain that was negotiated for you by Mr. Ross. Mr. Ross, you are relieved as Mr. McLaughlin's attorney. Five-minute recess."

The judge struck the sound block with his gavel. I didn't care anymore what Liam McLaughlin chose to do. Before anyone in the gallery could rise, and without even glancing at Clara, I walked out of the courtroom, through the hallway, and out into the blessed Bronx air. If I were really trying to free myself, I had to stop fearing a life without her.

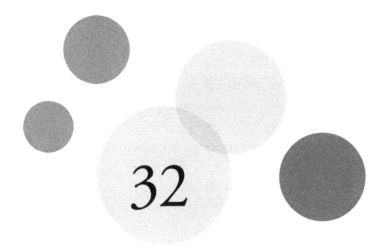

32

That night I met David's girlfriend, Felicia, at an Indian restaurant. We sat at a table near the bar where an oversized screen showed Bollywood clips. A bikini-clad seductress undulated and sang, waves roaring behind her as a strapping leading man made a dripping entrance from the surf. I hadn't seen Felicia since my mother's Shiva. She'd called, spur of the moment, to invite me here.

Sandalwood incense mixed with the smell of fresh poppadum on the table. I broke off a piece of the thin wafer leaving crisp, mustard-beige crumbs on the starched, white tablecloth.

"I didn't know you liked Indian food," I said to her as we perused menus. "You never had time for lunch when I was a lawyer."

She let out a breath of mock exasperation. "You think I wanted you hounding me about some drunk driving case while I was trying to enjoy my Chicken Tikka Masala?" She laughed—with her mouth not her eyes. Something was wrong. I searched her face for a clue.

"What's going on?"

She gave a weak smile. "Did you hear about the Norma Wilkes' case?"

No, I hadn't. But I thought about Joshua every day. "I'm pretty disengaged from that world," I said.

Felicia cleared her throat. "The case may never come to trial. The judge found her incompetent based on a psychiatric evaluation. She's decompensating. Not stable enough to testify. She's in a psychiatric hospital for rehabilitation. If rehabilitated, she'll be tried; if not, she's there forever."

I met Felicia's eyes trying to glean her motivation. Had she really invited me out to share news about the Wilkes case?

"That's probably what her lawyer wanted," I said.

"Some defendants prefer jail. More dignity. Less time." Her voice broke when she said *dignity*.

"Really," I pleaded. "What's wrong? It's all over your face."

She dropped her head back against the chair. "Are my eyelids still puffy?"

I looked closer and nodded. A hanging waterfall burbled on the wall behind her.

Felicia shook her head. "I'm trying to figure out what happened. It was like a game of chess with David. I started out with all my pawns. The focused career woman who needed nothing." She gestured with a fork. "No commitment. No kids. Insisted on paying her own way." She pressed her lips together. "David liked that fine. Then he asked me to spend a month in Switzerland this summer—which wasn't going to fly with my boss." Her lower lip trembled.

"I agreed, which was akin to relinquishing pawn number one." She reached for a pair of salt and pepper shakers perched on a small porcelain boat and moved the salt off the boat. "It also meant that I was tacitly signing on to his dream of eventually living in Switzerland. Second pawn surrendered."

She pushed the pepper off. It toppled over and sprayed flecks on the white cloth. She made no attempt to fix it. "The thought of leaving my career awakened an urge to have a baby. I told him. That was the third pawn." She turned over the porcelain boat itself.

The waiter arrived, ignored the damage done, and laid a bread basket of steaming *paratha* on the table.

"So, with my left flank wide open, he accused me of presenting a false veneer, a bait and switch." Her eyes burned. "Queen captured." She snatched a piece of hot Indian bread. "Check mate." She bit into it, chewed and swallowed. "I moved out yesterday. Thank God I had delayed selling the condo and giving notice to the D.A."

I nodded, careful not to break eye contact.

"The reason I agreed to all those things —" Her voice trailed off and face crumpled.

I finished her sentence. "Was that you love him."

"Yeah." She dabbed an eye. "I'm a *How To Lose A Guy in 10 Days* kind of girl. Did you ever see that movie?"

I hadn't even heard of it.

She smiled through her tears. "If you can get past the disturbing assumptions about gender roles, there's an absurdity to it that's comforting. It's my macaroni-and-cheese movie."

I pointed at her with a wafer of *poppadum*. "At least you found out something—you want a baby."

Felicia's eyes narrowed. "I'll put it on my car's bumper. See if I get any offers." Tears welled again. She compressed her lips as if exerting an act of will. *No more David talk,* she said with her eyes.

Now I wasn't sure what to do.

"Seriously," Felicia said with forced ardor, "she'll probably never get out of that place."

"Oh, Norma Wilkes?" I was relieved.

She was the last thing on my mind. I was more interested in the seeming coincidence of my brother's breakup with Felicia following so closely on the heels of my rift with Clara. My relationship with David wasn't ideal, but he was my only brother and I hoped it was just happenstance.

"So how are you?" asked Felicia.

"Meh." I held my palm toward the table and rocked it slightly.

"Tell me," she said. So I explained about Liam's battery case, the plea bargain, and how I'd blown Clara off after she begged me to take the case to trial.

"Yeah, I can see how she might be disappointed," Felicia said.

That wasn't what I'd wanted to hear. More like, *she'll get over it—you did her a favor whether she knows it or not.*

"But it's not fair," I said. "She refuses to take my calls."

"She was vulnerable," Felicia said. "She was desperate and you said *no*."

"It would have been bat-shit crazy to take that case to trial," I said, almost shouting.

"The facts don't matter, Will."

I remembered that old lawyer's saying—If the facts are against you, argue the law. If the law is against you, argue the facts. If the law and the facts are against you, pound the table and yell like hell. Neither mattered if you turned down a woman.

"Do you think that David knows about my rift with Clara?" I asked.

Her eyes widened. "You're asking if David left me to go after Clara?"

That *was* what I was asking. They'd been very close friends, or more, before I ever met her.

"No," I retreated. "Not really, but do you think they're in communication?"

"I'd be the last one to know," she said.

If they got together, I couldn't imagine anything short of never speaking to either of them again.

It was late, but I called Ray when I returned home. Maybe there was something I wasn't seeing—that my jealous mind couldn't grasp.

"Ray, how's the bride?"

"I'm not married yet," he said. "That's a year away. Four hundred people invited. I'll probably know about seven of them."

"I really loved the engagement ceremony." I was gushing but it was true. I had enjoyed it. It was also inextricably linked with my proposal to Clara, the memory of which I felt in my stomach.

"Yeah," he agreed. "It was all pretty cool."

"Hey," I asked. "Can I get your take on something?"

I imagined his wry smile.

"Call me Dick Diver." He could have invoked Dr. Phil but that would be too pedestrian.

I related the whole story of Mr. McLaughlin's crime, my dilemma about whether to take the case, our agreement, Clara's last-minute plea, and my opting out of trial.

"Well, you said it yourself," he concluded.

"What's that?"

"She wanted you to go to war."

"That's it?" I asked. "That's your whole analysis?"

"Her father's a brawler, and she wants someone who'll fight."

"But I got her dad the best result possible. The plea bargain was truly miraculous."

"Ah, Will," he said. "You've always put far too much emphasis on the rational. Most people make decisions that support their sense of self, regardless of good sense."

I knew talking to Ray would be a bummer. But he was right. Mind creates self-concept based on experience. Different experiences, different self-concept. It was all pretty random. There had to be a truer self beneath the constructed one. I remember going to sleep with that thought, not knowing that the next day it would be revealed to me.

33

Wednesday, May 7, 2010 Colonie, NY

I stepped onto a stage, strapped on my Taylor, curled my headset mic around my ears, and bent to untangle the wire trailing from the guitar. The Colonie Library, near Albany, NY, was packed. Children everywhere. Usually, the sight of excited kids got me ready to play. To see their faces light up, and the little ones, barely walking, moving to the music—there was nothing like it.

But I wasn't feeling it. Clara had been on my mind since our day in court, and all I could do was think about her compulsively. Which is why I started with the driving chords of "Happy" by Pharrell. If it got the kids up and dancing, maybe it would get me off this jag.

The crowd started clapping and moving, but one curly-haired girl stood out. As if propelled by fairies, she danced past the cross-legged bodies on the rug and slipped nimbly through the slim passages.

Clara had once asked me how it felt to entertain little kids. How did I get them to dance to the music like there was no place they'd rather be? The best way I knew was joining in with them. But even among all these happy children, I felt numb.

As the curly-headed girl twirled toward me, the light in her amber eyes did something. A place opened inside that hadn't existed before—space to feel the joy of this spindly, tangle-haired jewel. Certainly, by now, I'd encountered a slew of ethereal kids. But this sprightly dancer, moving to her own muse, drew out the song inside me. As it streamed through my voice and guitar, I knew beyond doubt that I was being used as an instrument for something radiant, beyond my comprehension.

Now, boogying down to Pharrell, I reveled in the chaos—tattooed father hoisting son, mother breast-feeding infant under sweater, grandfather spilling popcorn, and nanny bouncing siblings on her knees. I realized that I was in exactly the place I was meant to be—a community library on a weekday morning, instead of a courtroom.

When the song ended, I sat on the rug and motioned for the audience to do the same. It was a colorful tapestry, divided into squares, some bearing shapes, some letters or numbers, dots or checkerboards. Mothers and toddlers, grandparents and preschoolers, even a smattering of fathers, sat about me, as if around a campfire. Some parents held babies. One little girl had a Berenstain bear as big as she was. A big sister planted a surprise kiss on her little brother's cheek. A toddler, newly walking, kept stepping closer and closer to me, staring like an extraterrestrial. There were about eighty people in all, some very near, others further back.

Certain audiences were like dry kindling, play or sing anything and they'd light up. You had to hold back to avoid premature combustion. Some were Sphinx-like, inscrutable, needing to be wooed, lured onto *terra firma,* before they felt safe.

With this audience in Colonie, I felt an intimacy, a tenderness, that I didn't want to breach. I had stolen fire from the Gods and spread it around. Now it was time to pull it back in. Something familiar and quiet would do. I began fingerpicking Old McDonald. Not everyone sang, but they listened.

There were a number of parents with tots on their laps, so I trotted out some lap-riding tunes: "Mother & Father & Uncle John, Going to Boston." I was coming to the end of the show.

Some folks had already noticed the new, original CD that I had on display. It had taken me a weekend to record in the funky Hudson River town of Kingston. I assumed I might sell one or two here. That morning in suburban Albany, I sold twenty. But it wasn't the same without being able to tell Clara.

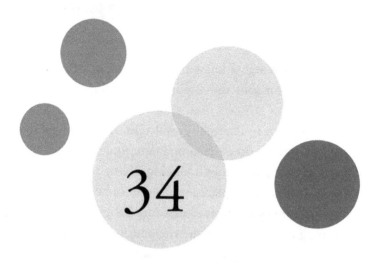

34

Sunday May 18, 2010 Manhattan, West Side

I wanted to talk to my mother. Usually, I preferred Dad. But in this case, a female perspective was needed. I knew Mom was dead. She couldn't be reached by telephone and was no longer occupying David's spare bedroom. I also remembered that David had blamed me for her death, claimed I'd broken her heart by not taking her into my cottage. Mom might be angry at me wherever she was. We had not been that close. But that was surface stuff. She was my mother.

The Spiritualist Church. I wanted to be in a place where others around me shared the belief of an afterlife. I was due there this morning. But this time, I would go to the service, not the children's room.

Despite the fact that I'd been playing there for many months, I was not entirely sure of the Church's dogma. Google said the core belief was that people survived the death of their bodies by moving into a non-corporeal existence. Typically, a medium conducted the service. Since my mother died, the afterlife had taken on new significance.

The church on the West Side was a gated, three-story, white building with bell windows and a black, arched-top door. I arrived twenty minutes early for the service. My mother, I knew, hadn't bought any of this "shit" but death might change that. In truth, I was hoping to communicate with her. Maybe, from her lofty perch, she could allay my worries about Clara, who I'd not seen or heard from for thirteen days.

Of course, it had occurred to me that I might see Clara herself.

I sat halfway back, next to the aisle, so as not to be hemmed in, though only a smattering of congregants occupied the three sections of white pews. Clara wasn't one of them, which spawned both relief and disappointment. More were already trickling in, advancing on the wall-to-wall crimson carpet. A black baby grand stood in the front left corner.

I felt out of place. As an adult, I'd scarcely set foot in a synagogue, and church had been reserved for rare occasions involving girlfriends singing in the choir or some such. Not knowing even one person in the sanctuary made me feel like an imposter.

At eleven o'clock, a woman with long red hair settled in at the piano. Before she could strike her first chord, Clara, holding a satchel, scooted through the door, and slipped into a front row seat. She was wearing a beige dress that hugged her contours from shoulders to knees. Smooth dark brown hair fell free down her back. She hadn't even glanced up.

An older woman, dressed too casually to be the minister, stepped to the altar and asked the congregants to open their songbooks. By this time, there must have been eighty or so present. They dug noisily into the racks for hymnals. I turned to the page posted on the hymn board slide: "Peace Like a River," an African-American spiritual. The pianist played the opening chords and the assembly launched into song.

I liked "Peace Like a River." For one thing, there was no religious language in it. I felt more comfortable with a God unbroken into faiths and sects. The less dogma the better.

Next, the minister stepped up to the lectern. She was a slim lady of about fifty with a ring in her finely-shaped nose. She started by reading the principles of Spiritualism. A chill moved up my spine. *Please don't let this be bat-shit bonkers.*

"We believe in Infinite Intelligence," said the minister.

Good so far. Especially since it was clear she wasn't talking about a white-robed judge in the sky.

"We affirm that the existence and personal identity of the individual continues after the change called death." Since my mother's passing,

I could swear I'd felt her. During one of these episodes, I'd gotten so hot as to strip off my sweater in a chilly movie theater.

My mind drifted. Only vaguely was I keeping track of the sermon. Afterwards, nine women and one man took places behind "healing" chairs hastily set up in front. The pianist played. People filled the healing chairs and more waited on line. The practitioners standing behind the chairs did Reiki or some similar energy work. I felt pulled toward a healer with long white hair and a tie-dye dress. When my turn came, her station was open and I claimed it.

"May I touch your shoulders?" she asked when I sat in her chair.

"Yes."

I closed my eyes on contact, and serenity washed over me. My body settled into the chair as if it were recomposing itself.

"You're drawing in a lot of energy," she whispered. I didn't answer so as not to take the chance of stopping it. Maybe it would happen now, an astral connection with my mother. I could almost feel it. But after a few minutes, the healer withdrew her hands.

When the service ended, I made eye contact with Clara and she approached. For a moment, a fledgling hope burned that she'd fling her arms around me, but she kept a safe distance. I wondered whether she was still working at PS 463, because I'd received an email from Ms. Rodriquez that my weekly guitar lessons with Charley had been terminated. I stared at Clara and said nothing.

"Are you okay?" she asked.

"No," I said. "I don't understand why you won't return my messages. I miss you. I love you. I did exactly what I said I would do with that case."

"I begged you to do one thing for me," she said. "You refused. He's doing his fifteen days now. You're lucky I'm talking to you."

The crowd was thinning out. My butt hurt from sitting on the hard bench. "Can we talk?" I asked. "Can we go somewhere private?"

"I'll walk with you," she said. "I don't want to sit."

"That's fine." I took a deep breath and felt alive again. She followed me out of the church.

We entered the park at Tavern on The Green and peeked in on

couples dining al fresco on this warmish day in early April. There was a celebration, balloon centerpieces, waiters in yellow shirts and black trousers serving patrons giddy to be outdoors after a long winter.

Walking south, I saw an artist sketching the portrait of a young girl. Behind them on a stretch of grass were children dancing and teens tossing a frisbee. We walked toward Columbus Circle.

"What did I do?" I asked her. "What did I do that was so horrible?" I'd felt plenty of sadness over the past few days, but now I experienced an anger that frightened me.

"You're a man with limits," Clara said. "You put limits on how much you would help your mom when she really needed you, and limits on how much you would help me. Maybe, on a practical level, it made sense. Your mom staying closer to the hospital. My dad doing weeks in jail instead of a year. But the truth is spelled out in capital letters right in front of me. You don't fully give of yourself. You hold back. I don't want to be with a man who holds back."

"I'm allowed to set limits," I argued. "Do you want to be with someone who is so boundary-less that he doesn't know where he ends and you begin?"

"You're a better talker than I am," she said. "But I know what I want. I liked that guy who jumped into the sound to save me from a shark. You make doling out love in dribs and drabs sound rational, but I want the kind that isn't rationed."

There wasn't a lot I could say to that. I was hoping that there'd be a chink in her armor, a crack I could slip through. This seemed pretty damn final.

She said nothing more as we strolled uptown through the park. When we got to Strawberry Fields, there were cut flowers scattered around the psychedelic-tiled circle with the word "Imagine" in the center.

"I wanted to ask *you* something," I said. "Are you still at the school?" That was not what I really wanted to ask, but I was curious.

"The DOE reinstated Ms. Pano after Ms. Rodriquez fired her," Clara said. "They want me to finish my project."

"So you're still there."

"Still there," she said.

If I stayed with her any longer, I was sure to betray further neediness. And that seemed sure to be met with more heart-wrenching finality. Or even worse, a measure of sympathy which would be hard to take on top of everything else.

"I'm going to cross over to the East Side." My voice was husky. I couldn't trust what might come out next if I stayed—if I asked her what *really* happened in Bangkok.

35

Sunday, May 18, 2010 South Salem, NY

I sat in my living room thinking about Clara, how she'd led me to the Spiritualist Church, and helped me speak to Joshua on Hart Island. I still wanted to talk to my mother. But Clara wasn't here to show me how.

I wrote a sentence right-handed in a blank diary.

Why did you leave, Mom?

I placed the pen in the crease and waited for an impulse. Upon feeling it, I began to write with a shaky left hand.

I wish I could have given you everything you needed. I love you—have always loved you.

Tears welled and rolled down my cheeks. I donned the pen with my right hand.

Mom, I wish that I had brought you into my house when you were sick or at least offered. I owed you that.

Much later, I heard knocking at the door to my cottage. I waited, hoping whoever it was would give up and leave. Mercifully, it ceased, and I could hear "Friends" again. I was in the midst of a sixth-straight episode. The hammering resumed, and a voice called out. It was my brother, David.

"Answer the door, Will. I hear the television."

I hoisted myself from the couch with great effort.

The show made it impossible for me to think about Clara. That was the beauty of it. Its pervasive frivolity obstructed my neural pathways like an anesthetic.

"Open up," David said through the door.

I let him in.

He walked past me inspecting the place, holding his flip-face helmet by the chin bar. He wore a red-and-black motorcycle jacket that served, I gathered, as a buffer to the world. His thinning hair was minimized by a short cut.

I found my well-warmed place on the couch and kicked back again.

"Reese's Peanut Butter Cups," David said, collecting the orange wrappers from the coffee table. He emptied them into the kitchen can, then leaned over me, placing a hand on my shoulder.

"Felicia told me about your breakup with Clara," he said. "I'm sorry."

"You mean Clara didn't tell you herself?"

"No," he replied. "She didn't."

I nodded. Better to fix my eyes on the set. If I were to keep talking I'd be in danger of feeling something.

Eventually, David helped himself to a candy. He sat back and watched the program. That was a relief. If the two of us watched Joey pretend to own a Porsche, I could pretend that everything was fine.

He turned to me. "Do you remember, as kids, when those guys chased us on Halloween?"

I remembered but willed myself not to respond.

David pressed on. "It was dark and we were walking up Barry Avenue with our trick-or-treat bags. A car going the opposite way on Barry stopped and called out to us. I veered toward him but you grabbed my collar and pulled me across the street."

My eyes wandered a moment and I offered a faint nod.

David's face grew animated. "The car tore down Barry, raced around the circle. We were going backyard to backyard with the guy running after us, ripping through the bushes. You pulled me under the Brusicks's deck and we didn't hear anything. You wouldn't budge. I had to go to the house, get Dad, and bring him to you."

A tear streamed down my cheek. I met his eyes.

David's attention strayed off to the corner of the room.

"Will, I can't get Dad now. He lives in Florida. But I don't want you hiding anymore."

My phone beeped on the table near him and he glanced at it.

"This reminder says you're playing at a pajama birthday party in thirty minutes."

I'd totally forgotten about it.

I said goodbye to David, drove like a maniac, then slipped into the celebration a minute or two late, after browsing the chords of two requested songs. Not surprisingly, I was on my game. Anger served me. I needed the party to feel better, so I focused that much more and cranked it up a gear. The birthday girl gave me a spontaneous hug.

"Bravo," said the girl's grandpa, clapping his gnarled hands.

I smiled but couldn't help thinking of the French hostess in Larchmont who had exiled me to the basement with the uniformed servants.

"Just a hired hand," I told the grandfather.

"Oh no," the old man replied, "I don't see it that way. You create a world of make-believe. You're a sorcerer. I've never seen kids react to a performer the way they did to you. I'm not sure *you* even know what you're doing. It's magic. I don't see you as a hired hand, more like a treasured guest."

When I got home, David was no longer at the cottage. I called Clara and she picked up.

"I have something to say," I began.

"Okay," she said. "I'm listening."

"I think we're breaking up for the wrong reasons. I am still the man who jumped into the Long Island Sound and I'd do it again."

There was silence on the other end of the phone.

"I thought we were something that we're not," she said.

"What do you mean?"

"Like a child who thinks she's holding a trusted hand but looking up it's a stranger."

Her answer was infuriating. I took a breath and waited for my anger to abate. Instead, it surged up my chest to my throat. I just watched it, knowing it was poison.

36

Friday, May 23, 2010 Somers, NY

I was still stewing almost a week later as I launched into the goodbye song for a class of two-year-old's at a daycare center in Somers. Without any prompting from their teachers, the toddlers lined up to hug the Guitar Guy. One after another, I felt their gentle embraces, the weight of their bodies leaning in. There is no such thing as an insincere tot cuddle. Each was as fresh as the dew on a lily, as intimate as a kitten's purr. To be clinched repeatedly by wobbling tykes made the notion of sin seem hallucinatory.

If I could generate such a response from those closest to God, all was not lost no matter what had happened. With each squeeze of tiny arms, and rub of downy cheeks, I felt renewed. Once disengaged, the babes immediately went on to other things, hardly cognizant, it seemed, of what had transpired, the rise of consciousness I'd experienced. Like a purple sunset, a symmetrical spider's web, or a brilliant shaft of sunlight extending from the clouds, a toddler's hug was a rare and precious thing.

What I got was this: It didn't matter what reason Clara had for leaving me. I needed to find out if I could take this journey for myself, not to please her, or prove anything to anyone. I'd had this date with myself from the beginning.

37

The phone rang. Alessia. It had been nineteen days since I'd spoken to Clara. I put down *The Complete Sherlock Holmes* and looked disapprovingly at the lonely supply of chips, dips, and wrappers spread across my living-room coffee table. The detective stories had cast a spell, distracting me from all I didn't want to accept. But tonight, I was losing focus. The book, like a cloud face in the sky, had lost shape, identity, and interest. I'd regressed to my slob persona, delaying the crackdown on my clutter in favor of reaching for any diversion that promised to make me feel incrementally better. Worse, it was my birthday.

"Remember you said you'd be happy to spend time with Charley whenever possible?" Alessia asked.

This was exactly what I needed. Except I wasn't sure in my present state whether I could be the Will that Charley knew. I could try to bluff it. The kid looked up to me. And I genuinely liked him.

"Absolutely." I noticed that my voice was too pumped up.

Alessia lowered hers. "I could have arranged that he go to soccer with a teammate's mother, but he says he'll only go with you." I could sense a smile on her end of the line. "It's this afternoon."

Better to be that mysterious white man in the South Bronx than Clara's hapless fool with too many limits.

"I'll be right over," I said and hung up, realizing that I'd failed to say goodbye.

One quick look into the selfie mode of my iPhone camera revealed that I hadn't fully grasped the state of my grooming.

I quickly showered, didn't bother to shave, swigged some Listerine, and escaped the cottage. It was early June. The air outside felt fresh. I imagined myself a Capuchin monk newly freed from working the catacombs.

Alessia was wearing a white poet's shirt over black leggings. Artistic and sleek. My heart sank. The outfit surely meant she was going out. I asked her as much.

She pressed her lips into a smile. "No. I could have taken him. But Charley wanted *you*, and," she purred, "I kind of miss you myself."

She what? Missed me? Warmth surged into my hollow places. I realized how lost I felt. What was I doing here anyway? Clara was the woman I loved. But she'd torn my heart out and I couldn't help wanting someone else to put it back in place.

Charley came from the kitchen in his soccer shorts—narrow shins, bony knees. Behind him, the kitchen floor and counter tops shined. The whole place was meticulously clean.

Charley smiled eagerly. "Are we going to drive in your car?" he asked. I nodded.

The boy's voice rose in pitch. "Can we pull up close so the kids see me get out of it?"

Ah, Charley had ulterior motives for demanding my company. This boy's challenges, I realized, were not easily imagined from the outside. If being seen with me in my car did the trick, that was more than fine.

"Sure," I said.

Charley handed me his purple soccer bag. At the Spiritualist Church on Sundays, I recalled children giving their parents all manner of things: candy bar wrappers, snotty tissues, banana peels. I chuckled, tucking the bag beneath my arm like a football. It made me feel less a misfit to join the club of adults relied upon by a child.

Once in the car, Charley wanted to sit in front, but I told him it was against the law. I set the GPS on my iPhone. We were about halfway there when I noticed tears dampening the boy's splotchy face in the rearview mirror.

"What's wrong?" I asked him.

"A guy punched me last time," he moaned from the back seat. "They say I'm not good enough."

I figured this was part of growing up male in the city, or really anywhere, and ignored him. As we drew closer, his pleas grew desperate: "I'm not going. You can't make me!"

I pulled over along the grass shoulder of Crotona Avenue adjacent to the soccer field. "Please don't force me," he wailed.

I understood. I often felt like I'd been led kicking and screaming through life.

Turning to meet the boy's eyes, I said, "Charley, all of us are scared sometimes." This from a guy who had been sitting paralyzed on a couch an hour ago. Funny how one jumped into a role and assumed it. For the first time that day, I felt calm, steady.

Charley lifted his chin. "What are *you* scared of?" he asked.

I stared out the window. "The same things you are. People leaving me all alone, saying I'm not good enough."

A team wearing Charley's purple uniform was on the field practicing. I opened the door, got out, and reached for the boy's hand.

He made a fierce face, cheeks out, eyes bulging. "Don't make me," he shouted.

"I'm not." What was I going to do? Carry him onto the field crying in front of his peers? I remembered a father at the church had told me that he paid his daughter twenty-five cents each time she kicked the ball in a game. That had sounded ludicrous, but not so much now. I didn't want to take Charley home early and risk losing face with Alessia. Plus, the kid had to deal with this or it would never end. That was how boys operated. They'd pick on you until you fought back.

I took a breath. "What if I bought you a soccer ball?"

"No!" he howled.

"Charley," my tone softened, "if you can't face these boys now, it will be harder to do later."

I could see him thinking about it, trying to dig beneath his hysteria. He swallowed hard and looked up.

"Are you still offering the soccer ball?"

"Yeah."

He gave me his hand. "I'll do it."

I felt connected to him. It wasn't easy to defy kids who are ready to whip your ass.

I watched closely as Charley took the field with his teammates. There was no outright hostility that I could detect. But I saw what he was up against. Many of the kids were immigrants from Africa and South America, skilled soccer players—entertaining to watch. Charley was not a smooth ball handler, but he didn't back away from contact. I kept one eye on the practice and the other, I admit, on my Chevy. When practice ended, Charley joined me and we walked across the field to the car.

"That white guy your father, Charley?"

A teammate's voice. Neither of us turned around. I had no idea how to define our relationship. It frightened me when I sensed Charley's hand reaching for mine. Even so, I felt my fingers dipping to meet his, and holding on.

When we got into the car, Charley asked if we could get the soccer ball now.

"Can I get it for you first thing tomorrow" I asked. "Your mother wanted us home for dinner."

"You don't really have to get it." It seemed like he was testing me.

I raised a palm as if swearing in before a judge. "First thing tomorrow."

When we got back to the apartment, Alessia had fixed a green salad, not just lettuce but tomatoes, avocado, red onion, cucumber, Kalamata olives, chick peas, and croutons. I adored Kalamata olives—and croutons *made* a salad. A cruet of homemade dressing stood near the wooden salad bowl and three place settings. This woman knew how to make a home.

I stood looking over the table. "You eat so healthy!" I gushed.

Alessia put a hand on her hip. "What'd you expect?" she asked. "Kool Aid and KFC?"

I put up my hands and took a step back. "No, no."

She smiled. "It's alright. I'm not touchy that way. Sit down." Her eyes found Charley. "You sit too."

"Do you think of yourself as Venezuelan or Puerto Rican?" I asked.

"I think of myself as Puerto Rican," she said flatly.

I tilted my head toward her. "You were born here, right?"

"In Brooklyn. The Jewish ladies were always really nice to my mom. You wanna hear my imitation of Debbie, the JAP, from Brooklyn?"

I nodded.

She made her eyes as big as possible. "Jeffray? Jeffray? The cawfee is cold but don't tell ya motha. If she stawts tawking to the waitress we won't get outta heah 'til Thuhsday." Alessia beamed a photographic smile.

I laughed too loud. Where was I taking this? Had Clara been right that the best I could offer was conditional love?

The three of us sat down at the kitchen table and Alessia served. We all dug in.

"How was practice, Charley?" she asked, glancing at me.

Charley spoke through a bite of salad. "It was good, Mom."

I inferred that neither the crying nor the bullying was to be mentioned.

"Charley was badass," I said.

Alessia's lashes fluttered. Under the table—had I just felt her hand brush my knee?

"I always tell Charley it's a higher order to be sensitive than badass, don't I?"

Charley smiled weakly.

I considered mentioning that sensitivity wasn't always feasible for a boy in the South Bronx, but decided against it.

A cat made an appearance, rubbing against Alessia's leg. She picked him up. "There's nothing for you in the salad." She eyed me. "This is my other child, Roscoe, former street cat. He'd prefer us to be more carnivorous." She stroked his head. "Nobody starves here."

Something about Alessia made me feel shy. Later, when Charley went to bed, and we sat together on two living room chairs, I wondered if I'd overstayed my welcome. She asked me about Clara and I told her.

Then she steered me to the love seat. She was a good kisser. Like Roscoe, the street cat, I had been taken in from the cold.

38

Saturday, June 8, 2010 Bronx, NY

Charley was sitting in the back of my car with his new soccer ball. It was cobalt blue with a big Adidas logo and black-graffiti splotches designed to look spray-painted. He had not put it down once on the ride to Crotona Park for soccer practice. Placing it atop his head, he let it roll down his shoulder then repeated the action. It was blocking my visibility, but I looked out the side mirrors rather than correcting the boy. People didn't like to be told what to do, even children, especially children. It wasn't the way to connect.

We passed PS 463. "That's my school," Charley said.

A new sign in front of the building read: "School No Asthma Zone. No idling." Who were they kidding? A bus stopped every ten minutes or so and each one ran its diesel engine. It was a lofty goal to declare a busy Bronx street a "No Asthma Zone." More public relations than public policy.

I noticed that they'd also changed the color of the bus lanes from yellow to a dark, gory red. Little things, like the color of bus lanes, had begun to bother me since Clara left. She had let me go so easily. Was there such a thing as real love, real friendship, I wondered, or was it all conditional?

"Look at my stomach," said Charley. I glanced at the rearview mirror. Charley had stuffed the soccer ball beneath his shirt.

I was scouring the side streets for cops. I had an inordinate fear of being stopped by a policeman in the Bronx.

"Charley," I said, "maybe put on your seatbelt."

"Wolf got out of jail," he replied.

Wolf? Oh yeah. His absent father. I cringed involuntarily.

Charley leaned forward. "He needs my help."

What man needed a nine-year-old's help? Besides myself.

"Oh?" I tried to sound non-committal. The traffic was slowing on a Saturday morning for no reason I could imagine. Except maybe cops. I gazed ahead and saw a stream of cars glistening in the June sun.

"Charley, the seatbelt?"

He fidgeted with the ball, passing it back and forth from one hand to the other. "He wants to live in public housing in Manhattan. If I come to his interview, he'll have a better chance of getting in."

So he ignores Charley for nine years, and then when it benefits him to put a dependent on his housing application, it pops into his mind that he has a kid.

I could feel myself frowning. "Is he a nice guy?" I tried to keep my tone free of judgment.

Charley was now sitting on the soccer ball so that his head was flush against the roof lining. This meant no seatbelt.

He pursed his lips. "Not really a nice guy. He never wanted to see me."

I rubbed the back of my neck. "What does your mom say?"

We passed that same mold-green live market—"Chickens, Goats, and Rabbits."

Charley slid off the ball and sat up a little straighter. "Mom says it's up to me."

Why would she say that, I wondered? It didn't make sense for Charley to get involved in this man's life. But clearly it was her call.

"Seatbelt," I said tersely.

It took a saint to play a part in a child's life without wielding any authority. I didn't think I was up to it. Squinting into the rearview mirror, I saw him finally digging for the belt.

We were turning onto Crotona Avenue. The park was a bright green oasis, a welcome respite from the clogged streets and relentless apartment buildings.

Charley raised his jaw. "I'm gonna do it," he said.

I glanced anxiously back at him. "Why?"

He crossed his arms. "I don't want to be like him. I want to be like *you*. *You* would do it."

Warmth surged from my chest to my throat and I couldn't speak. Nine years of neglect and Charley was doing a favor for this man who refused to be his father. *Because he thinks I would do it.* If I needed proof that relationships matter, this was it.

I knew that I was not as Charley perceived me. I held grudges, nursed prejudices, and did not consider myself overly generous. Truly, I was the limited man that Clara had described. But Charley saw something else. What would I *do* if, in fact, I were as Charley supposed? A man who easily excused others. Who would I forgive?

On the field, the whistle blew and the coach called the boys, including Charley, into a circle. A black lady with a turban sidled up to me.

"Are you with that boy with the bony knees?" The woman herself was painfully skinny and spoke with what I took to be an African accent.

"Yes," I said.

She immediately reported the news to a group of friends, who looked as though they were sizing me up. I waved and two of them smiled shyly.

After dinner, Alessia asked me if I would stay the night. She was wearing a red midriff shirt and jean shorts frayed down to the light-blue threads. The faded needle marks on her arms were old news in light of this vibrant woman whose smile radiated a warm glow. If anything, the tracks seemed to ground her with hard-won wisdom.

Alessia's eyes brimmed with an almost-embarrassing life force. If she were my daughter, I might admonish her never to look at anybody that way. I thought of Clara. We'd been apart now for more than a month. I could be loyal to a woman but not a phantom.

After Charley went to bed, we sat on her couch talking. Alessia's fingers wandered over my upper arm, my knee, the small of my back. I loved her gentle, almost imperceptible, touch.

"When did you know you liked me?" she asked. Her mouth was

just below my earlobe. She smelled of jasmine.

I took a breath. "The first time I saw you I thought you were beautiful." I inhaled again and exhaled slowly. It frightened me to make this confession. "When you came with me to Pottery Barn Kids, I knew I liked you."

She smiled coyly. "Not when you saw me perform at the club?"

I frowned. "No, you scared me half to death."

She tilted her head toward me. "Does my history frighten you?"

I thought about it. "Not right now," I said.

She rolled her eyes. "That's because you're thinking with your little head not your big one. You've probably never had a girlfriend like me."

I knew what she meant but hadn't really considered it. If I were going to treat this like it mattered, and God knows the child inside wanted that, I should go in with my feet on the ground.

I squinted at her. "You mean a former heroin addict?"

She widened her eyes. "The whole thing. Hispanic, mother, former addict." She lowered her voice to a purr. "I'm planning on sleeping with you tonight, and I don't want to hear later that I was out of contention from the very start."

"Alessia," I protested.

She maintained her steady gaze. "It's a fair question."

I could feel my knees shaking. Alessia was blunt. It was part of her attraction, this take-no-prisoners honesty. Of course I wanted to have sex. But her question was reasonable. I kissed her as an excuse to hold her close. Steadying myself, I looked over her shoulder toward Charley's room.

She drew away and scrutinized me as if to ask *who are you really?*

I don't know, I answered telepathically. *I'm finding out right now.*

Her voice got low and raspy. "I don't want you thinking you're a hero for slumming it with an ex-heroin-addict. You think you're a hero? I want to know."

It was a hard question to answer. I'd rarely thought of myself as a hero, but I knew what she was getting at.

"Okay," I admitted, "You *do* scare me."

She said nothing, watching me closely with *miel de abeja* eyes, as if watching colors passing through a prism. I thought she would tell me to leave. But she slid closer.

I woke in a night sweat beside a sleeping Alessia. The digital clock was blinking one-thirty-two. There must have been a power outage. I looked at my watch but couldn't make out the dial. I'd been so drawn to Alessia, but now my mind was reeling, spewing doubts, terrors.

How foolish I'd been to have unprotected sex with her. If you'd call it sex. I hadn't maintained my erection. What diseases might she have? Could someone ever *really* come back from what she'd talked about in her comedy club act? Living out of a motel room, selling her body like a blow-up doll? Craving junk more than life itself? More to the point— could I resist branding her with "A" for addict? My T-shirt was wet with perspiration. I felt nowhere near as enlightened as I had imagined myself to be.

I was so worked up now I wanted to leave. But eliminating Charley from my life would be worse than failing Joshua.

Oh, I was such an idiot! She'd warned me up front to let her know if I couldn't deal with her past. What a hero.

I squeezed my eyes shut wanting to burrow ten feet underground. Why was I so hung up on a life she'd lived a decade ago? It wasn't fair to permanently damn her for it. Would it be reasonable to blame *me* for my part in Joshua's death *in perpetuum*? I understood the injustice of it. But reason wasn't getting through to me. I was feeling an increasing urgency to escape her apartment. How would I phrase it to her? What could I say that wouldn't wound her to the core?

I misjudged my ability to accept your past.

That sounded bland enough in my head, but how would it go over out loud? Sometimes, hearing words spoken was an entirely different thing than thinking them. I didn't bother to check the regularity of her breathing before I mumbled the phrase to myself.

"I misjudged my ability to accept your past."

Lying beside her, only hours post-coitus, ensconced in her comforter, I realized the words didn't really fly. They spared no pain at all.

I heard a quick intake of breath.

"Get out this minute. Don't say another word. Leave now."

Her throaty growl, as if issued from a Minotaur, intensified my fear. It was like the Devil had honed a red laser to the center of my being and revealed me to have no soul. My heart beat in my throat. Without putting on shoes or socks, I grabbed my shorts on the floor, felt them for my wallet and keys, sped through the bedroom, living room, and foyer, escaping the apartment, shutting the door hard behind me. Downstairs, I found my car, unlocked it, slid into the driver's seat. By this time, I was hyperventilating. It was only after my breathing slowed that I felt the shame from my gut to the tips of my ears, sitting at 3:09 am on Bathgate Avenue.

In the next week, I showed up at all three of Charley's practices. I didn't try to talk to either Charley or Alessia, who was present at all of them. Neither did they approach until the last day when Charley ran over after practice and gave back my guitar and shoes. He looked at me with eyes sheltered by an unforgiving brow, lips pursed, cheeks puffy. Then he spun on a dime and ran the other way.

I now had two women and a boy furious with me for different reasons. The fault, I understood, was not in the stars. It wasn't easy to repel two lovers in just over a month's time. It took a certain *Je ne sais quoi*.

39

Friday, June 14, 2010 South Salem, NY

By the end of the week, soccer practices had concluded. The school year was almost done. I felt mortified about what had come over me that night. I sympathized with Alessia's desire not to see or even talk to me. She needed a lover who could acknowledge who she was now. It was not as if she were hiding anything. Hell, she'd transformed it into performance art.

I sat at home before my altar of Jesus, Divine Mother, Sekhmet, and Ganesh. Please, please, I prayed, don't allow me to hurt anyone else. Stop me. Intervene. Prevent me if I am about to do harm. Amen.

For a week or more, I felt so disjointed that I burrowed underground except to show up for the gigs already on my calendar. When I thought I'd reached bottom, I discovered a package in the mail containing both the statue of Sekhmet and the engagement ring carefully swaddled in bubble wrap. Initially, I brought them home and placed them on the kitchen table, then went about my business. After a few passes through the kitchen—to take out the garbage, make a peanut butter sandwich, and find my checkbook—I saw that I couldn't tolerate them being in the kitchen, or in any other room. I gathered the driest kindling I could find in the backyard, stacked it tall over newspaper, and set it on fire with Sekhmet and the diamond on top. The wood burned extravagantly, covering the ring and statue with ash. A few days later, sifting through the rubble, I dug up both, singed but intact. They'd paid for their misdeeds, so I put them in a sacred place: the dresser drawer containing photos of my college girlfriend. That was the right place for them.

Even so, for a number of days, I could not stop writing long rants in my new diary. I needed to talk to somebody. But every time I'd confided something to Ray, his interpretation proved so troubling that it reduced me to kneeling at the living-room altar. This time, though, I considered myself beyond disenchantment—no one could cast me further adrift.

"Ray here."

"Hey," I said. "Guess what?"

"How many guesses?" he asked playfully.

I was irritated by the pleasure he seemed to derive from my misery.

"First guess," he continued. "Clara has not come back to you."

I acknowledged this by grunting.

"Next," he proclaimed. "After due time wallowing in the mire, you rekindled your sense of self by sleeping with someone else."

I knew I was far from sphinxlike, but it was humiliating to be transparent as air. I coughed my resentment.

"Have you managed to alienate your new lover yet?" he asked.

Was he tapping my phone, my brainwaves? I felt like an amoeba, observed under a microscope, any sense of self-importance demolished. But I filled him in on the details anyway, the return of the figurine and the ring.

"Go easy," he said. I could hear the smile tugging at the corners of his mouth. It wasn't exactly a Ray thing to say.

He continued. "You're beating yourself up. It wasn't just Alessia's past that spooked you. Your real fear was damaging any hope of being with Clara. Don't worry. The women haven't talked. It would breach the most basic girls' rule."

"Which is?"

"Don't steal your co-worker's man right after a breakup with your kid in the next bedroom."

Ah, the byzantine world of girls' rules.

"So what do I do?" I asked, feeling relieved to lay the burden at his feet.

"I would leave Alessia alone. You were on the rebound. She ought to have known that."

"What about Charley? I feel like I was filling an important role in his life."

"You blew it. I don't see you as Joe Gargery—showing Pip the meaning of love and all that."

"So just stew in my own shit?"

"No. Not at all. You've got to talk to Clara. She's not as far gone as you think."

"But how? She won't answer my texts or calls. Not even a return address on the package."

"The package itself was a form of contact." he said. "I have an idea."

It wasn't very complicated when he explained it to me. Get into PS 463 by offering to give a free kindergarten concert or two. Then ask someone to arrange a brief meeting with Clara. It was a godawful plan, flat out pathetic to confront a woman at her workplace. If that didn't set her off, she'd cringe at the demand for an urgent one-on-one.

"Alessia is a teacher's aide in one of the kindergarten classes," I said.

"Then ask *her*."

"To set up a meeting with Clara?"

"Why not?"

Such a scheme could only be devised by an itinerant musician who, despite his perfect pitch, was tone deaf on social norms, an idiot savant. But I didn't have a better idea.

40

Thursday, June 27, 2009 Bronx, Tremont neighborhood

The morning of the concert I woke early and dressed as if I were doing any spring gig, shorts and a cotton T-shirt. Then it struck me that I'd better suit up like a teacher at PS 463 or at least wear trousers. Shorts might be a flag of disrespect.

When I reached the school, there was a sign in the adjacent parking lot welcoming patrons from a nearby Spanish restaurant. I wondered if I could still park there. An orange-vested construction worker told me that he'd seen George, the attendant, about an hour ago. He wasn't there now, maybe in bed with one of the women from the apartment complex, as he'd once boasted to Clara. The valet operation was based on George having the keys to rotate the cars. But there was no sense in parking further away. I was carrying a forty-pound speaker, two guitars, a mixer, wires, a microphone, instruments, and puppets.

After squeezing into George's lot, I headed toward the deli when Charley crossed my path. He wore sneakers, black chinos and a denim jacket. In my embarrassment, I almost let him pass, calling out at the last minute.

"Hey, Charley. Good to see you!"

The boy ran a few steps toward me then stopped. "Why did you hurt my mother?" He threw up a hand and made a diagonal to the school entrance.

I followed him, pulled open the door to the school, and adjusted my eyes to the relative darkness. He was gone. A teacher was chatting with the uniformed guard upstairs as I climbed toward them.

Ms. Rodriquez was just inside the main office. She eyed me while tapping a microphone. The sound resonated through speakers in the hallway. Morning announcements.

"Remember Mr. Ross? A few of you may know him," she said. "He has volunteered his time to perform for our kindergarten children today. We welcome him to PS 463." She beamed, then began listing the day's affairs, "ESL meeting fourth period, Special Ed meeting sixth period," and so on.

The principal finished and came out to greet me. A flattering haircut framed her face. Her light salmon belt cinched the waist of a blue-and-white polka-dot dress. She looked quite human, not at all like the demon Clara despised. I wondered what Clara would think of me fraternizing with the enemy—the principal from hell who fought her at every turn.

"Thank you for coming today, Mr. Ross. What time would you like to start?" Ms. Rodriquez smiled. There was, admittedly, something barracuda-like about it.

"Nine-thirty like we planned," I replied.

"You know," she said, "you could play in the cafeteria. There's a buzzing in there. We've done it before, but it's —"

"Not ideal. The classroom is better."

Clara had once filled me in that the school had no real auditorium or gym.

"Let's go then," she said, pivoting to the tile wall and sticking her key into the lock of the pea-green elevator. It was a tiny, crate-like lift. Stepping into it with Ms. Rodriquez was an intimate experience. I was forced to edge close—only a foot between us. The mechanical door closed with a startling slam but Ms. Rodriquez, plainly accustomed to it, didn't flinch.

"How are you and Ms. McLaughlin?" She pitched her voice an octave. There was a muted rocket-ship sound of the old elevator taking off.

I knew how protective Clara was about her personal life. And Ms. Rodriquez was surely the last one she'd want privy to it.

"Both of us have been so busy," I said. "Life is so . . . busy."

The elevator climbed the short distance to the second floor, squealing under our weight.

"She loves making that documentary," I added. Ms. Rodriquez winced.

We landed with a bam and a muted hydraulic grunt.

Liberated from the compartment, she took me to an unoccupied kindergarten classroom decorated with a flow-of-the-day chart, calendar, posters, the alphabet, and a number line.

"Perhaps we could fit all five classes into this room," Ms. Rodriquez suggested. Was she trying to be accommodating? "Then I could send Alessia on an errand." She flashed me a meaningful glance. We had spoken about two shows but she wanted to spare her daughter discomfort. I wondered if they spoke about such intimate matters.

"Moving the equipment is fine," I told Ms. Rodriquez. "Let's go with two performances. You'll just have to give me about 20 minutes between classes."

"How much time do you need now?" she asked.

"Maybe twenty-five minutes." It was 8:55 a.m.

"Okay, so 9:30," she said. "We'll start at 9:30."

You're probably thinking that the last person I'd want to see would be Alessia. And that was true. But none of the other teachers or aides knew me from Adam. It made no sense to ask them to set up a meeting. Of course, Alessia might demand why I imagined she'd do anything for me. A good question. So I was bearing gifts. A new Fender guitar for Charley, complete with case and electronic tuner. Okay, it was bribery. Plus, I wanted Charley to know that I cared about him. Even so, I abhorred confrontation. But I was willing—if it might get me through to Clara.

Once I'd transported my equipment from car to classroom, I tuned my guitar, adjusting the tension of each string until it vibrated at exactly the right speed. Turning the pegs, I wondered how it would be to see Clara. Would she smile at me, treat me like an alien? Or simply refuse to see me?

When the children arrived, they settled on the floor. Teachers and aides stood above them handing out my colorful chiffon scarves. Alessia was not among them. I started with "Who Says" by Selena Gomez. The song, about self-worth, was out just a year then, and I suspected every elementary school girl in the South Bronx knew it. The beat was march-time, similar to the left-right, left-right, rhythm of feet. It translated to up-down, up-down, with the scarves. The kids caught on quickly, filling the room with waves of color. Alessia had still not appeared.

I ratcheted up the tempo with "Firework" by Katy Perry, asking the children to wave their scarves high during the chorus.

Girls shimmied their hips and did mermaid dips, colors aloft. A few were already attaching scarves to their belts as fashion accessories. Some of them, not only girls, mouthed every word. Boys competed to shake their scarves the highest. Some were snapping them like towels at their friends. The rhythmic patterns of the song suggested a particular scarf choreography. The verse was staccato shakes, the build-up long sweeps, and the chorus ecstatic gestures toward the sky. Then, from nowhere, Alessia sashayed into the classroom moving her shoulders, arms out, provoking a burst of laughter from the kindergartners. I broke into a smile. She did not return it.

Alessia and the staff collected the scarves and distributed rhythm sticks for the song "Dynamite" by Tao Cruz.

I counted out a beat. Instantly the kids were pounding sticks on the linoleum floor to the song's strong, articulated pulse. They shared the fervor of hungry inmates clanging spoons at chow call.

They were so in-sync, it was like they'd been jamming together for-ever. A group of girls put down their sticks and danced—holding their noses, diving under, swimming, surfacing, and repeating. They were smooth, these little girls, their movements precise. They had me feeling it: the joy of their dance.

It gave me just enough confidence to approach Alessia and present the guitar to her.

"It's new," I said. "A gift for Charley."

She stared at me reproachfully.

"Please," I begged. "Take it."

"Only if you'll leave me alone," she whispered.

"Yes, I promise. But just one thing. Could you ask Clara to meet me? Somewhere in the school. Just five minutes."

"Why should I?" she asked, frowning.

Another aide interrupted.

"Alessia, you still got that one-on-one?"

"Oh yeah," she said. "That kid is something. I pop into the principal's office and say 'Hi, Mom!' And she says, 'I'm tired of seeing you.' 'Then why did you give me this kid?' I say. The last few days she sends me upstairs with him alone. And I get him calmed down. But once he's back in class, it's always the same."

"Where's he now?" the other aide asked.

Alessia laughed. "In my mother's office!"

I looked into her caramel eyes with the co-worker standing by. "Can you help me?" I asked.

"I'll see what I can do," Alessia said.

Minutes later, before I could even pack my equipment, she led me through the hallway into a janitor's closet. Clara was sitting on a low stool, eyes penetrating, arms folded, a crease splitting her forehead. Beautiful as always. I stepped inside and Alessia closed the door.

"Why do you do this to me?" she asked.

Okay. Not a great opening. But she was here.

"Please come back," I said.

She just stared at me.

I added, "I miss you so much."

She looked at me like she didn't believe me.

"I'm falling apart," I said. "Whatever keeps me focused—it's gone. I stop putting my clothes in drawers and my dishes in the sink. Nothing means anything. I can't make sense of the world. That's the way I feel now—without you."

I watched her, and strangely enough, my speech seemed to have landed. It's amazing what going naked will do. She glanced down at her hands, and when she finally focused in on me I could tell that she was coming from a different place.

"I didn't —" She scanned the closet as if the walls had ears.

"You didn't what?"

"I didn't tell you the facts about me." Her eyes penetrated mine. "I can't have children." She covered her face. "I screwed up. I did something wrong."

"What did you do?" I asked gently.

For a moment it looked as if she would bolt from the stool and run. "I can't tell you," she said.

She had clearly imagined that this was a big deal to me. My attitude toward all living things, these days, was that they were trouble. I was lonely. But even a pet you had to feed and clean up after. I'd compromised on a jade plant, and it was enough to have to water it once every two or three weeks.

"Do you know how insignificant that is to me," I said, "that you can't have children?" I forced my eyes wide for emphasis. "I mean—tying my shoes today was a big deal. The last three mornings I've woken up with headaches so fierce that all the Aleve in the bottle wouldn't help. I go to Trader Joe's and I eat a whole bag of dried mango pieces. And the texture calms me down a little before my body goes into sugar shock. Please come back so I can *sleep* again."

She laughed. I made her laugh. And I almost repeated the line so that she might laugh once more. Our eyes met. A silent dialogue. Better than words. Eyes plead and commiserate at the speed of light. Sound is tethered to matter and so easily misunderstood.

She sat on that low stool, legs together, elbows atop jutting knees, hands supporting her face. I wanted to kiss her lips. There was a mop and bucket between us, which made the task difficult, so I edged around her and leaned over from behind. Placing my hands on her shoulders, I craned my neck above her forehead and puckered up, vying for her mouth. She smiled, broke into a stifled laugh, steadied her hands on the floor, and angled her head up just enough for me to graze her lips. I gripped her waist, pulling her toward me. The kiss that we couldn't quite execute now came quick and smooth. The wetness of her mouth. How dry and lifeless I'd felt. It was like escaping from sarcophagus to Blue Lagoon.

The click-clack of heels on waxed floors came perilously close to our closet, then passed. Clara's eyes expanded.

"Please," I said. "When can I see you again?"

"Tomorrow night. Alessia is doing her performance art at that club in Yonkers. She needs me to come."

"Okay," I agreed. "Tomorrow night."

As I retreated down the shiny tiled hallway, I felt elated. But I'd be lying if I didn't admit to pondering the human predicament—mine. Why was it that the love I felt inside had to be provoked by another? How was it that one minute I was depressed, albeit functional, and then next, I danced twinkle-toed, skimming along the buffed floor? It had all changed on a word, and though I experienced it, I had no ability to turn the switch myself. But then I remembered I had a second show to do, and started to run.

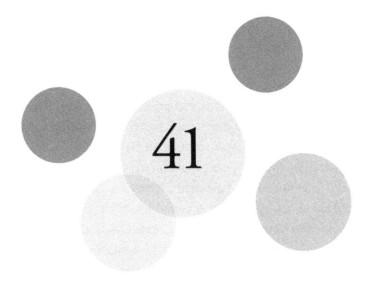

41

Friday, June 28, 2010 Manchester, Connecticut

It rained the next day. I was scheduled to do a library show in Manchester, Connecticut. Approaching Exit 50 on Interstate 84, the Malibu began to buck and lose power. I managed to limp off the exit, and flooring it, crawled into a Walgreens lot.

I called Triple-A and a taxi. The taxi came first and agreed to wait. When the tow arrived, I persuaded the driver to deliver my car, unaccompanied, to the nearest service station so I could dash to the library.

Halfway there, I realized my guitar was still in the car. The cab delivered me, empty-handed, five minutes to show-time. The host librarian was able to locate a 12-string Yamaha, the only guitar left in their instrument lending program. I tried it out. The closely-set strings left no gaps. Playing finger-style was cramped. There was no pick.

None of it mattered. I used the entire program room as my stage, the kids trailing me like the Pied Piper. Props, it turned out, were secondary. The Guitar Guy did not need a serviceable guitar. The show was me.

Afterwards, I let that sink in. I had just shown up, unadorned as the lilies in the field, and the world had adapted.

Getting back to South Salem was another matter. Sadly, the mechanic needed to order and install a new transmission, and my car would not be ready until Tuesday.

I somehow needed to get home, change, eat, and set off for the Yonkers show. Bus service was spotty. No chance of going anywhere fast. I managed to hail a Greyhound to Danbury and flag a taxi from there.

At home, I showered, dressed, and ate. It was raining. The cabs were backed up. Two Katonah dispatchers balked at banishing a vehicle to the boonies of Lake Kitchawan on such an active night.

I changed into shorts, T-shirt, sneakers, and wheeled my old Schwinn ten-speed out of the basement. There was nothing to do but put my head down and pedal. Rain pelted my back. Cold torrents. I needed to make it to Katonah in an hour to catch Metro North. Fifty or so minutes later, in a chilled sweat, I wheeled the bike onto the train. By the time we reached Mt. Vernon, it was after nine, and the downpour had emptied the streets. I ran lights, took a short cut against traffic on a one-way. It was dark enough so that I could see the cars, but they couldn't see me. Scaling the hills left me gasping and bleary-eyed. At twelve years old, I could have made short work of it, but the previous month I'd turned thirty-eight. Finally, as I rolled my Schwinn up the sidewalk to the club, it was past ten, probably too late. No option but to leave my bike on the street in a pretty rough neighborhood.

Alessia was under the lights. It was another "bringer" show, mean-ing the performer had to drag in a paying customer to get on stage. Clara sat alone at a table. I moved toward her.

"I admit that I saw a lot of penises when I was an addict," Ales-sia said. "Penises are more to be trusted than their owners. People are complex. Some tell you what they want. Some make you guess. People can be scary. But penises—just want to be sucked. At a McDonald's for penises, you could eliminate the pickles, onions, lettuce, cheese, special sauce, and sesame-seed bun. The customers would drive through and every order would be the same."

A man in the back stood up. He was young with brown hair cut close to the scalp and a trimmed Fu Man Chu.

"You've seen so many dicks—what man could ever want you?" he shouted.

"Sit down." My words startled me. It was as if a replacement-self had emerged, wet and disheveled from the streets.

A waiter took a step forward to intervene but thought better. The heckler pivoted and stared. He charged. I hooked him by the neck with my arm and he fell backward. A chair broke his landing then buckled as he collapsed to the floor.

The man rose to his feet. I raised my hands to protect my face.

The waiter chimed in. "We've already called the police." He spoke the lines like a bad actor and I doubted it was true.

"Is he your friend?" the heckler asked Alessia, placing a hand on his hip as if he had a right to know.

Every cell of my body was on high alert. Alessia paused on stage and took in the scene. "No, he's not." She curtsied then turned.

"That's the show tonight!" she sang. Voiced ironically as if it had been scripted. She stepped behind the curtain and disappeared. Clara ran after her, visibly upset. Fu Man Chu kicked a chair and headed for the exit. I waited patiently for Clara and Alessia outside the ladies room. Eventually, I asked a female customer to check. They weren't there. I searched the premises futilely, punishing myself once more for that night. Backstage, Clara must have asked Alessia why she had disavowed me. That was the only thing that made sense.

When I went out into the drizzle, my bicycle was still there, testifying to God's mercy in the face of epic failure. Being left with nothing, not even an explanation, seemed unfair considering the extremes I'd endured. But that wasn't really their problem, was it? Now, unless I wanted to find a motel, I needed to pedal fast enough to make the last train up-county.

My bike lurched side to side as I pushed forward. Back and forth, an argument raged in my head as to what I could have done differently to avoid this outcome. But then I found myself musing on the nature of romantic love—how it was so easily torn to shreds. It wasn't as if I had slept with Alessia while actively with Clara. I cursed the fragility of it all. Depending on another person for love didn't work.

My long-planned summer tour of libraries was to begin in a couple of days, and I'd be on the road July and August, playing a gig almost every day. A summer awaited me of campgrounds, swimming in lakes, cooking dinners on a portable propane stove. Maybe I could forget who I was. Imagine myself as someone else. I caught the last train out of Mt. Vernon West.

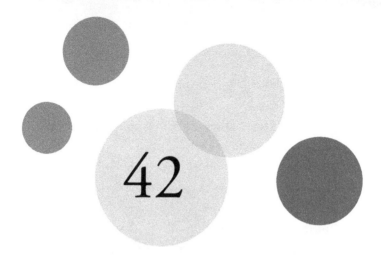

42

Sunday, June 30, 2010 South Salem, NY

The Malibu was packed and ready, so eager was I to get on the road. No groceries in the house. I planned to order take-out the final day before my first performance in Litchfield, Connecticut. Food had emerged as my primary focus since Clara vanished from the comedy club that rainy night. It was four in the afternoon and already I was thinking about dinner.

My cell rang. Oh no. Alessia's number. What could that mean but a harangue?

"Hello?" I answered.

"Will?" A boy's voice.

"Charley?"

"I'm at the hospital. Mom can't wake up. I'm really scared."

"Who are you with?" I asked.

"I'm with Mom." His voice got croaky. "I'm with nobody." He stopped as if absorbing that. "Mom can't hear me."

"What hospital?" I foraged for a pen in a kitchen drawer crammed with junk.

"It's in the Bronx," he said.

There had to be twenty major hospitals in the Bronx. Charley had to do better than that.

"It sounds like monopoly."

"Monopoly," I repeated. "Montefiore?"

"Yeah. Please come. Can you get here in one minute?"

"I'm coming now, Charley. The drive will take an hour."

"Not an hour," he said. "Go fast." Immediately he hung up.

I went fast. If I could reach him before the start of rush hour so much the better. I wondered what happened to Alessia and considered ringing Charley back for more information but decided against it. She was not yet thirty, an apparently healthy woman. An overdose was out of the question. She wouldn't relapse after all these years. In fact, her hasty rejection of me that night had testified to her mental fortitude.

I got to the hospital, lied about my relationship to Alessia, got issued a pass and directions to the room. Charley ran to me, throwing out his arms. I surrendered to his embrace, squeezed his shoulders in return. Alessia was unconscious, laid out with a trachea breathing tube, a feeding line, and an IV in her arm. A nurse bent over the plastic bag, replenishing the drug which flowed into a catheter. The ventilator in the corner showed three sets of graphics labeled pressure, flow, and volume. I didn't know what they meant.

"What does she have?" I asked the nurse. Charley was now hanging from my arm. The nurse straightened and pivoted gracefully toward us. She seemed to size up my role in this drama by Charley's obvious affection for me. "Hepatic encephalopathy," she said. "A coma induced by late-stage cirrhosis of the liver. She apparently suffered from asymptomatic, undiagnosed Hepatitis C."

Charley clawed my elbow, clinging as his feet slipped out beneath him. "Will she die?" he asked.

"I don't know," said the nurse in a clipped tone, perhaps realizing that she had already divulged too much.

The ventilator sounded an alert. Three quick shrill beeps and two slower ones.

"That's a high-pressure alarm," she said, immediately grabbing a suctioning tool and digging into Alessia.

A doctor ran in. "Did you inject saline?" she asked.

"There wasn't time for that," said the nurse, stepping aside.

"Prepare 150 micrograms of fentanyl and 80 milligrams of lydocaine," ordered the doctor. She was a thin, blonde woman, hair pulled back, wearing white scrubs. She bent over Alessia, inspecting closely. "Part of the tracheal tube is gone," she said. "Bite marks on the remaining portion." A quick glance back to the ventilator. "The oxygen saturation level is only 60 percent. Cardiac arrest."

A fully-masked doctor had quietly entered the room. "Try reintubation," he ordered. "I'm going to begin resuscitation. These people will have to clear out."

Charley fought to remain in the room but the nurse gripped his hand firmly and dragged him into the hall, closing the door. She gave me a pointed look which I took as an admonition to keep him out. Charley didn't try the door again. Instead, he streaked down the hall running as fast as he could. I broke after him. When he reached the end, he turned and ran the other way. This continued for some time as I trailed closely, breathing hard.

It was sometime after I stopped wheezing that the male doctor left Alessia's room with his fingers steepled over his chin. The nurse and other doctor followed closely. They sealed off the door for, I feared, a post-mortem.

Charley took a moment to observe their body language. Then, he streaked down the hall, pushed open a door labeled "Stairs" and vaulted two-at-a-time as I trailed him. When he reached the top floor, he climbed an iron ladder over the landing, pushed open a hatch, and lurched through. Not so easy for me. Best I could do was to squeeze my torso into the portal, and shimmy, with great effort, until I surfaced on the pebbly roof. When I'd risen to my feet, Charley was already atop a wall at the edge, looking down.

"Get away from me!" he said, not even glancing back. "I don't even know you."

There was a faint quarter moon in the darkening sky.

"Can you get yourself down?" I asked.

Charley shook his head. "No, I want to be dead."

"Are you sure?" I wanted him to think about it.

Charley pointed one foot over the wall to the other side as if testing the water. A gust of wind caught his shirt causing him to teeter on the brink. He had the boniest knees and the hair on his head stuck out like a porcupine. It must have been nerves that made me laugh. He wheeled around, then strangely joined in, until we were both convulsing helplessly.

When we had settled down, I asked if he was okay.

"I'm dead now," he said matter-of-factly. I was still a good ten yards from him.

It reminded me of being a kid with my brother when one of us would say, "You're the bad guy and I shot you."

It was quiet—the street noises masked by the hiss of the wind. I wanted to run and grab him but the sound of crunching pebbles might set him off.

"There's a way to tell if you're really dead," I offered.

Charley shifted his weight on the ledge, again peering over the other side.

"How?" he asked faintly.

"If you're not hungry at all." I was hungry myself.

"I'm a little hungry," Charley admitted.

"There's a machine downstairs with cookies." I'd seen it in the visitor's lounge.

"What kind?" He squatted down on the wall, knees protruding toward me.

"Famous Amos chocolate-chip."

He extended a hand to me and I helped him down.

We retraced our steps. Once in the visitor's lounge, I coaxed a small package of chocolate-chip cookies from the vending machine.

A half hour later, we were finally admitted into Alessia's hospital room. Her lifeless body was arched upward in a gaped-mouth, yogic backbend, as if that were the posture necessary to dispense her spirit.

She was beyond naked—without her soul she was maximally exposed. Instinctively, I blocked Charley's view. But he skirted around me, peering at his mother with less terror than fascination. This wasn't a goddam science experiment. I glanced at my watch, signaling I wanted out. Charley ignored me, viewing the body from one angle, then another.

Exasperated, I finally asked, "Can we leave?"

He turned away from me. "I won't see her again—I want to re-member."

Embarrassed, I shut up. When we finally retreated to the corridor, a nurse approached us. "Please keep the boy here," she instructed, "his father is on the way."

"Wolf?" asked Charley. "Wolf is going to take me?"

"He said he'd be here in ten minutes," the nurse affirmed.

Charley narrowed his eyes and made prayer hands.

"Please let me go with you." His arms shot up like a wisteria, fling-ing out tendrils, long sprouts which wound around my heart.

I considered grabbing him and fleeing like I'd done with Sekhmet. I'd gotten away with it then. My hand was already fastening around Charley's, and adrenalin was pumping. But wait.

The crime would be kidnapping, no, not kidnapping exactly, be-cause that required the threat of force. But certainly, abduction. Per-suasion would be assumed, because Charley was too young to consent. In New York, the minimum jail sentence was five years. Maybe I could get the charge knocked down to mere custodial interference, but that still meant up to a year. Taking him out of this hospital was out of the question.

"Is there someone you'd prefer to stay with?"

"You," he said, raising his quivering chin.

"Other than me."

"My grandmother."

"Ms. Rodriquez?"

"Yes." His eyes caught sight of someone over my shoulder.

Wolf walked toward me in a jingle-jangle flurry of erratic hands and elbows. He had a unique style. Was it calculated to keep me off-bal-ance? If so, it was working. He extended a hand and showed his teeth—not so much a smile as a warning.

"Thank you for bringing him this far," he said, "but I'm his dad and I'll be taking him home now."

He wasn't a particularly intimidating man—short and slight, his eyes intelligent. But he'd dealt with dangerous people and done time, too. Charley flashed one more pleading look before Wolf took his hand

and turned him about-face. They walked out the double doors of the hospital corridor. Once again, I had let down a boy in trouble and I felt like a ghost, a thin, diaphanous vapor with no claim on solidity.

It was a welcome change to be in the Chevy tearing up Route 684 toward Connecticut. The hospital, with all of its tubes and wires and sanitary smells, was already fading like a bad dream. I was on the open highway, keen on the purpose of all road trips: running from mortality. I wondered if I should have taken Charley. I remembered how I used to fall asleep lying on my father's lap as he drove. He would remove his wallet and comb from his pocket, and though my head would occasionally buzz up against the vibrating steering wheel, that was where I felt most secure.

The first night I planned to stay at a campsite in Litchfield in preparation for my show the next morning. Stowed in the trunk were my tent, portable gas stove, sleeping bag, musical equipment, food, and clothes.

An hour or so later, I rolled into the campsite while it was still light. The clouds were muscular cauliflowers, fabulously three-dimensional in grand Old Testament style. Gradually, they grew charcoal underbellies as if an invasion of gloom had routed their southern slopes. The sky opened and it poured. It would be futile to pitch the tent or try to cook dinner.

Soon there were rumbles and bright streaks of lightning. I counted the seconds between the lightning and thunder. The lightning was four miles away. I was sleeping in the car tonight. As I watched nature's show, I left an email message for Charley's grandmother, Ms. Rodriquez, expressing my condolences and offering to help her petition for Charley's custody—free of charge. My resolve was firm. I would cut short the tour if needed. I owed that to Alessia. Law would let me know when it was done with me. Immediately upon that resolution, I finally felt some freedom—not freedom for myself, as I had always sought, but freedom from myself.

Just then, the nurse's words echoed in my mind, that Alessia had suffered from undiagnosed Hepatitis C. I'd had unprotected intercourse with her. Hepatitis C could be wreaking havoc with my own liver. Had my strange dread that night been an inchoate sense of exactly this? I took the deep dive from freedom to utter terror. Scrolling through my iPhone's search engine, comparing various web pages, it became clear that contagion required trauma and bleeding. I scoured my memory for either the feel or smell of blood but couldn't recall either the presence or absence of it. As the intervals between lightning and thunder drew nearer, part of me ached for a well-placed bolt from Zeus. At the same time, I was aware of an observer within watching my anxiety mount, noticing that while I no longer sleep-walked, I remained neurotic as ever. Following my bliss had not truly touched my obsessive nature.

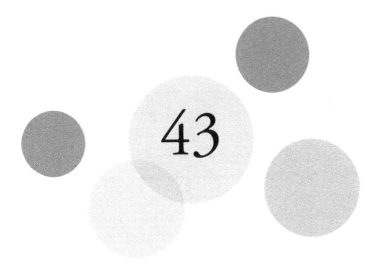

43

Tuesday, July 6, 2010 North Canaan, CT

Several days later, I drove through some beautiful country on my way to North Canaan—well-groomed farms with rust-brown barns set in by stone walls. I passed a large house built in the style of a log cabin, although it was clearly pre-fab. As I approached the library, the homes nestled close to each other, thickly-settled, as they call it in New England.

My attention was divided. I had pressed down my Hep C dread deep enough so that it only surfaced periodically, like when I cut myself shaving. Then I'd play whack-a-mole and knock it back down.

Somehow the repression of that fear made me yearn for Clara. Like a lawyer, I framed an argument to her in my head. Did you ever consider, I might say, that husbands are made in the crucible of relationship, not just delivered on a half-shell? Imagine a couple who has rolled up twenty, thirty, forty years. The guy seems to possess all the sought-after qualities: loyalty, generosity, a patina of success. But was he like that in the beginning? Or, was his wife a sort of high school baseball scout who saw potential and took a chance?

North Canaan was the smallest town I'd toured so far. Three thousand people. Douglas Library was open only three full days, Monday, Wednesday, and Friday, along with Saturday morning. After eating a fried egg sandwich and coffee outside a little brick deli in town, I drove a short distance to the venue.

The library was nothing more than an old house, and the librarian, likewise, a small but elegant old woman. She showed me where to set up, and also pointed the way to a museum lodged under the same roof. It took just a few minutes to carry the guitar and puppets from my car to the corner of the main room. Now, with almost an hour to spare, there were two choices. Either I could log onto my laptop, or visit what was billed as the C.H. Pease Museum of Natural History.

A man named Charles Pease had amassed a collection of Connecticut animals about a hundred years ago. Faded but not decrepit, they lined the walls in glass cases. Above, there was a mounted, trophy moose head with antlers soaring above it like eagle's wings. A real eagle occupied one of the displays, trapped back in 1920 and kept alive for seven years before being stuffed. I took a macabre interest in some of these specimens, pressing my nose against the glass to get a close view. Even so, it only took a half hour to get my fill of taxidermized carcasses.

Upon returning to my guitar and puppets, Clara was sitting, right leg over left, on the chair placed in the corner for me. She was wearing a white dress, her long dark hair in loosely falling curls with thin braids threaded through and tied together. The shaved legs, lacy frock, and eye makeup seemed too formal for a morning singalong but it gave her an aura of otherworldliness, as if she'd beamed down, Star Trek-style, from another planet. Despite my morning deli coffee, I'd been feeling lethargic, even lead-footed. Now in a millisecond I was super-charged. I felt as light as Hermes running through the Elysian fields. The part I couldn't wrap my head around was that she'd come for *me*. But who else did she know in North Canaan, Connecticut?

"You," I said, "you're here!"

I'd missed her so much and not dared to feel it.

"I saw a picture of you in a Danbury newspaper," she began, smiling. "It showed the back of your head, tilted at a certain angle, and the faces of children in the audience. That tilt, that angle, had carved a place in my heart without me knowing it. How does that happen do you think?"

I didn't know. But it made me wonder whether events on earth were a lot less haphazard than they appeared. Maybe the sacred geometry of that angle of tilt had been impossible until now. And no prayers, supplications, maneuvers or strategies could have made it come sooner.

Clara screwed her mouth to the side and arched her brows in amusement as if she were also enjoying the cosmic joke. Her eyes shimmered with specks of gold.

"I wanted you to come so bad," I said. "In fact—"

She interrupted. "Alessia's dead."

"I was there," I said.

"How?" she asked.

"Charley called me. He wanted me to take him afterward."

"You slept with her once," she stated matter-of-factly.

Any qualification or obfuscation of this point would work against me.

"Yes," I agreed, letting my hands drop weakly to my pants pockets.

"Why did you do that?"

Her question opened the door to a lot of pain, including Clara's lack of communication, but my gut warned me to steer clear of that. "I don't know. I'm sorry."

Her cheeks swelled up squeezing her eyes into almond slivers. A tear lingered on her lower lash. She pressed her lips together in a strained grin.

"How is your father?" I asked.

"He's out," she said, brightening. "Feeling a lot better."

While I had attributed her return to the mysteries of the Universe, it might have been as simple as family pride. She hadn't been fully free to be with me until her father got out of jail and was standing on his feet. I'd heard of an Irish saying, *A daughter is a daughter all of her life*. If Clara had come to me sooner, it would have been a betrayal. I got it. Deep down, I had a lot of respect for people with that sort of propriety, who existed within solid family walls.

"You're not in school today," I observed.

She nodded. "Ms. Rodriquez called me into her office Tuesday."

"And she —"

"No, I didn't get fired," she said, dismissing that with a toss of her hand. "Charley ran away from his father, and took a bus to his grandmother's apartment in Manhattan. Charley's father has petitioned the court for custody. Ms. Rodriquez wants you to represent her." Clara paused, gauging my reaction. "Shocking that the old bat actually loves someone."

"Oh," I said, biting my lip but secretly thrilled—both that Charley had made a getaway, and that I might get to discharge an old debt.

I lowered my head, remembering my refusal to go to trial for Clara's father. There was a faint glint of sarcasm in her eyes. "Believe me, I get it," she said. "You have to do this."

"When is it?" I asked.

"Tomorrow afternoon. Ms. Rodriquez just found out what it was going to cost to actually hire an attorney."

"I'll do this show," I said, "and drive back."

"Do you have anything tomorrow?" Clara asked.

"It doesn't matter."

She made an expression of mock admiration, then smiled and held out her arms for a hug. I got on my knees and embraced her.

"You know," she said, as I kneeled before her, "I lied about Bangkok. I was raped. I got pregnant and miscarried. My parents never knew and neither did any of the other models. Since the miscarriage was prior to the twelve-week mark, my doctor suggested dilation and curettage to clean me out. It caused scarring of my uterus. The chances that I can get pregnant are slim to none."

She stared brazenly, almost daring me to pass judgment with a gasp or some uncontrolled facial muscle.

"I wouldn't change anything about your past," I told her. "All of it has gotten you to me."

44

Wednesday morning, July 7, 2010 White Plains, NY

I was getting a little help from my friends, David and Felicia, who had patched things up enough to be willing to meet in David's office together. Felicia was using some nifty investigation tools through the District Attorney, including an ongoing search of the records and data compiled by Wolf Pappas's parole officer.

"Wolf is really getting his act together," she said. "He's set up a spare bedroom in his apartment. He's enrolled Charley at a local charter school in the Bronx. Most importantly, he's holding down an actual job. His lawyer has developed a parenting plan."

"How do you know this?" I asked.

She flashed a big, cheesy grin. "All of this must be monitored as a requirement of Wolf's conditional release from Sing Sing."

Felicia placed a hand on my shoulder. My exhales evened out as I tried to slow everything in my mind. "What do we need to prove?" I asked.

David glanced down at some notes.

"When a judge decides custody between a parent and a non-parent," he said, "the key phrase is 'extraordinary circumstances.'"

I nodded. This was a familiar term.

Felicia twirled a highlighter between her fingers. "Yeah, that's the standard. Otherwise, it's a slam dunk win for the biological father."

"Don't we have that here?" I asked, focusing my attention first on Felicia, and then David.

He nodded toward Felicia. "Madam Investigator," he drawled, in a falsely deferential tone.

"Well yes," Felicia nodded. "We've got his stint in jail, obvious parental neglect, no child support payments over ten years. If that isn't extraordinary circumstances, I don't know what is."

"So, we've got a case," I said.

David scratched his forehead. "Yeah, but Wolf is still the father. And that plays a part, especially if the parent has taken measures, which he obviously has."

I steadied myself. "So you're saying he still has the edge?"

Both nodded gravely.

I mourned Alessia. The birth of Charley had induced her to kick heroin. She'd repaid that miracle by adoring her son and forging a loving home. How could she have had known that what she built was so fragile? It haunted me that she'd been a good friend and I'd let her down.

"Take a deep breath." Felicia said. "You'll do fine."

45

Wednesday, July 7, 2010 White Plains, NY

David and I wore blue suits and Felicia sported a J. Crew type red blazer. We were as ready as we could be under the circumstances.

At the stairs to the courthouse, Wolf was standing with his attorney, a woman who I didn't recognize. Wolf's counsel gently prodded him toward us as Felicia, David, and I approached.

Wolf's lips started working before any sound came out. His suit was a conservative charcoal. It looked new. "I will settle for fifty thousand dollars," he said. We had called Ms. Rodriquez about such an eventuality, and she'd given us a number.

David butted in. "Ten," he countered.

"Forty-five," said Wolf. "And that's as low as I'll go."

This answered my questions about Wolf in Solomonic fashion. We were under instructions not to go above twenty-five, which was all Ms. Rodriquez said she could afford. Sadly, I shook my head.

Wolf's lawyer chimed in, "The petitioner withdraws his offer. Shall we proceed?"

The courtroom was dignified, solemn, and nearly empty, with a lofty dome-like ceiling, handsome gallery of wooden benches, and the stars-and-stripes on the side wall.

The judge entered in her robe. Since there were only a handful of people, Wolf, his lawyer, Ms. Rodriquez, David, Felicia, and a nurse from Montefiore Hospital, the sergeant-at-arms merely raised his hand instead of calling all rise. Everyone stood. Then I sat down with David and Felicia at the respondent's table.

All of this was familiar to me except the stakes. I had to win for Charley. It was unnerving for the consequences to feel so personal.

As petitioner, Wolf took the stand first. His lawyer methodically established the foundational details. Wolf's name was on Charley's birth certificate as father. He'd lived with Charley and Alessia until Charley's second birthday. Recently, he'd secured an apartment and a job. His lawyer introduced that Wolf had done prison time in Sing Sing for grand larceny. That way, there would be no appearance of hiding anything when it came out in cross-examination.

His lawyer told a story of redemption. Troubled man. Good intentions. Until now, he'd not been able to get his act together sufficiently to be a father. After the tragedy of Alessia's death, he was seeking another chance. America's the land of second chances, right? I might have fallen for it if Wolf hadn't offered to settle for cash. But settlement-related evidence, like the offer, was not admissible to impeach a witness. Otherwise, who would ever offer to settle?

I rose to cross-examine Wolf Pappas. Even on the stand, his body never was still. Fingers tapped, shoulders twitched.

"Mr. Pappas," I said, "Did you visit Charley during the course of his seven years with your former wife?"

Wolf hesitated. "I did occasionally."

"You're under oath," I reminded him. "Charley may be called as a witness." We had decided to spare Charley the trauma but the other side didn't know that.

Wolf cleared his throat. "Only twice."

I feigned surprise. "In those seven years, you visited him twice?"

"Yes," the witness agreed.

"Why?" I asked. Always a risk. The rule is to never ask a question about anything you can't verify.

"I was incarcerated three of those years," he said.

"And before that?"

"I did not think that I would be a good role model for him," Wolf said with tender sincerity. "But now, I've developed into the type of man who can be a good father. And I am," he paused, "Charley's father."

Wolf had made me pay for asking an open-ended question. I acknowledged this by retreating a few steps.

"In the nine years of your son's life," I began, "did you ever send Charley a present?"

"I was living hand to mouth."

"Did you —"

"No," Wolf said. "I didn't send anything."

"Did you pay child support?"

"I told you I was living —"

"Witness will answer the question," said the judge.

"No," said Wolf.

"You said that during the first six years of Charley's life, you were not a good role model. The next three, you were in prison. Now you're ready to be a good father? What guarantee do we have that you'll stay that way?"

"Guarantee?" Wolf asked. "Like when you buy a used car?" He laughed at his own joke. "I don't know," his voice trailed away.

"We really don't know, then, whether this *new you* is permanent or temporary, do we?" I asked. "You don't have much of a track record."

"Objection," cried Wolf's lawyer.

"Sustained," ruled the judge. "Counsel asked no admissible question."

I felt myself getting emotional. "Can you cite any interaction with this child in his nine years of life that shows an iota of devotion to him?"

"I have always loved him in my heart," said Wolf. "A father's heart."

"You were depending on Charley to be a mind reader? A heart reader? Is that it?"

"Objection!"

"Sustained."

"No further questions, your honor."

David's eyes met mine as I returned to the respondent's table. That last jab had connected.

After a short recess, the judge swore in my first witness, a nurse from Montefiore. She was heavyset with a pretty face and hair tied in bun. I made a few preliminary inquiries establishing her credentials and schedule on the day in question. Then we got to the heart of it.

"What exactly did you say to me at the hospital directly after the death of Alessia Perez?"

"It wasn't directly after," the nurse said. "Maybe an hour past." She paused. "I told you to keep the boy here. His father was coming to get him in ten minutes."

"So Charley knew that Mr. Pappas was coming soon?"

"Yes, he did."

"What did Charley say when he heard his father was on his way?"

The nurse frowned. "He said to you, 'Please let me go with you.'"

"No further questions for this witness," I said. "I call Principal Irma Rodriquez to the stand."

I shepherded Ms. Rodriquez through the preliminaries, that she was the principal of an elementary school in the Bronx and lived in Manhattan. We touched upon the death of her daughter and covered Alessia's period as a heroin addict, both to explain the asymptomatic Hepatitis C that developed into late-stage cirrhosis of the liver, and because we expected it all to be brought up on cross examination. I felt a twinge in the general area of my liver, which I suspected was psychosomatic.

"Tell me, Ms. Rodriquez, about your relationship with your grandson, Charley."

"People tell me that I'm a tough principal, and I'll admit that I was tough with my daughter," Ms. Rodriquez said. "But I'm a soft grandmother. From the time Charley was born—anything that boy wanted. I've never raised a hand to that child. Not one *pela* or *bofeta*. Nor did his mother. So when his father smacked him —"

"Objection. Hearsay."

"My grandson ran out of Wolf's place and took a bus to me in Manhattan."

"Objection sustained. The court will disregard the testimony."

"The boy had never experienced any physical abuse and I'm so proud that he didn't tolerate it. Of course, I took a photo."

"Objection, your honor."

"Sustained. Disregarded."

"And we've been living happily together ever since." Ms. Rodriquez smiled theatrically.

Nobody wanted Charley to have to testify against his father, so this was our way of slipping in Wolf's assault on the theory that the judge couldn't really un-hear what she'd heard. The photo, unfortunately, wouldn't be admissible without Charley's testimony to lay a foundation.

"Can you tell me about some activity that you and Charley have shared recently?" I asked Ms. Rodriquez.

"We happened to see the movie, "Big," on TV, you know, with Tom Hanks? They dance on that giant piano? Charley wanted to see the piano at F.A.O Schwarz. He goes for anything with music. I happen to love their doll collection, the Newborn Nursery it's called. I live on the Upper East Side, so we walked down there, and split a double-chocolate brownie on the way. Charley got so excited when we saw the gold and orange F.A.O. Schwarz sign, just like the movie. When we walked in, an employee with a red shirt was dancing "Chopsticks" on the piano. I held Charley's hand as we watched. The feeling was so delicious. Then we went to see *my* favorite—the dolls. The saleswomen wear white nurse uniforms and the idea is that you're adopting a baby, rather than buying a doll. There's even a sign saying "Do Not Enter – Hospital Staff Only." It's a little schmaltzy, *meloso* we would say, but it gets me every time."

We covered other ground such as the regular frequency that Ms. Rodriquez had enjoyed seeing her grandson throughout his life, and an account of the exhaustive number of presents she'd bought for him. Ms. Rodriquez finished by saying, "In the Puerto Rican culture *la abuela* is an honored position, and it should be seen that way by this court."

The lawyer for the petitioner stood for cross examination.

"Ms. Rodriquez, are you aware that there have been thirty-seven teacher complaints filed against you with the union, most alleging some form of cruelty?"

"I told you," she said, "I'm a tough principal but a soft grandmother."

"And you admitted to also being tough with your daughter. Did your treatment cause her heroin addiction?"

"I'll admit," Ms. Rodriquez said, "that I'd like the opportunity to make up for some of my failings as a mother. But I'll also point out that Alessia had been clean almost ten years when she died. She turned out to be a good person and a good mother."

Ms. Rodriquez's humility surprised me. This was not Clara's bombastic bully.

"No further questions." Wolf's attorney sat down beside her client at the petitioner's table.

The judge called a short recess. Upon our return to the courtroom, counsel for the petitioner commenced final argument. She stood at her table and spoke directly to the judge.

"The parental preference rule," she emphasized those words, slightly popping her P's, "stipulates that custody of a minor child should usually be decided in favor of a fit parent—as opposed to any other party." She paused to let that sink in. "That means, an adequate parent who is prepared to care for the child should gain custody, rather than a non-parent. Legal parents have strong rights.

"If a non-parent, such as Ms. Rodriquez, challenges a legal parent for custody, she must be able to prove that the legal parent, Mr. Pappas, is not fit *right now* to gain custody of the child. Proving that Mr. Pappas was not a suitable parent *in the past* isn't enough.

"Right now, Mr. Pappas has a reliable income. Right now, Mr. Pappas has an apartment in the same borough where Charley has always lived. There is a bedroom for Charley. Mr. Pappas has enrolled him in school. Wolf Pappas is a fit parent.

"Parental preference means that a parent who shows willingness and preparation has superior rights. Whatever other aspects of character, capability, and experience that may seem relevant must be secondary.

"The parental preference rule should be followed in this matter, and my client, Mr. Pappas, should be awarded custody of Charley."

I immediately stood up to respond.

"Ms. Rodriquez has demonstrated more love for Charley as his grandmother than Mr. Pappas has shown as his father. The core standard remains: What caretaker would be in the best interests of the child? Charley has shown his unwillingness to live with Mr. Pappas not once, but twice. The first time was at the hospital when Charley asked me to take him away before his father arrived. The second time was when Charley traveled across two boroughs to move into his grandmother's apartment. A nine-year-old knows what's in his best interests. This court should as well. It would be reprehensible to take Charley away from a caretaker who he's obviously bonded with in favor of a father who has never before showed much interest. My client, Irma Rodriquez, has proved her fitness. Granting custody to the petitioner would be a cruel experiment."

That ended the hearing. No verdict would be announced. The judge would consider the case, and when she had arrived at a decision, deliver the result to the attorneys.

46

Wednesday, July 14, 2010 South Salem, NY

A week later, I received it.

In the matter of *Pappas v. Rodriquez*, the petitioner is the natural father of the nine-year-old child, Charley. The father petitions for custody of the child from respondent, the grandmother, who took illegal custody of Charley for a period of two weeks. The court rules for the natural father, Mr. Pappas, based on parental preference and the father's documented willingness and readiness to take custody of the child. The father, having served time in prison for a non-violent theft crime, now has shown sufficient evidence of being a responsible parent. This is consistent with the decision in *Matter of Mohammed v Cortland County Dept. of Social Servs.*, 186 AD2d 908, 908, which found that incarceration alone does not diminish a parent's custodial rights. Ordered that the petitioner be awarded custody of the minor child, effective Wednesday, the twenty-first of July.

"How could they give Charley to that guy instead his grandmother?" I asked David over the phone.

"It's unfair," he agreed. "But he's the father. That's hard to beat."

"Did you see what the judge said about Ms. Rodriquez? Illegal custody?"

"Yeah, she was blunt. But how can you argue with it? Looking from the outside in, that's what happened."

"Were we stupid to even attempt this?" I asked him.

"No," he said. "We had to go for it."

"He's going to hate me."

"Who? Charley?"

"He's going to think I didn't fight hard enough."

"Did you get your blood result?" He was purposely changing the subject.

"Negative," I said.

"You might want to tell Clara about that." I could hear his smile.

47

Wednesday, July 21, 2010 South Salem, NY

I've never liked cleaning house. Only when agitated do I actually enjoy scouring and scrubbing. This was one of those times. I was leaving for Manhattan soon. The day of Charley's court-ordered transfer had arrived. Ms. Rodriquez wanted me to drive him to his father's in the Bronx. "I might murder him if I see his face," were her words.

I knelt on the tile floor of my bathroom with a spray can of Scrubbing Bubbles, abrading the tub with the green side of a heavy-duty sponge. It felt good. Tiles digging into my knees gave me grim satisfaction, self-effacing, like a hair shirt. I finished the tub, then buffed the toilet bowl like a shrine.

In the kitchen, I scrubbed pots, stacked dishes, and wiped countertops. I was a cleaning dynamo until minutes before it was time to go.

Charley sat on Ms. Rodriquez's Manhattan stoop with his grandmother standing behind him. His red suitcase rested on the sidewalk. Ms. Rodriquez's cheeks were puffy. Charley dug a stick into the concrete stair, refusing to look up. He had stolen a peek of me as I neared but now feigned blindness.

"Stand up, Charley," Ms. Rodriquez instructed, her voice washed thin. She wore a peach blouse and three-quarter-length cotton pants. I doubted she owned a pair of shorts.

On this hot July day, Charley looked stifled in his starched Sunday best. But I couldn't blame his grandmother for wanting to add a touch of decorum.

He stood up, looked at me, raised his hand half-way as a greeting and let it fall. Ms. Rodriquez stepped between us, then hugged Charley to within an inch of his life.

She shook her head, saying, "I know right and wrong, and this is wrong."

Charley tentatively cupped his hand toward me and I took it.

"Let me take a picture of you two," Ms. Rodriquez said, fidgeting with her phone for an unnecessarily long time before nodding that she was done. I lifted the suitcase, waved goodbye, and we took a few steps toward my car.

"Oh wait," said the principal, and she produced from a paper bag the blue Adidas soccer ball I'd once bought for Charley. He readied his hands and she tossed it to him. With the ball tucked under one arm, Charley reached for the passenger seat door, but I nodded toward the backseat and he complied. We were on our way.

Before we'd driven out of Manhattan, my cell rang. Ms. Rodriquez, I guessed, with some final detail, but no, it was Wolf. His voice rang through the car speaker.

"Can you bring him to Ossining?"

"Ossining?" I said. "Are you kidding? I'm crossing the Third Avenue Bridge."

"I'm hung up here," he said pleadingly. "I'll make it worth your while."

"Where?" I asked.

"The train station. I'll meet you at the Metro North."

"Why the hell should I meet you at the train station in Ossining?"

"Because I'll be on the train that arrives at 2:30 pm."

None of this made sense.

"I'm taking him back to Ms. Rodriquez," I said.

"Pleeease," he begged. His tone was so pitiable. It tugged at an unexpected sense of mercy. I looked back at Charley and he shrugged, widening his eyes.

"Okay," I agreed. "I don't know why I'm doing this." I shut off the phone, cutting short Wolf's thank you.

"Do you think he'll be on that 2:30 train?" I asked Charley.

"No," he said.

"Why?"

"I can tell when he's lying."

Waiting on the platform in Ossining, we polished off some burritos I'd bought in town. Charley was still young enough to be excited about trains. I hoisted him on my shoulders so he would see it first.

"Do you see it, Charley?"

"No," he said.

"Now?" I was standing on my tip toes.

"No." He gripped my shoulders to steady himself.

The kid was heavier than I'd expected.

Now!" he shouted.

As if looking through his eyes, I saw a steel dragon, pulsating and hungry, growing as it approached, until the brakes screeched, and Charley clapped his hands over his ears.

There was a pause and the doors opened simultaneously. People bolted as if from cages, hastened off, and vanished into the two stairwells, some slipping into an elevator.

"Do you see him, Charley?"

"No. I told you he wouldn't be here."

"Oh God," I said. My knees hurt from carrying him on my shoulders. I let him down, but without his weight, felt bereft. He looked up at me. I phoned Wolf. No answer.

"Should we wait for one more train?" I asked.

"Okay," he said. "But I've got to pee."

We walked halfway up the hill that funneled into the station and found a coffee shop with a men's room.

"There's ice in this urinal," he said.

"Melt it, Charley."

He did.

"I wish —" he stopped in the middle of the sentence.

"You wish what?"

"I wish I had more pee."

After we walked back down, Charley and I paced on the platform. People were accumulating across the tracks on the southbound side to board the Hudson Line to Manhattan.

Our train swung into view with the inky river behind it. It made a shrill stop, and people filed off purposefully, up the staircases, into the elevator. Again, I didn't see him. Everyone dispersed into cars, cabs, or sidewalks, and we were left, once again, abandoned at the station.

"Some people are irresponsible!" I complained to Charley.

My phone rang. "I'm sorry," Wolf said. "They didn't let me call 'til now. Bring him to the visitor's waiting room at Sing Sing." The call broke off. Sing Sing. It had never occurred to me.

The prison which had defined Ossining since the early 19th century, still loomed large, perched on high ground along the banks of the Hudson. A cabbie told me to follow the river south from the station and I'd get there. But it wasn't quite that easy, and I found myself marooned in a shopping center. I stuck out my hand and stopped a woman cruising by in a Saab.

"Can you direct me to Sing Sing?" I asked.

She, a well-coifed lady of about 65, looked into my Malibu, assessing us.

"You don't want to bring a child to a prison," she advised.

Embarrassed, I replied, "But it's his father."

"Do you want to give him nightmares?" she asked. "It would be irresponsible of you."

"Charley has been there before," I said. "Several times. It didn't give you nightmares, did it, Buddy?"

"No," Charley said solemnly.

"If he's been there before how come you don't know the way?"

I couldn't answer that.

"Low life!" she declared, rolled up her window, and drove away.

That fizzled my energy. I hung my head, still impeding the lane of traffic at the shopping center. Someone honked from behind, then maneuvered around me.

"Sing Sing?" I appealed to his open window with my palms turned up.

"Follow me," he said.

Weaving through a series of narrow dingy roads, he brought me past one of the tall towers of the fortress prison. As we climbed higher, I could see that there were four such towers, connected by castle walls. At the second campanile, the Jeep stopped, and I pulled in behind him.

"Visitors is *that* way," the man motioned down a road.

"Thank you so much," I replied.

I escorted Charley out of the car, and we made a byzantine trek, around a hillside, down stairs, past a parking lot, and through the prison gates.

"Is it a castle?" Charley motioned to the fortress.

"It's a dungeon," I replied.

We walked beyond the employees' entrance where a sign read, "Through these doors pass some of the finest corrections professionals in the world." I saw the "Visitors" sign near an afterthought of a side door. It opened into a barren room that looked temporary but might have been there since the 19th century, still awaiting some care. The walls were lined with battered wooden chairs but only a few people sat. There was a counter with some forms, and beyond that, uniformed guards at a high wooden desk. I walked a wary Charley to the desk in front.

"People wait here," I explained.

"To do what?" he asked.

"Visit the prison."

"Ohhh," he said, his eyes wide as moons.

I gave the guard Wolf's name and asked if he was an inmate. The guard scanned a computer screen, then nodded. Must have violated his parole. That was the only thing that could land him here this fast.

"Can he receive visitors?" I asked.

"Yes," the guard said. "Take a seat."

"Do you want to see him?" I asked Charley.

"Do I have to live here with him?" He trembled visibly. It had been a long day and I couldn't help laughing. "No, you're going back to your grandmother. But do you want to see him?"

"Okay," he said.

We waited forty-five minutes and I was glad we'd scarfed down those burritos. Then a guard motioned to us and led us down a corridor with white brick walls. "This is the medium security sector," he explained. He unlocked an iron gate to a housing unit and ushered us through. Guards in tan uniforms and caps, armed with batons, stood outside the cells. As we passed one cell, Charley's head swung around responding to his father's call. But the guard hurried us along to the visitor's room.

Inside, there was a painted mural of a seagull soaring high above the Hudson, Manhattan in the background. A slim, sealed window was imbedded close to the ceiling, out of reach. We sat at a table, and again waited. Wolf walked in without the guard. No handcuffs or restraints. Immediately, he hugged Charley who remained rigid but did not flinch.

"I'm very sorry," he said. "I really wanted this time together with you and it ain't going to happen. I'm so sorry." His eyes were wet.

He glanced at me. "I was afraid if I told you where they were taking me you wouldn't come." He kneeled, his head dipping below his son's. "I had to see Charley one more time."

Charley's eyes looked hollow, his skin pale.

"How can you live in here?" he asked his father.

"Oh, I've done it before and I'll do it again. I don't find trouble here. Model inmate."

"Was it my fault?" asked Charley. "Were you trying to steal something for me?"

"No, it ain't never been your fault," Wolf said. "The best you can learn from me is what not to do."

"But what did you doooo?" Charley pleaded.

"I —" Wolf hesitated. "I got fired last week. So I held up a bodega for rent money."

He gave Charley another quick hug and rapped on the door for the guard.

On our way back to the City, I called Ms. Rodriquez and gave her the news. She was waiting on the curb when we arrived. Charley got out of the car and wisely skirted past her. This time her hug might truly smother him. I brought the suitcase and soccer ball to the top of the stoop.

"Wolf was different in jail," Charley said to me.

"Yes, he was," I agreed. "More —"

"Real." Charley finished my sentence.

"My novenas," crowed Ms. Rodriquez. "My novenas brought you home."

Charley held out his arms to me and I gave him a hug. Then Ms. Rodriquez stepped forward, lifted her arms, and we embraced.

"Is this legal now?" she asked, motioning to Charley.

"I'll send an email to the judge's clerk explaining the circumstances," I said.

48

At lunch on Saturday, Clara and I ate *al fresco* at an elevated garden table. There was a bed of Red Spider Lilies on one side and a fountain on the other. One bottle of Moet & Chandon Nectar Imperial Rosé sat at my feet, another between us, with two poured glasses of the apricot-shaded liquid. Clara had once let it slip that it was her favorite, and I had convinced the maître d' at Bernard's to allow us this one trespass on her special day. She had gotten her film into the Woods Hole Film Festival on Cape Cod.

Clara wore white, open-toed sandals, with her toenails painted the color of the Moet. Sitting on the bar chair, she could barely reach the ground below. Kicking off my Birkenstocks, it felt good to feel the grass between my toes. On Clara's wrist was my mother's old watch which no longer told time. A way to include Mom in the festivities. May the circle be unbroken. Clara proposed a toast, "To the unexpected."

"Woods Hole," I said. We raised our glasses.

"Ms. Rodriquez, the loving grandmother," added Clara. Another sip.

"C.H. Pease Museum of Natural History in North Canaan, CT," I said.

More swallows ensued.

"Here's something you're not expecting," Clara teased.

"What's that?" I asked.

"You're coming with me to Woods Hole for a weekend." Her eyes gleamed hopefully.

I did not want to cancel anymore summer gigs.

"Going solo will open you up to meet more colleagues," I suggested.

"What if I were to say that I really want you to celebrate this with me?"

I got it. My choice would be something she'd always remember for better or worse.

I took a breath and made peace with it. "To Cape Cod," I toasted.

She pressed her lips together revealing that one charming dimple. We clinked glasses and drank. She kissed me tentatively, as if testing whether I was truly coming to Woods Hole. Her lips were plump and soft and just a bit chapped, which excited me, and made me feel protective at the same time. I wanted to consume her, like a double-chocolate brownie, but held back. If you are the double-chocolate brownie, I reasoned, scented and luscious, you might not want to be scarfed down in one enormous bite. We were dining at a fancy courtyard restaurant, after all. But Clara's tongue dug in deep, relinquishing me to passivity, as I absorbed her lunges, surrendered to her fierce jabs. No doubt I was already wearing her lipstick. God, I loved her overbite.

Even as I bathed in Clara's love and approval, and the corresponding endorphins flooded my brain, it occurred to me that these thoughts and emotions were just part of the passing show. There would be changes of temperature, ups and downs, hers and mine. Not to disparage human love, but it ain't solid ground.

Epilogue

Thanksgiving, 2010 South Salem, NY

I wish I could say that delivering Charley to his grandmother changed my life, redeemed the tragedy of Joshua, and left me to live happily ever after, or more happily, or changed forever in some important way. That's our religion, right? That something you do on the outside can have a drastic effect on your insides, cause you to swim rather than sink. Sure, I'd rather play music than argue cases. Clara did come home to me. Charley is adjusting to his new school in Manhattan. All of it helps. But, at core, am I still the same neurotic? Absolutely. Just ask Liam and Mary McLaughlin, who are hosting Thanksgiving today. They still think I'm bad news.

What did I expect, freedom? From law—I thought. But really from myself. What I found is that nothing you do on the outside frees your insides. Not even the grand gesture of trading wing-tips for clown shoes.

Worse was faking it for Clara—that my career change had truly made me whole. She was doing the same. As if getting her film into a few festivals had altered her core existence.

I'm still playing music for kids. Clara's working on a new documentary. And guess what? We got a dog. Timmy is enjoying an early morning snooze on the couch beside me as I tap on my laptop. I aspire to be more like him in his delight when I return home, or grab the leash.

I'm proud of what I did. Music and children carved a channel through to my heart. Not bad. But really just a first step.

ABOUT THE AUTHOR

Robert Markowitz has written personal essays for the *New York Times*, released three children's music albums of original songs, and played thousands of shows. He holds a law degree from Duke University, and has worked as a teacher, an attorney, and a clown. *Clown Shoes* is his first novel.

Author Photo©Dennis Lee 2022